SEA OF LIES

RACHEL MCLEAN

JOIN MY BOOK CLUB

If you want to find out more about the characters in *Thicker Than Water* - how they escaped the floods and arrived at the village - you can read the prequel *Underwater* for free by joining my book club.

Go to rachelmclean.com/underwater to read *Underwater* for free.

Happy reading!

Rachel McLean

AUTHOR'S NOTE

This book is a standalone sequel to *Thicker Than Water*. It's designed to be read alone but you may enjoy it more if you've read the first book.

PROLOGUE

Sarah slid the patio doors open quietly, careful not to wake her parents. She'd seen him out there, a flash of white on the grass behind the house. She had no idea how he'd got out.

"Snowy!" she hissed, pulling the door shut. She wrapped her arms around her chest; the wind was rough on the clifftop in September, especially this early in the morning.

She peered back up at the bedroom windows, checking that her parents' curtains were closed. Nineteen years old and still treated like a child. But it was nothing compared to the way her father treated her mother.

Satisfied, she rounded the side of the house, heading for the village square. Snowy liked to head for the bins at the back of the pub in search of scraps. He rarely got lucky; their isolated refugee community was obsessed with minimising waste.

"Snowy!" she called again, wishing the cat would reappear. She wanted her bed. The air was damp and the thin blouse she'd dragged on to come outside – it wouldn't do to risk being seen in her nightclothes – was getting soaked.

She reached the front of her house and stopped. Someone was coming out of the Dyers' front door, four houses along.

She pulled into the shelter of the wall and watched, her heart pounding. There was a reason she only came out here early in the morning or late at night. They stared at her, she knew they did. They gossiped about her. She was a freak, the only girl her age who didn't play a useful role in the village. Her father rarely let her leave the house, so she had little choice.

A figure backed out of the Dyers' door. Tall and lean, struggling with something he pulled behind him. What was Ben Dyer doing dragging things around at this time of day? She shrank back into the wall, her breaths shallow. Could it be something to do with the men that his sister Jess had insisted on rescuing from their stricken trawler two nights ago? Her father had been raging about tit, full of disdain for the actions of Jess Dyer, their new steward. The village had taken the men in, temporarily at least. Ted didn't trust them, but he was powerless against Jess and the rest of the village council members. It was what this community did; take in the dispossessed, the desperate. They'd all been that way once.

The man had mousy blonde hair that looked like it hadn't seen a comb for a very long time. He wore a pair of jogging bottoms that were a couple of sizes too large. He turned and heaved his burden up, supporting it against his side.

Sarah gasped. He was dragging Ruth Dyer, Ben's wife. She leaned on him precariously, her arms flopping at her sides.

But Ben Dyer had dark hair.

Sarah took a step forwards, her heart hammering against her ribs. She opened her mouth but nothing came out.

She heard footsteps behind her. She closed her eyes. Her father had caught her.

She turned, ready to face the tongue-lashing. Snowy would have to make his own way home.

A man advanced on her. He was heavily built with dark, greasy hair and wore a creased blue shirt with the sleeves rolled up. No coat. He had a tattoo that snaked from his wrist into the folds of his shirt.

This wasn't her father.

"Who are you?" she breathed. She looked back towards Ruth. Another man had joined the first now. They were hauling her away, towards the beach. Sarah felt a cry stick in her throat.

She felt movement and turned to see the man close to her, his face hard. He pushed his hand towards her face and she let out a whimper.

"Shut up, lass," he said. He sounded impatient, irritated. She'd caught him and his friends taking Ruth. Would they punish her, silence her?

He had something in his hand. A cloth. It smelt sharp, medical. She pulled back as he shoved it into her mouth.

She felt his arms go round her as she collapsed, the sound of birds above her head echoing in her ears. Then there was nothing.

CHAPTER ONE

FIVE DAYS LATER

SARAH STARED AT THE APPROACHING BEACH, HER HEART thumping in her chest. She could make out dim figures waiting for them.

She raised a hand to wave then dropped it. She was tired. More tired than she could ever remember. The adrenaline had got her out of that festering cell and to the beach with Martin, then back again after her second capture. Now all she wanted to do was sleep.

She felt her father's weight shift next to her. He was clutching his wounded shoulder, muttering under his breath. She looked at him and felt ice run down her back.

She looked back at the beach, searching for her mother. *Mum, have you come out? Did you dare?*

The boat was nearing the shore now, its occupants shifting, preparing for landing. Ruth was sitting in the boat in front of Sarah. She stood up, her face pale as the sea and her lips trembling. She smoothed her hands on her blood-stained trousers and sniffed the air.

Ruth had been in the cell next to her, and Sarah hadn't even known it. Sarah had even run off without taking her.

Ruth was the wife of the village steward – former steward, Sarah corrected herself – and the doctor to their village of refugees. Sarah was nobody.

She hoped the village would forgive her. Their community had been through enough; each of them making their way here after the floods six years earlier, and demonised and attacked by the residents of nearby Filey ever since.

Ruth turned. "Sarah, can you help me with Roisin?" Roisin had been imprisoned in another cell; she'd lost blood.

Sarah nodded. She wasn't used to being asked for help, but her ordeal made her one of them now.

She leaned over Roisin and, together with Ruth, took her weight. The boat's keel scraped on sand, slowing as they crept up the beach. People came forwards, arms outstretched. No one spoke.

She saw a pair of hands reach for Roisin and looked up. The girl's mother.

"Oh my God, my poor girl. Michael, come here. Help her."

A tall stocky man pushed his wife out of the way and leaned into the boat.

"Sweetheart. What have they done to you?"

"It's not as bad as it looks," said Ruth.

The man looked at Ruth and nodded. His lips were tight and his face lined with worry.

"Thank you," he whispered.

Ruth nodded. She helped him manhandle his daughter out of the boat, Sarah flailing to help.

Ruth turned to Sarah. "I need to check you over too. Your face. And your foot."

Sarah put a hand to the knife wound on her forehead. Her foot throbbed but she'd managed to ignore it for the last few hours.

"My dad first," she said.

"Of course. Ted, can you stand?"

Sarah's father grunted and pushed himself upright. His dark coat was stained with blood and his face was ashen.

"Will he be alright?" Sarah whispered.

"Shut up, girl. I'll be fine."

Ruth threw her a sympathetic smile. "Can't argue with that. I'll need to take you up to the pharmacy though, Ted."

"Can't be doing with that. Fussing's for women."

"It's also for a man who's been stabbed in the shoulder. You'll need antibiotics."

"Then bring 'em to the house." He put a hand on Sarah's shoulder and stumbled out of the boat, all but falling onto the sand. No one came forward to help him.

"Where's your mother?" Ted muttered.

Sarah clambered out of the boat, ignoring the pain in her foot, and went to his side.

"She'll be at home, Dad. Waiting for us."

"Good. Let's go."

Sarah looked up to see the crowd parting to let them through. A few people threw her awkward smiles but no one spoke. In contrast, behind her Ruth was being thronged by well-wishers wanting to welcome her home.

Sarah shrugged and pushed on. She was used to this.

"Stop." Ted stopped walking.

"What?"

"Wait."

"Come on, Dad. Mum will be worried."

"No. The boat's going back out. I need to wait."

She felt her stomach dip. "No, Dad. Let's get home."

He glared at her, panting. "I need to talk to that little bastard. Find out what he did to you."

She looked out to sea. The boat was heading south

again, silhouetted by the reflection of the low sun on the waves. It would return soon, with the rest of the villagers who'd gone to the farm, their rescue party. Plus one extra passenger.

"Dad, can't this wait?"

He shrugged off her hand. "Go home. See your mother. Tell her we're back."

He turned to the beach. Harry would be on that second boat, her father's friend. Would he restrain him? Did she want him to?

Ruth was level with them now. "Sarah. Come to the pharmacy, will you? Bring Ted."

"I've already told you," said Ted. "I'm fine."

Ruth put her hands on her hips. "You can intimidate my husband, Ted Evans, but it won't work on me. Your wound needs cleaning up. You need drugs."

"Talk to Dawn. Give her the drugs. She can clean me up, too."

"Very well. Can you ask her to come to the pharmacy, when you get home?"

He grunted and walked past her towards the sea, not making eye contact.

She turned. "Ted, you're going the wrong way."

He waved a hand in dismissal. "Stop telling me what to do, woman. I can look after meself."

Ruth looked at Sarah, her expression one of exasperation. "You'll come?"

Sarah nodded. "Will it be quick?"

"I have to see to Roisin first."

"In that case, I'll wait with my dad. Come on later."

Ruth shook her head. "You need rest, Sarah. Your forehead could get infected."

Sarah raised her fingers to the welt on her forehead, remembering. The knife. Ted hurtling through the door, throwing himself on her attacker. Martin coming at him, plunging a knife into the man's throat. The sucking, gurgling sound of blood leaving his body.

She swallowed a wave of nausea and spread her arms to steady herself. "Alright."

"Thanks."

Ruth picked up pace, catching up with Roisin's family who were almost at the village square and the pharmacy beyond. Sarah looked back at Ted. He stood at the shoreline, fifty feet from the crowd that had stayed behind to wait for the second group. He stared out to sea.

Don't hurt him, Dad, she thought. *Let me deal with him.*

CHAPTER TWO

THE BOAT DIPPED UNDER THE WEIGHT OF THE FIVE MEN AND one woman. It wasn't built for a load like this; a family craft, it would have been designed for a couple of adults and two kids, four adults at a push.

It wasn't the first time Martin had sailed in it. The first, he had been barely conscious, hardly aware of the storm raging around them. The second – well, best not to think about the second.

Across from him, Ben stared at the sea, his eyes dark. Ben Dyer. The reason all this had happened. In the farm-house kitchen, there'd been shouts and recriminations. Robert, the leader of the men Martin had been living with until a few hours ago; he and Ben had history, and Robert had taken his revenge by snatching Ben's wife Ruth. Three others, too, including Sarah.

From what Martin could see, Ruth didn't belong to anyone. She'd managed to get herself out of her cell and to the beach with no one's help. When she'd been recaptured, she'd retaliated in the most definitive of ways. He blinked, putting the memory out of his mind.

The sun was high in the sky now, or as high as it got off the North Yorkshire coast at the end of September. It pulsed down weakly, as if aware of how little he deserved its warmth. He shifted to face it, hoping he would dry out. Not much chance of that, with the constant spray.

They rounded a dark, heather-clad cliff and the village came into view. He held his breath. The windows of the houses at the cliff edge glinted in the sun. He wondered if one of them belonged to Sarah's family.

The group at the front of the boat – two men, one young with pale weather-worn skin, the other plump with dark skin, along with Jess, the village steward – had stopped talking. They spotted him watching and looked away. Ben, sitting at the back, was staring at the village now, muttering under his breath. And Harry, next to Ben, was staring at Martin, his disdain undisguised. All Martin knew of Harry was that he was an ally of Sarah's father. And that Robert had locked him and Ted up together when they'd attempted to rescue Sarah.

Was he thinking about what Martin had done, or about what might happen to him when they arrived?

"Nearly there," said the dark-skinned man. The boat leaned and turned for the shore.

They made for the boathouse, passing a crowd on the beach. The villagers watched, some running after them. No sign of Sarah. Ted was there though, looking like he wanted to disintegrate Martin with the force of his stare. Martin stared back, his heart pounding.

This was a bad idea. He should have stayed behind with Bill and the other men. Without Robert, the men would be directionless, but there a chance they'd change their ways. That was where he belonged, not here. Bill would be in charge now; would things be different?

Then he remembered the way they'd crept up on him

as he followed Sarah back through the dunes, intent on fleeing with her. The twine that Bill had tied round his wrists to restrain him.

Martin didn't belong anywhere.

The boathouse doors were pulled open and they chugged in. The dark-skinned man grabbed a rope and Harry jumped out to tie the boat up. One by one, he guided his fellow passengers out of the boat. Each of them headed out of the boathouse at speed, looking for someone from the first boat no doubt.

Harry and the other man stayed behind, securing the boat and unfolding a cover they pulled out of a hatch. They left Martin in the boat.

He watched them, his mouth dry.

"Where should I go?" he asked. His voice echoed in the empty space. Water lapped at the boat and reflected green and blue off the roof.

Harry shrugged. "Back to your mates, if I were you."

"They won't take me back. You saw what happened."

Harry tensed. "I was at the beach, helping the women. The women you took. I saw nothing."

"I helped Sarah. I helped her escape. They came after us, tied me up with twine."

"If you say so."

"It's true. Honest."

"Don't waste your breath. It's Ted you need to convince."

"I want to talk to Sarah first."

Harry let out a low laugh. "Fat chance, mate."

Martin hardened his jaw and put a hand on the side of the boat. He heaved himself out, half expecting one of the other men to jump him. They didn't.

"I'm going to find her."

"Good luck with that."

He slid past them to the boathouse door and eased it open. Outside, the air was cold and still, the only sound a flock of gulls above his head. A path led to the left. To the village.

He clenched his fists and started walking. The sea thrummed to his left and a bird cawed in the hedge to his other side. Clouds scudded overhead, pushed southward by the wind.

It was a climb up to the village, but he could see houses ahead, facing out to sea like a rebuke to the elements. Which one was Sarah's?

He tried to remember what Bill had said, the night after the abduction. *She walked right out of that bloody great house, looking for a cat or something.*

Sarah lived in a large house, then. Probably near the sea, if taking her had been so easy.

The houses were close now. He couldn't go knocking on all of them. Maybe he'd find the pharmacy. Would Ruth help him?

"Oi, you little fucker!"

Ted appeared out of nowhere, his left shoulder in a sling. Blood seeped through it. Martin let himself be distracted by it; it gave Ted the chance to swing at him with his good arm.

Ted grabbed Martin's neck with his hand and dug his fingers in. Martin cried out.

He brought his hands up and prised Ted's fingers off his flesh. The older man's hand was shaking but his grip was firm. He was panting.

"I helped her!" Martin grunted. Ted shrieked and pulled his hand free. He dug his fingers into the flesh of Martin's cheek.

Martin was ready this time. After his experiences on the road as a younger man, he'd learned to defend himself.

He was taller than Ted, and uninjured. He shifted his weight back and sideways, sending Ted tumbling to the ground. Ted's grip loosened. Martin grunted and caught Ted as he fell. *Don't hurt him*, he told himself. *However much he wants to hurt you.* This was Sarah's father, after all.

Ted pushed himself up, arm flailing. He threw Martin a look of pure fury and launched himself again.

Martin side-stepped. Ted threw his good arm out to grab Martin's waist but it wasn't enough to stop him crashing to the ground. He landed on his shoulder, screeching in pain. He turned and heaved himself up, prodding at his bandage with a tentative finger.

Martin turned to him, waiting. His breathing was shallow and his senses on fire. Above him, a gull cried out.

Ted stood up. "You bastard. What did you do to my girl?"

"I helped her escape."

"You were with them. The distress call, that trawler you had. The one that weren't in distress at all."

"I had nothing to do with that."

Ted leaned in. His eyes were dark green with flecks of yellow. His breath was sharp and pungent. "Don't lie to me!"

"What's going on?"

Martin turned at the sound of the voice. *Sarah?*

It was Jess, hurrying towards them from the village. She'd led the rescue party the village had sent to find the women. She'd told Martin he could come back with them.

Martin relaxed for a moment, giving Ted an opening to swing at him, catching his chin with his fist.

"Aay!" Martin threw his hand up to his chin. It was bleeding.

"Ted!" Jess shouted. "Stop it. We have ways of dealing with this sort of thing."

Ted stood between them, his chest rising and falling. He looked like a man possessed. "You're not dealing with me, you bitch."

"I don't mean *that*. I mean Martin here." Jess glanced at Martin then approached Ted. "He was involved in the abductions. Just because I let him come back with us doesn't mean I don't recognise that."

"So what you going to do about it? Set an example, I hope."

Martin watched her. How much was she going to tell the village, about what had happened? "The village council will have to meet," she said. "Come to a decision."

"You're not going to call the police?" said Martin.

She eyed him. "If you know anything about this community, you'll know that we don't trust the authorities. They haven't helped us in the past, and I don't expect them to now. But surely you knew that, or why else would you have come here?"

He shrugged. "I just did what I was told."

"Seriously? That's your defence?"

"I'm no—"

She threw up a hand. "Save it. You're badly cut. You need to come to the pharmacy. I'll take you. And Ted, you need Ruth to take another look at that shoulder."

"Bugger that," said Ted.

"Thanks," said Martin.

Jess stared at Martin for a moment, as if sizing him up. She nodded and turned to Ted. "I can't force you to get treatment. But please, keep the law out of your own hands for a while eh?"

"Why should I?"

"Because that's the way we do things round here. If you want to stay in this village, you stick to the rules."

"Fat lot of bloody good the rules have done so far."

"Save it, Ted. There'll be a council meeting tonight. You'll have plenty of chance to raise objections there. And go and see Ruth. Please. At least ask Dawn to get you clean bandages."

She turned for the village, throwing a *come with me* over her shoulder to Martin. He followed, half wishing for and half dreading the prospect of finding Sarah at the pharmacy.

CHAPTER THREE

Sarah watched as Ruth helped Roisin out of her blood-stained skirt. The girl was shivering, her teeth chattering despite the relative warmth of the pharmacy. Her mother Flo stood next to her, a hand on her shoulder. She took the skirt off Ruth and slid it over her arm.

The door burst open and two small boys ran in in a jumble of voices, limbs and tangled blond heads. Ruth's mouth widened.

"Sean! Ollie!" She bent to clasp them in a tight hug. She planted a kiss on each boy's cheek.

The boys huddled into their mother. One of them started to cry while the other stared at his mum, unblinking. Ruth smiled back at them through tears.

"I'm sorry, my loves. But Mummy has to work for a bit. You know how I help people who are poorly?"

The boy who'd been staring into his mother's eyes nodded. His brother burrowed further into Ruth, whimpering.

Ruth's eyes were gleaming. Sarah stepped forward. "I'll watch them, if you want."

Ruth looked up. "Just into the shop, please. Wait out there till I'm ready for you."

"I'm fine. I promise."

"I just want to check you over."

"Isn't it more important for you to be with your boys?"

"Sarah. Please, just let me do my job."

Ruth wiped a hand across her face. Her hands were scrubbed clean now, free of the blood that had stained them on the journey back.

Sarah shrugged. "Come on, boys. Let's play in the square."

"Sarah."

"We'll be just outside, Ruth. Promise."

Ruth frowned at her but didn't object. Sarah bundled the boys through the village shop that fronted the pharmacy, then into the cold air outside. She was glad to be away from the claustrophobia of the Murray family's worry over Roisin, the smell of blood and stale urine.

Outside, the air was fresh and salt-tanged, but dry. She could hear the sea beyond the village hall and smell cooking from a house just across the road. Her mouth watered. When was the last time she ate?

"How about a game of tag?" she said to the boys. They jumped up and down, each clamouring to be 'it'.

"You go first, Ollie," she said.

"I'm Sean."

"Sorry. You go first, Sean. This bench is den."

She lowered herself to the bench, glad to be off her feet. She hadn't slept for over eighteen hours and that had been on a filthy mattress in a dingy cell.

"That's cheating."

"Not for grown-ups, it isn't. Look, your brother's started running. Go after him. And don't leave my sight!"

She looked past them to see a door open in one of the houses. Her own house. She stiffened.

A figure appeared in the door. Sarah stood and started running.

"Mum!"

Dawn's face broke into a smile. She looked around the square then started to run. They collided not far from where Sean and Ollie had fallen into a squabbling heap on the tarmac.

Dawn held Sarah so tight she almost lifted her off the ground. "I never thought I'd see you again."

"I know, Mum. I'm sorry."

Dawn stood back. She wiped her eyes. "It wasn't your fault, sweetheart. Those men. They should never have gone out to that distress call."

"I know, Mum. But it's not as simple as that."

Dawn clasped her again. "Why isn't it as simple, love? What happened?" She pulled back and her voice darkened. "They didn't – do anything to you, did they?"

Sarah swallowed. "No." She tried to push out the thought of the man who'd visited her cell on the second night. He'd been young, and enthusiastic. But she'd held him off, upturning the table next to her mattress and using it as a shield.

"You're home," Dawn said. "That's what counts. Come inside. I'm never letting you out of my sight again."

"Sarah! I need you in here! Oh."

Sarah turned to see Ruth at the door of the shop. Flo Murray, Roisin's mother, was leading the girl away. Roisin wore a clean blue dress and looked older than she had at the farm. Sarah watched her, wishing she could ask her if the men had visited her, if they'd threatened her too.

"I'm taking Sarah home," said Dawn, her voice so quiet the breeze almost carried it away.

"I only need her for a moment," said Ruth. "Check on that wound. Boys, come into the shop for a minute."

The twins groaned before righting themselves and sprinting over to their mother. She hugged them again before bundling them inside.

Sarah clutched Dawn's arm and looked into her eyes. "It'll be alright, Mum."

Her mother seemed to have aged ten years since she'd last seen her. She wondered how her father had reacted to her disappearance; would he have taken his anger out on his wife?

Dawn nodded and let go.

"Have you told her about Martin?" Ruth asked as Sarah reached the doorway.

"Not yet."

"He'll be back soon, with Ben. God knows what'll happen."

"I know."

Ruth motioned for Sarah to sit on the pharmacy's solitary chair. She took a thermometer out of a metal container and shook it. She put it into Sarah's mouth.

"I hope you know what you're doing."

So do I, thought Sarah. *So do I.*

CHAPTER FOUR

"WAIT THERE."

Jess pushed the pharmacy door open and Martin hung behind, doing as he was told.

This wasn't the first time he'd been here; Ruth had brought him to the village pharmacy on the night he'd first arrived. He'd fallen off the trawler, the boat that Robert, Bill and he had convinced the villagers was in trouble. Jess and some others had saved him then Ruth had brought him here to treat him for hypothermia. That was before they had taken Ruth and Sarah, and the other two he'd never met. Before Ruth had let him stay in her and Ben's house, where he'd taken advantage of her hospitality by drugging her and taking her away in the villagers' own boat.

The pharmacy was in a room off the village shop. Behind the counter of the shop, a large woman with a prominent mole above her lip and a disapproving frown watched him.

"Ruth, I've got Martin," said Jess, out of sight. "Ted's split his chin open."

"He did *what*?"

"It was going to happen sooner or later. Better sooner."

The frowning woman pulled some vegetables out of a box and placed them on a shelf, but Martin knew her attention was on him. He listened to Jess and Ruth's conversation, wishing he could disappear.

Jess emerged. "She's busy. Wait here."

He shrugged and bent his head. His shoes were torn and full of wet sand and his clothes were stained with grass and mud. He thought of Ben's trousers that Ruth had given him when he'd fallen overboard, his first night here. He'd still been wearing them when he drugged Ruth and dragged her from her bedroom to the waiting boat.

He stared at the door, his chest tight. Ruth would have to be some sort of saint to treat him. Regardless of what he'd done for Sarah.

"I have to go and deal with… never you mind what I have to do. Just wait there," said Jess.

He nodded.

"Don't move a muscle, OK?"

He nodded again. She screwed up her mouth, glanced at the woman behind the counter then thought better of speaking. With a sigh she pushed the shop door open and disappeared outside. Martin watched her through the glass, the incongruous ting of the shop bell ringing in his ears.

He took a deep breath and waited.

Sarah wanted to be home, to check that her mother was all right, to know if her father had arrived yet. If he'd gone home. If he'd found Martin.

She fidgeted as Ruth dabbed at the cut on her forehead.

The disinfectant stung but it was nothing to what was going on inside her head. She'd asked Jess to let Martin come back with them. She'd convinced them to trust him, recounting the story of how he'd helped her escape. But what she hadn't told them was how she felt when he'd admitted to being there when she was taken. That he'd been a part of it.

She'd seen the look in his face after Robert, the ringleader, had fought with her father. She'd heard him shout that he loved her, and listened to him careering across the table towards Robert. He did it for her; at least that was what he believed.

Robert was dead. There was no way Martin could stay at the farm after that. On impulse, she'd told him to come back here, with her.

And now they were home. Had she made the right choice?

The door opened and Jess appeared.

"I've got Martin."

Sarah felt like her heart would stop. *Don't bring him in. Not here. Not now.*

Her hands were clammy and her face hot. She stared between Jess and Ruth, listening to their conversation.

I have to face up to him sometime.

But not yet. She wanted to go home. She wanted her mother.

Jess closed the door – what had they decided? – and Ruth smoothed the dressing on Sarah's forehead.

"There. Just a surface wound. It'll be fine. But let me know if you start feeling off-colour."

"Off-colour?"

"I want to be sure you haven't got an infection. You spent three days in filth. Heaven knows what you've come into contact with."

Sarah resisted the urge to remind Ruth that she too had spent three days in filth, on the other side of the wall.

"Is there another way out of here?"

Ruth frowned. "What?" She looked at the door. "Oh. I see. I'm sorry, you're going to have to go past him. But he helped you, didn't he?"

Sarah nodded. "He took you," she said.

Ruth's face darkened. "I know. I don't think it was his fault though."

"Really?"

Ruth's throat shifted as she swallowed. "Not entirely, anyway. It was Robert Cope. He forced them to do it."

"All of them? Even the other older one?"

"Bill?" Ruth let out a shaky breath. "Who knows. I'm glad he stayed behind, anyway."

"He buried Robert's body. With Martin."

Ruth put a hand on Sarah's arm. "If you need anything, I'm always here."

"I'll be fine."

"I don't mean just physical. It'll be hard talking to your mum about what's happened, I imagine."

Sarah felt her cheeks warm. She blinked back tears. Ruth squeezed her arm.

"Come on. I'll take you out. You can ignore him, if you want. You're going to have to speak to him at some point though. It was you who wanted him with us."

"I know. Thank you."

She stood up. As Ruth put a hand on the door, Sarah stopped her.

"How can you forgive him?"

"Martin?"

"Mm."

"Like I said," Ruth replied. "It wasn't his idea. That was all on Robert. I certainly don't forgive *him*."

Sarah dropped her gaze to the floor.

"Come on then, let's get you out of here." Ruth pushed the door open. "Wait there, Martin. Sarah is just leaving."

Martin stood up. Sarah could smell him; sea and sand mixed with the mud they'd crawled through together. She clenched her eyes shut.

"Sarah?"

She ignored him and bustled past, letting Ruth guide her to the door.

"Hello, Dawn," said Ruth.

Sarah opened her eyes to see her mother entering the shop. She looked worried.

"Is she going to be alright? That cut?"

Sarah's fingers went to the dressing on her forehead. She could feel Martin's stare behind her. Did her mother know who he was?

"She'll be fine," said Ruth. "Just a surface wound."

"Are you coming home then, love?"

Sarah nodded. She felt the air shift behind her. Martin cleared his throat.

No. Stay quiet. Don't speak to her. Please.

"Hello." Another cough. "I'm Martin. You must be Sarah's mum."

Sarah felt her legs weaken. Dawn turned to Martin, puzzled.

"I wanted to apologise, for what happened to her. I helped her escape. I hope she'll recover."

Dawn shrank back. "Oh. Thank you. Who are you?"

"Martin."

"Do you… do you live here?"

"I hope to."

"Oh." Recognition crossed Dawn's face. Sarah felt as if her stomach was turning itself inside out. She grabbed her mother's arm.

"Come on, Mum. Take me home."

"Of course."

Ruth flashed Martin a look then held the door open. Behind the counter, Pam looked on, not even pretending to be working. Sarah wondered if the whole village would be talking about her within the hour.

If they weren't already.

She shoved her mother out of the door and hurried towards the house.

"Slow down, love. You'll do yourself an—"

"Come on. Please. I want to get home."

She kept her head down, unsure if there was anyone around to watch them. Dawn hurried to catch up. They reached the path outside their house and her mother put a hand on her arm to stop her.

Sarah looked up. Dawn was looking at the house, her face pale. Was she scared?

"What did they do to you, Sarah? Did they hurt you? Did they – oh, I don't know how to say this – did they force themselves on you?"

"I don't want to talk about it, Mum."

"Please, love. I want to help you. That Martin lad. Back there. Was he one of them?"

Sarah stiffened. "Yes."

"Did he hurt you? Why is he here?"

"He told you, Mum. He helped me escape. He came back with us."

"He came back with you? Why?"

"He wasn't safe, there."

"Why ever not?"

"Mum! I've told you I don't want to talk about it." Sarah let out a shaky breath. "I'm sorry. I didn't mean to shout. Let's go inside, yes?"

Dawn cast a worried glance at the house. Sarah wondered if her father was home yet.

"Yes. Let's," said her mother.

Dawn hurried along the path, leaving Sarah behind, and turned her key in the lock.

CHAPTER FIVE

DAWN PULLED SARAH INTO THE HOUSE AND CLOSED THE door behind them. She was like a startled animal, breathing in sharp bursts and looking around her with small, quick movements.

"Mum? What's wrong?"

"Did your father come back with you? Did he find you?"

"Yes. Yes, he caught up with us. He didn't find me though. Jess and the others, they had to let him out."

"*What?*"

"Robert and his men. They found Dad and Harry on the beach, coming after us. They put them in the cell I'd escaped from." She backed into the wall, her limbs heavy. "Dad's injured, Mum."

Dawn paled. "Dear God." She crossed herself.

"His shoulder. But he's going to be alright. He's already shouting at people." Sarah tried to laugh.

"You're making no sense," said Dawn.

"I'm sorry. Look, I need a lie down. Can I talk about it later?"

"I've got someone to see you first."

"Who?"

Sarah pushed past her mother into the living room, wondering who might be there. They never had visitors.

As usual, the room was tidy to the point of sparseness, the sound of the sea faint through the tall windows at the back.

She turned to Dawn. "Who?"

"He's outside. On the grass."

Sarah crossed to the window and peered outside. The sun had disappeared behind thick clouds now and the sky above the sea was blurred. It was going to rain.

There was no one out there.

"Who, Mum?"

"Wait."

Dawn pushed the sliding door open a crack. "We're here. Come in."

Sarah watched, frowning, as a shape appeared from beside the window where it had been huddled unseen against the wall.

He stepped inside, shaking himself out and glancing down at his shoes as if worried he'd bring mud in.

"Sam?"

It was Sam Golder, one of the Golder twins. His brother Zack had gone out in the boat with Jess a week ago, to answer a distress call. The mission that had brought the men to their village. He'd gone with Jess on the walk south to find Sarah and the other women, too. Leaving Sam behind. She wondered how Sam felt about that.

"Hi, Sarah." He ran a hand through his messy hair. He was almost a foot taller than her, and similarly broad. A stranger would never know there were only four years between them.

She turned to Dawn. "Why is Sam here?"

"I thought you might want to see him. After what you've been through."

"Sam?"

"He's your friend, isn't he?"

"Yes, but…" She turned to Sam, aware she was being rude. *Friend* was hardly the word she'd use. She'd spoken to Sam on a few occasions, on the beach. They both liked to go down there for early morning solitude. She had no idea they'd been spotted.

She turned to Dawn. "Have you been spying on me?"

"I just saw you talking. He's a nice boy."

Sarah blushed. She blinked at Sam. Was her mother trying to play Cupid?

"It's good to see you home," said Sam. He looked down at his feet again. He hadn't moved them since stepping inside.

"Close the door," said Sarah. "It's freezing." She reached round him to pull it shut. They both jumped as her arm touched his back.

"Nice house," he said.

She looked around them. The living room was dull in this light, with nothing except her mother's crucifix on the wall. The coffee table was bare except for a single spray of flowers picked from the dunes, in a cracked cup. The kitchen, beyond, was equally bare; nothing on the surfaces except a teapot.

Dawn hurried into the kitchen. She picked up the teapot and put it in a cupboard. "Excuse the mess."

Mum, it's spotless, Sarah wanted to say. But she'd lived with this all her life. It was as if her mother was scared to leave her mark on the world in any way than through her faith.

"Have you been out there for long?" she asked Sam.

"Not long. Twenty minutes or so."

"That's ages, in this cold."

A shrug. "I'm used to it."

She knew he was. Sam was one of several young men who regularly left the village in search of work. It was their community's only way of getting cash for those things they couldn't grow or make themselves. They worked on the land reclamation near Hull, trying to grab back land the sea had taken in the floods six years ago. Floods that had made Sarah's family homeless and forced them to make the journey north to this village. Everyone here was like them, a refugee from the floods, provided with temporary accommodation in this former holiday village but not, as yet, able to leave. She doubted they ever would; the authorities seemed to have abandoned them.

"Why did you come?"

"To see if you were OK, I guess." He shifted his weight without moving his feet. She longed to tell him to step inside, to ignore the mud on the carpet. But her mother would be horrified.

"Well, I am. Thanks for coming."

She put a hand on the door, ready to open it again. He gave her a shy smile as she did. She blushed.

"Quick, out!"

She turned to see her mother advancing on them, her face full of horror.

"What?"

"It's your father. He's outside." Dawn's eyes were wide. "He looks cross."

Cross would be an understatement. In the last few days, Ted had seen his daughter abducted, had gone after her, been locked up himself, and then almost killed the man responsible. Yes, he would be *cross*.

Sarah had the door open. Dawn pushed her and Sam

through it. Sarah grabbed her arm, not wanting to go out herself. Surely only Sam needed to leave?

The pressure made Dawn stumble into her. They tumbled to the grass, Dawn gasping in surprise.

Sarah turned back to the glass door. Through it, she could see the front door to their house opening. Without thinking, she yanked the door closed then pushed her mother and Sam to one side, out of sight of the interior.

"What are you doing?" breathed Sam. "Are you coming with me?"

"No, silly." Sarah looked at Dawn. "I don't know what I'm doing. But can you leave me and my mother alone, please. We need to talk."

Sam threw her a sheepish smile then shook his boots out and slipped around the side of the house. Sarah assumed he would head home, to see his brother Zack, who would only just be back himself. She realised she had no idea where he lived.

She turned to Dawn.

"What was all that about?"

"Why did you pull me outside? It's starting to rain." Dawn moaned and tugged her pale blue cardigan up over her head. It was threadbare at the elbows and there was a thin trace of black cotton where she'd sewn up a tear in the hem.

"Sorry. It was an accident. Let's get back inside."

"Yes."

Dawn reached for the door. "It's locked."

"What?"

"You closed it from the outside. I can't open it."

"Damn."

"I *beg* your pardon?"

"Sorry, Mum. Let's go round the front. Dad'll let us in."

Dawn peered round the door. "No."

"It's raining. We have to get inside."

Dawn turned to her. Heavy drops of rain fell, darkening the village and the view out to sea. "I don't want to alarm him."

"Mum, please. He'll let us in. We can tell him we just got back from the pharmacy."

"No, love. We'll shelter for a bit, wait for him to go out."

"What good will that do? We still can't get in."

"Do you have your key?"

"Mum, I just got back from three days being locked up in an outhouse. Of course I don't have my—"

She fumbled in the pocket of her skirt. She had taken her key, on the morning she'd been snatched. Her parents had been asleep and she hadn't wanted to disturb them. She'd been looking for her cat, Snowy. She hadn't seen him since returning.

"I've got it," she breathed. Dawn looked like she might cry with relief.

"Mum, what's he been like? While I've been gone?"

Dawn shook her head. "He's hardly been here. He came after you, remember."

"Dad does things like that when he's angry." She lowered her voice. "Did he take it out on you?"

Dawn looked away. "He shouted at me a bit, that's all. Nothing I can't handle."

"You shouldn't have to handle him, Mum."

Dawn leaned in close. Her eyes flashed at Sarah, the pupils dilated. "With God's help, I handle him. I always have and I always will. It's what I do."

"It's not right."

"Sarah. This is not for you to judge. Now let's get inside. You're the one complaining about the rain."

"I'm not complaining." But Sarah's body *was* complaining. About the wet, and the cold, and the aches deep inside as well as her throbbing head. She wanted to sleep for a year.

They rounded the house to the front. The village square was deserted, rain chasing everyone inside. Sarah slipped past Dawn to get to the front door.

She raised her key to the lock. Theirs was one of few houses that were locked in the daytime.

She paused. "What was all that with Sam?"

Dawn shook her head. Beads of water sprayed into Sarah's eyes. "He's a nice boy."

"I know he's a nice boy, but why did you bring him here?"

"He'd be good for you."

"He'd be *what*? Mum, I don't need a matchmaker."

"You need to lead your own life. Sam could give you that."

"I don't. I'm nineteen years old. I'm not leaving you. Not with him."

She looked back at the door, imagining Ted inside. Would he be pacing the room? Watching from an upstairs window, wondering where his women had got to? Listening to them through the door?

"Just let me make my own decisions, please Mum," she said, as she turned her key in the lock. "I can look after myself."

CHAPTER SIX

MARTIN COULD BARELY BRING HIMSELF TO LOOK RUTH IN the eye as she patched up his chin. She bustled around the pharmacy, grabbing surgical glue, disinfectant and cotton wool, then tending to his wound without looking into his eyes.

At last she was finished. She stood back and wiped her hands on her apron. He jumped down from the table on which he'd been sitting.

"Thanks."

She shrugged.

"I'm sorry."

Her eyes moved upwards to meet his gaze. "Yes."

"If I'd known you, if I'd known what you were like, I'd never have—"

"But given that I was a stranger to you, you were happy to go along with it?"

"Not happy. I was scared. Scared of Robert." His hands were sweating. He hated himself. "I'm sorry, is all. If I can make it up to you in any way…"

"Go home."

"Sorry?"

"I have no idea what possessed you to tag along with the boat. I think the best thing is for you to go back to your friends, at the farm."

"You saw what they did to me. They'll never take me back."

"That's hardly my concern."

"And Sarah wants me here."

Ruth arched an eyebrow. "Does she?"

He thought of Sarah shuffling out of the pharmacy, refusing to look at him. "Maybe I should go back."

"Sensible boy. Just take care of that chin. Keep it clean."

"I will."

He pushed the door to find Jess outside, making stilted conversation with the woman running the shop. Martin knew that she'd only become village steward a few days before he and his friends had taken Sarah and the other women. He'd seen her struggling to assert her authority. Especially with her brother Ben, who'd held the job before her.

She turned at the sound of the door.

"All fixed?"

"Yes. Thanks." He ignored the puzzled stare of the other woman. "I think I'd best be on my way now."

"On your way where?"

"I'm not welcome here. It was stupid of me to think I might be."

Jess shook her head. She opened the shop door and guided him outside.

"That's better," she said. "Pam does like to listen in." She smiled. "Don't tell her I said that."

"I can't if I'm leaving."

"About that. Are you sure?"

He looked around the square in front of the shop. Heavy drops of rain were falling, and there was no one in sight. The air was dark and heavy and he could barely make out the houses beyond.

"Yes," he said. "I should go back to the farm."

"I saw what you did, back there."

"I didn't do anything."

"Yes, you did. You stopped that man in his tracks. And you did it for Sarah."

"If by that man, you mean Robert, well it wasn't me who stopped him. Not in the end."

She shook her head. "Not a word about that. Ruth is the beating heart of my family, and indispensable to this village. If anyone found out what she did…"

"I won't tell."

"Good. Now, the flat your fr— that Robert and Bill were in. After we rescued you from your boat that wasn't really sinking."

He blushed. "Sorry."

"Stop saying that. The flat's still empty. I'm putting you in it for twenty-four hours, while we come to a decision."

"You really don't need to do that."

She stopped walking. A gust of wind blew her red hair in front of her face and she shoved it to one side. "I said you could come. I've only been steward here for a week. If I change my mind, I'll look weak. I'm sticking up for you, whether you like it or not."

"Err—"

"Come with me."

She started walking. He followed, unaware now which direction they were going in. Towards the sea, or away from it? Towards the road back to the farm, or away from it?

"Where are we going?"

She didn't break stride. "I told you. The flat. One night. Then you'll either stay, or you'll go."

They reached a low red brick building. She handed him a key. "Here you are. That door there. It's upstairs, first on the left, once you get inside. It's basic, but it'll do."

"I don't deserve this."

"That's for the village council to decide."

"Thank you."

She hesitated, as if about to say something, then decided against it. She turned away from him and started walking back towards the square. He realised he had no idea where in the village he was, no idea how to get back to the farm even if he wanted to.

When she was twenty yards away, she turned. "Sit tight," she called. "Stay in the flat. And lock your door."

CHAPTER SEVEN

Sarah sat against her bedroom door, listening to the voices downstairs. Ted had been irritable when she and Dawn came in, snapping about the fact that his lunch wasn't ready and the house was cold. Dawn had fussed about his shoulder but he'd pushed her away. So she'd slipped into her usual mode of attempting to reach him through his stomach. They couldn't be too fussy about food here, not with the rationing and the limitations on power. Soup, made from carrots grown in the allotments, wouldn't have been Ted's preferred meal. But he'd learned to live with it.

Sarah had slipped upstairs as soon as she and Dawn had finished the washing up, anxious to get away from her father. And she was tired. She'd spent over an hour lying on her bed, blinking up at the ceiling, thinking about Dawn, and Sam, and Martin. She didn't understand why her mother was trying to hook her up with Sam. Dawn needed her here, to help ward off Ted's moods.

Now they were talking about the village council. It would be meeting in the morning to rule on whether

Martin could be allowed to stay in the village. Ted would fight Jess's decision hard.

But where was Martin now? He deserved to know that his future was in the balance.

She closed the door and crept to the window. It was set into the eaves, with a sloping roof she could jump off.

She reached into her wardrobe for a warm sweater. Her coat was downstairs, on the hook by the door. She would have to do without.

Wrapped up in the sweater and two scarves, she opened the window. Cold air blew in; it had stopped raining but the evening was a bitter one, with a harsh wind coming in off the sea. She wrapped the scarves more tightly around her neck.

She pushed the window as wide as it would go then felt outside, her fingers searching for a place to stand or sit. There was a flat section immediately below the window. It would be somewhere to start.

She took her book from the chair next to her bed and put it on the bed. She picked up the chair and placed it under the window.

She stepped back and put one foot on the chair, then the other. She was next to the window now, nothing between her and the drop.

Downstairs, she heard Ted's voice raised.

"I'm going to bed."

She stared at the door. He never checked on her, but tonight, after everything that had happened…

Quickly, she closed the window and stepped down from the chair. She pushed it back to its spot and dived under her duvet, pulling it up to her neck. She lay there, watching the door, her heart pounding.

The window swung open. She hadn't secured it. She heard footsteps making their way up the stairs.

Did she have time?

The footsteps arrived outside her door. No. She could claim she wanted fresh air while she slept.

The footsteps stopped. She imagined her father outside, listening. She bit her lip.

The window swung to and fro, rattling softly. She stared at it, her heart pounding. *Shut up*.

There was a creak from outside the door, then another door opening and closing. He'd gone to his and Dawn's room.

She put her hand on her chest, breathing heavily. She was no good at this.

She pushed back the duvet and crossed to the window. With Ted in bed, Dawn would be sitting in the living room, staring out to sea through the darkened glass doors. She went into a kind of trance at this time of night, as if reaching into herself for the will to go up and join her husband in bed.

She wouldn't notice Sarah leaving via the front door.

She closed the window, checking the catch, and padded to her bedroom door. She leaned on it for a moment, listening. Nothing.

She turned the handle and pushed the door open, peering into the dark hallway. No light filtered up the stairs; Dawn was sitting in darkness.

At the bottom of the stairs, she grabbed her coat and opened the front door. She slipped outside and pulled the door behind her, twisting the handle to make it close silently. Her key was still in the pocket of her skirt; by the time she returned, both Dawn and Ted would be asleep.

She surveyed the village square. The only light was from a half moon shrouded by fast-moving clouds. Lights-out was hours ago and not one house was illuminated.

Where would he be? In the JP, maybe? At Ruth and Ben's house again?

No. Last time Martin had slept there, he had taken Ruth in the night.

She headed for the JP. The pub was dark, no sign of movement through the windows. She leaned on the glass, trying to make out shapes.

"Sarah?"

She turned to see a shape heading towards her. She closed her eyes, searching for a story. An excuse for being out here at night.

"Sarah, what are you doing out?"

"Sam?"

He joined her next to the window. His eyes were hooded and he looked puzzled.

"What are you doing here?" she asked him.

"Can't sleep. Thought I'd take a walk. You?"

"Looking for my cat."

She cast around them as if searching for the creature she knew was curled up on a chair at home.

"Is that wise?" Sam asked. "Zack told me you were out looking for it when they took you."

She resisted the urge to tell him not to pry. "He's probably over by our house. See you in the morning."

She started walking.

"Can I help you?"

She turned. "No. No, its fine. Look, there he is." She turned towards her house. "Snowy!" she hissed.

"Where?" he asked. The cat was all-white and would have been distinctive in the darkness.

"He's gone round the side of our house. Probably trying to get in."

"Oh."

She gave him a smile. "Thanks, then. See you around."

He looked dejected. *Don't be hard on him*, she told herself. *It's not his fault.*

"You're working tomorrow, right?" she asked.

"Yes."

"You need your sleep then. Maybe I'll see you when you get back."

His face brightened. She cursed herself for leading him on but held her ground. "See you tomorrow."

"Yes," he said. "Yes, of course."

She watched him run away, towards the northern edge of the village. He must live over there, with Zack.

If Martin wasn't in the JP, then maybe Jess had put him up at her house. She had plenty of space, after all. Jess lived in the last house before you reached the main road, as far from the centre of the village as possible. Sarah's family lived in the big houses overlooking the cliffs, the houses allocated to council members, handy for the village square and community centre. Jess still hadn't moved out of the house where her mother had died, before Jess was elected. Not long after the Dyer family had arrived here.

Sarah squared her shoulders and set off along the Parade.

CHAPTER EIGHT

DAWN WATCHED THE DARK CLOUDS FLOWING ACROSS THE sky out to sea. It was windy tonight; mild by the standards of this coastline but a howler compared to the breezes where she'd grown up in Somerset.

She could hear Ted moving around above her, his heavy tread unmistakable. She always knew who was on the move in this house, who was coming down the stairs and who was entering the room. Sarah's footsteps were light and quick; she tried to disguise them but Dawn could always hear. Ted's, by contrast, were heavy and slow. He would lumber down the stairs each morning, prolonging the agony of anticipation as she waited for him to appear in the kitchen.

It was only when Ted was angry that his gait changed. His steps would lighten and he would be fast, nimble even. She dreaded the sound of that tread.

Beneath the creak of Ted's footsteps, Dawn heard a second, lighter tread, so pale as to almost be a whisper. Sarah, coming down the stairs. This was how she sounded when Ted was in one of his moods; wary, hesitant. Scared.

Dawn drew in breath then held still, listening. The sound stopped as Sarah reached the bottom of the stairs. Dawn pictured the girl watching her, waiting to speak. She prepared herself for conversation.

Sarah didn't head her way. Instead, she pulled the front door open and slid outside. Dawn listened, her heart pounding, as her daughter eased the door closed again.

She turned. The door was closed. Everything was as it had been except for Sarah's coat missing from its peg.

There was a creak above her head; Ted falling into bed. She swallowed the lump in her throat. She would wait half an hour, as always. Until she heard his first snores.

She went to the hallway, running her fingers through the coats. She eased the door open. Outside, Sarah was crossing the square.

She toyed with the idea of running after her daughter, calling her back. But people would see. How many of them were watching Sarah from their darkened windows?

She closed the door again. Sarah would return in her own time. She wasn't stupid.

"What's going on? Why are you going outside?"

She turned to see Ted at the top of the stairs, rubbing his eyes with his good arm. His sling was tangled and spotted with blood. It made her feel queasy.

"Ted! You startled me. I was just locking up for the night. Go back to bed, please."

He rumbled down the stairs, almost tripping in his haste. She pulled back.

"What is it?" He yanked the front door open and stared outside. Dawn held her breath. There were a few seconds of agony as he stared onto the square, then relief as he closed the door.

He turned to her. "What's going on?"

"Nothing. I was locking up."

"I already locked up. I always lock up. You know that."

"I was just checking."

"You saying I didn't do it properly?"

"Of course not."

He pushed past her into the kitchen. He grabbed a glass and turned the tap on, splashing water on his sling. Then he leaned against the counter and took a long drink. Dawn watched, resisting an itch to look towards the door, to check that Sarah wasn't returning.

Ted slammed the glass on the counter and marched to the stairs. "Sarah! Sarah, get down here!"

Dawn stepped in behind him. "Don't wake her, Ted. Not tonight. Not after everything she's been through."

He turned, his eyes dark. His greying hair was messed up from being in bed and a strand leapt up from the top of his head.

"You're acting strange. She'll tell me why."

"She won't. She—"

He raised his hand and she flinched. "Thought I was asleep, didn't you?" His eyes widened. "Were you out there with that boy?"

He tugged the front door open. Dawn tried to look over his shoulder; there were no sounds coming from the square.

He slammed the door shut. "Where is that girl?"

Dawn put a hand on his arm. "Please Ted, just calm down. She needs her sleep."

He shrugged her off and bounded up the stairs, his footsteps light. He flung open Sarah's door, the first one at the top.

Dawn squeezed her eyes shut.

Ted disappeared into Sarah's room then emerged. Dawn couldn't see his face; he was nothing but a dark shadow at the top of the stairs. But she could imagine his expression.

"Where is she?"

He thundered down the stairs. Dawn stumbled back into the living room. She hit the back of the sofa and all but fell over it. Ted followed her.

"Where is she?"

"I—I don't know."

He leaned in. His eyes gleamed and spittle ringed his mouth. "Tell me!"

He rounded the sofa and grabbed the jug of flowers she'd placed there two days ago, while he was gone. She normally kept the surfaces free of anything sharp or heavy. She cursed herself for not removing it when he returned.

He turned the jug upside down and shook it out. The flowers fell to the floor in a spray of water. Ted raised the jug and wielded it over his head. His eyes were bright with pain and anger.

"Tell me!"

"She went outside. I heard her. I don't know why—" Dawn's voice was shrill.

"Why didn't you stop her?"

She shook her head. Her body felt cold, like she had frostbite, all sensation in her fingers and toes gone. "I—I don't know. I'm sorry."

He dropped the jug and stepped towards her. She backed away. He grabbed her wrist and pulled her towards him.

"There," he breathed. "That's better. Tell me the truth, Dawn."

She closed her eyes. She knew better than to meet his gaze when he was like this.

"Maybe she was looking for Snowy," she suggested.

Ted pointed towards the living room. "That cat there, on the sofa?"

Dawn felt her chest dip. "Oh."

Ted glared at her. She shrank back, not meeting his stare. After a few moments, he dropped her arm. He turned and yanked his coat from its peg, thrusting his good arm into a sleeve. He draped the other side of it over his shoulder.

"You stay here. I'm going after her."

CHAPTER NINE

SARAH STRODE ALONG THE PARADE, HER EYES ON THE BEND in the road where it led out of the village to the outside world.

It was a route that scared and fascinated her in equal measure.

She'd lived here for almost six years, since she was thirteen and the floods had forced her family from its home in Somerset. She had vague memories of a cottage by a stream, of being nestled against a hillside, hidden away from the world.

Here, she was just as hidden. Not only from the world outside the village, but from the village itself. Ted made sure of that.

And she would never leave the family home, never abandon her mother. Dawn had to know that. All her efforts with Sam were an irrelevance.

Tonight, for the first time since arriving five years ago, she walked towards the village entrance. She slid along the Parade, the main artery of their village, imagining people watching her through their windows. The village was quiet and dark; power was rationed here, like everything else, and lights-out had long since passed. And the people who lived here needed their sleep in preparation for the hard physical work they would be doing in the morning. Tending livestock; digging the allotments; baking bread; smoking fish.

Her steps felt heavy, as if she was being pushed back. She glanced from side to side, checking for movement in the darkened windows. An owl hooted somewhere and she nearly jumped out of her skin.

But she had to know how much involvement Martin had in the plan to snatch her. He'd pretended to be something he wasn't – her rescuer, her knight in shining armour. He'd helped her escape from the farm, and they'd fled together to the beach. But then he'd told her that he'd played a part in taking her. She struggled to reconcile that version of him with the one who had screamed out his love for her and thrown himself on Robert in the farmhouse kitchen, claiming he was defending her.

She had to understand. She had to know what he'd done voluntarily, and what he'd been forced to do. After that, he could leave the village. His presence only led to trouble.

She kept to the shadows and tucked her arms in at her sides, trying to be as inconspicuous as possible. When she heard a scraping sound, she ducked into the shadow of a bush.

"Sarah!" a voice hissed.

She looked back. The road was empty.

"Sarah! Up here!"

She pulled out of the shadows and looked up. A head was poking out of a first floor window above her.

"Shush," she hissed.

"Were you looking for me?"

She frowned; the arrogance. But he was right.

"Yes."

"Wait a minute."

The window closed and he disappeared. Moments later, a door opened below it. The tall, willowy shape of the man who'd abducted her, then helped her escape.

Her stomach contracted.

"Quick, come inside," he whispered.

It was too late to back out now. She approached the door, waiting for him to move out of her way. He obliged, disappearing up a flight of stairs ahead of her. She followed, half intrigued and half terrified.

No one knew she was here.

The flat's main room was lit by a solitary candle. It flickered off the walls, casting ghoulish shadows that only heightened her sense of dread.

"They put you in here," she said.

He gestured around the room, as if welcoming her to his luxurious home. "Just for one night. Then they decide if I can stay."

She nodded but said nothing. There was a small table in one corner and two hard chairs. She took one of them.

Martin took the other one, at right angles to her. She shifted away, the chair legs scraping against the wooden floor. She wondered who lived in the flat below.

"Will you vouch for me?" he asked. "Tell them I helped you get out?"

"I don't know."

Sarah had never even been to a village meeting, let alone a council meeting. The thought of standing in front of them, her father among them, filled her with dread.

"It would help, you know. Only if you want me to stay though."

"I don't know."

He nodded. "I understand."

She sniffed. How long before she could leave? But then she remembered; she'd come here for a reason.

"What happened, the night you took me?" she said.

"Sorry?"

"You heard. I want to know it all."

"Oh." He rubbed his nose. "Of course you do." He placed his hands on the table, fingers laced together. They were long and pale. He huddled over them. She leaned back in her chair.

He spotted her unease and withdrew his hands, placing them on his lap. She made herself relax, wondering if he could hear her heartbeat.

"Where do you want me to start?" he said.

"At the beginning."

"The distress signal?"

"No. Before that. When you agreed to take part."

"I didn't have much choice."

"Everyone has a choice."

"Sarah, you have to understand. Robert Cope, he had a hold over me. I owed him."

"You owed him? What for?"

"He—he helped me, after the floods." He shifted his weight; she watched him, unforgiving. "You know that. I owed him."

"I can't believe you got yourself indebted to that man."

"I know. But it's like I told you after we escaped. He saved me. From those kids who beat me up, took my ruck-sack. If it wasn't for Robert, I'd probably have died."

"Did that sort of thing happen to you a lot, on the

road?" She felt cold, pricked by her own memories of the floods and their aftermath.

Martin bowed his head. "Nothing like that. I managed to get as far north as Lincoln, before that happened. After that, things were OK. Safety in numbers. And then he told me that if I helped him with this mission, I wouldn't be in his debt anymore."

"*Mission*? That's what you called it?"

"That's what he called it. Not me."

"It's the word you just used."

"Sorry."

"Go on."

His Adam's apple bobbed in the candle light as he swallowed. "He didn't tell me much. Said there was a village, north of us. A family there, that he knew, from before. He said the man had lied about him to the police. That he'd gone to prison."

"And you trusted him, despite knowing he'd been in prison?"

"He said it wasn't his fault. It was this man's fault. That he should have been the one arrested."

"And you believed him."

"I had no reason not to."

"So what did he tell you to do?"

"We'd found a trawler, washed up to the south. Near Hull. A couple of the men knew their way around boats, they'd got it working."

She looked towards the door. "Get to the point."

"Sorry. We were going to go out in it, raise a distress signal. Get ourselves brought to the village."

"And then?"

"Then one of us had to take Ruth. Just Ruth, that's all I knew about."

"Why should I believe that?"

"Its up to you, Sarah. Believe me, or don't. I won't lie to you."

"So why was it you who took her?"

"It was supposed to be Robert. Maybe Bill. But I was closer, in the end."

"Ruth and Ben took you in, after you fell in the sea."

Martin rested his hands on the table again. Sarah didn't move.

"Ruth was kind to me," he said. "She treated me for my hypothermia, gave me a comfortable bed. Clothes. Food. You have no idea how I—"

"I get it. So why didn't you stop at Ruth? What about the rest of us?"

He slumped in his chair. "I don't know. Maybe they planned it, maybe they didn't. But I knew nothing about it until we were on the boat. I promise you."

She stood up. "So you think that exonerates you? That it's fine to do that to Ruth, even if it isn't to the rest of us?"

"No. I wish I could go back, Sarah. I really do. I wish to God I'd never got involved."

She shook her head and headed for the door. She'd heard enough. Tomorrow he would be judged, and she wouldn't be there to vouch for him. Never mind that he'd helped her get away from them. Never mind what he'd told her he felt for her.

"Goodbye, Martin."

"Sarah, please—"

She ignored him and trudged down the stairs. Her feet felt heavy. She was home now, but she had the memory of all that had happened to deal with. She had her mother's insistence on Sam to dismiss.

She pulled open the outer door. Outside, a figure was standing in the road, looking up at Martin's window.

She pulled inside and closed the door. "He's found us."

"Who?"

"My dad."

Martin backed up the stairs. "Shit."

She clenched her fists. Why had she crept out? Coming here had been pointless. She'd known what he was going to tell her, in her heart. He was bad news, and she'd been mad to ever think otherwise.

"You have to hide," Martin said. "He can't find you here."

The door rattled behind her. She felt her legs turn to lead.

"Sarah! Martin! Are you in there?"

Martin stopped at the top of the stairs. "That isn't Ted."

She sighed. "It's Sam."

"Who's Sam?"

"Long story. Be quiet, and he'll leave us alone."

She imagined what Sam would be thinking, standing outside, watching the window. The flickering candle, her alone up here with Martin.

It didn't matter. Sam didn't matter.

"I'll get rid of him," she said. "I'm going."

She opened the door again. Sam fell through.

"Sam, what are you doing here?"

He righted himself, glancing up at Martin. She sensed Martin shifting from foot to foot above her.

"Your dad's on the warpath."

"You've been spying on us."

"No. I was worried about you, when I saw you outside the JP. I went back, I saw him leave your house."

"How did you find me?"

He blushed. "I heard Jess talking to my brother."

She pushed him aside. Despite his bulk, he moved easily. "Don't follow me, Sam. I'm going home."

If Ted was out looking for her, she could slip into the house without him seeing. She had her key. And she had her lightness, her quietness.

"Sarah!"

She turned to see both young men standing in the doorway. She hissed at them to be quiet.

She ran for home, not caring what they thought.

CHAPTER TEN

THE NEXT MORNING, MARTIN SAT IN HIS BARE FLAT AND waited. Sarah didn't want him here, so there was no reason to stay. But he felt he owed it to Jess to at least wait for the outcome of the council meeting.

The only food in the cupboard was a half-empty tin of biscuits. He'd worked his way through most of them in the night, struggling to sleep. Now he polished the rest off. Robert had told him that the villagers were self-sufficient, which meant someone had baked these biscuits. Did they know they'd been left here? He suddenly felt guilty for eating them.

He'd lost his watch years ago and there was no clock in this flat, so he couldn't be sure what time it was or how long he'd been awake. Judging by the low sun hitting the houses opposite, it was about eight o'clock.

He thought of the look on Sarah's face last night, when she'd thought Ted was outside. He fingered the plaster on his chin, already curling at the edges. Did Ted ever do that to her?

He took one last look out of the window. Two men

passed, deep in conversation. One carried a garden fork and the other a wooden crate which looked heavy.

He came to a decision.

He waited for the men to pass, then unlocked the door and slipped downstairs, keeping quiet in case of curious neighbours.

He headed towards the village square. Sarah's house was that way; he'd watched her run off last night. And if Ted was a member of the village council, then he probably had one of the large houses that looked out to sea, on the same row as Ben and Ruth.

Ben and Ruth. He pushed down a pang of guilt.

He ran as stealthily as he could, passing under an archway next to a pub, his mouth watering at the thought of freshly-pulled ale. He found himself in an open space and remembered watching Robert and Bill walk across it, the morning before they took the women. He'd been standing in the doorway to Ruth and Ben's house, after they'd taken him in because of his hypothermia.

There was no sign of movement at their house. He scanned all the house fronts, looking for clues. The houses were identical, all having solid front doors and no windows facing the front. They'd be at the back, for the views. This had been a holiday village once and views were everything.

A door opened. He pulled back into the shadows, watching. The air was still, the sea beyond the cliff the only sound.

A woman emerged. She was in her early fifties, wearing a pink cardigan over blue trousers and an old-fashioned floral blouse.

Sarah's mum. He remembered her from the pharmacy.

He darted forwards.

"Hello."

Her eyes widened.

"Can you tell me where Sarah is please?"

She looked from side to side. "You can't be here!"

He approached her, being careful not to get too close. Her face was heavily lined and she had purple marks under her eyes. Tiredness, or bruises?

"We met in the pharmacy. Yesterday."

She stiffened. "Go. Now, please. Go."

She looked up at the house behind her.

"I just want to speak to her. Before they tell me to leave."

She folded her arms across her chest. "As well they should."

She took another look around the square then pulled the door closed behind her. "I shouldn't be talking to you."

"Is she in there?"

She squared her shoulders. "If she is, she's not coming out." A pause. "My husband's in there too. He did that to you, didn't he?"

He touched his chin. "Nothing I didn't deserve."

"Sarah's asleep. I suggest you go."

"Let me say goodbye to her first."

"She's not interested in you. She's engaged."

Sarah had said nothing about this. But then, she hadn't had much chance to speak, after he'd answered her questions.

"Engaged? To who?"

"None of your business." She pulled the door open just a crack and took a step backwards.

"Tell me who she's engaged to and I'll leave you alone."

Her eyes were hard now, glinting in the low sunlight. "Sam Golder."

"I met him."

"When?"

"Last night. When I… nothing. He seems nice."

"He is. Quiet. Dependable."

"In that case, I won't cause any trouble. Tell her I said goodbye."

She said nothing. He stared at her for a few moments, breathing heavily. He felt like his legs had been ripped from under him.

"Go on then."

He turned for the clifftop and started walking. He'd rather take the long route than be spotted in the village.

CHAPTER ELEVEN

Dawn slid back into the house, hoping no one had heard her talking to Martin. Ted had arrived home two hours after storming out the previous night, Harry with him. Harry, it seemed, had calmed him down.

Sarah had slunk back while he was out and crept up to bed. With Harry's help, Dawn had persuaded Ted to leave her to sleep, to wait until morning to punish her.

Poor girl. Dawn had no idea what she'd been through at the hands of those men, and her own father wanted to hurt her too.

And now this man, little more than a boy, was turning up on their doorstep, asking for her like he was a gentleman caller picking up his date.

His face had fallen when she'd told him about Sam. *Good.* Martin was bad for Sarah. Sam was what she needed.

She clicked the door shut. Someone was stirring upstairs; Sarah.

Dawn hurried to the kitchen and started slicing bread, anxious to look busy. As she sawed the bread knife to and fro, she heard Sarah's light steps cross to the living room behind her. The girl was holding her breath.

She paused in her slicing. The steps paused too. She continued slicing.

She heard the back door open. She spun round. Sarah was sliding it open, her eyes on Dawn. When she spotted her mother watching, she slammed the door open and threw herself outside.

Dawn ran to follow her. She pushed the door aside and reached out to grab her daughter's wrist.

"Where are you going?"

"I heard you. Talking to Martin." Sarah pulled away but Dawn's grip was strong.

"Stay here. Don't be stupid." She lowered her voice. "Your dad's livid as it is."

Sarah stopped pulling. "I want to know if they've decided to let him stay."

"Council can't have met yet, can it? Your dad's still in bed. He wouldn't miss that."

"I still need to speak to him."

Dawn tugged harder, pulling Sarah halfway through the open door. "Not yet. Wait. You need to be here when your dad wakes up."

Sarah looked towards the staircase. She curled her lip.

"Don't get on his bad side, love."

Sarah shook free of her grip. "I'll stay here, for you."

"Good."

Sarah stepped inside. She shivered and clasped her arms around herself. She was wearing a jumper Dawn had knitted for her last winter, and a striped scarf with unraveled ends.

"Come into the kitchen. I've got eggs boiling. Warm you up."

"Thanks."

Dawn gave her daughter a feeble smile then returned to the kitchen. Those eggs would be hard by now.

She heard Ted's heavy tread on the stairs and tensed. She carried on with her business, pretending she hadn't heard him.

"Morning," he said as he pulled back a chair. He'd lost the sling and was using his injured arm, his hands both on the table. Dawn stared at it: *so dirty*.

"Morning," muttered Sarah. She was at the chair opposite him, chewing a slice of bread.

Dawn smiled at her husband, trying to conceal her fear. She looked at Sarah; the girl had her head bowed, her almost-white hair brushing the table.

"Sit up straight, girl," Ted snapped. "That's unhygienic."

Dawn, her back to them as she lifted eggs out of the pan, heard Sarah's chair scrape on the floor as she shifted her weight. She waited, spoon in mid air.

"I've got council this morning," he muttered. "Getting rid of that bloody boy. I expect you to be here when I get back."

Silence. Dawn transferred one of the eggs to a plate and buttered some bread. Movement would calm her nerves.

"Speak to me!"

"Yes, Dad."

"Yes, Dad what?"

"I'll be here. When you get back."

"Good. Now, go up to your room. And stay there."

Dawn listened to Sarah retreat to the stairs and head up to her room. She closed her door just a touch more forcefully than she should have.

Ted grunted. "Where's those eggs?"

Dawn placed his plate on the table, her head bowed.

CHAPTER TWELVE

SARAH OPENED THE WINDOW AGAIN, WONDERING IF SHE dared climb out in daylight. There were no houses behind theirs, nothing but the clifftop and the sea beyond. But Ted might come round this way for some reason, checking on her maybe. Or one of the neighbours might look out of their window.

Maybe she could slip out when Ted had gone, make sure she was back when he returned. Or maybe she should stay where she was. If Ted found her gone, he would only take his anger out on her mother.

She leaned out of the window, taking great gulps of air. Being in this house made her claustrophobic. It was as if the air pressure was two bars higher than outside, and the temperature five degrees hotter.

Dawn wanted her to fly the nest, to be with Sam. She couldn't do that. She couldn't leave her mother alone with him.

She pulled back, glad of the scarf, and listened to the birds wheeling above the clifftop. She envied them their freedom. To ride on the wind, only needing to land for food. That would be the life.

She frowned as she heard an unfamiliar sound. A car engine. No, two.

No one in this village had a car. There weren't the resources. Fuel was scarce and they didn't have a mechanic. Sam and Zack got a lift on a works truck down to the earthworks every morning.

So whose cars were they?

She leaned further out of the window, trying to see around the house and cursing the fact that her window was at the back.

This house had just one window facing the village; a high one over the stairs.

She eased her door open, listening for her parents' voices. They were quiet. She crept out, heading for the stairs. She leaned over the top steps, placing her palms on the windowsill.

At this angle, she couldn't see down to the road. But she could see lights reflecting off the buildings opposite.

Blue lights.

She shrank back, almost falling down the stairs. She leaped back towards her bedroom as her father crossed the bottom of the stairs and opened the front door.

She slid into her room and held the door open. Her heart felt like it might escape from her rib cage.

"Can I help you?" Ted sounded impatient. "I take it you've spoke to our steward."

She heard another voice; a woman. She couldn't make out the words. Something about *authority*?

"You got a warrant?"

More words. There were two voices now; the other a man, older.

"I think we should let them in." Her mother was

behind her father, at the door. She had a tentative hand on his back.

Ted turned to his wife. "Leave it to me."

The woman took the opportunity to push the door further open. "Your wife's right, sir. It would be easier if we could come inside."

Sarah pushed her door further closed, leaving it open just a crack. How long before they summoned her?

And where was Martin?

"Thank you, Sir. Madam. Mr and Mrs Evans, is that correct?"

"Yes." Her father, his voice sharp.

"Can we all sit down, please?"

Dawn muttered something and there was the sound of feet shuffling into the living room. Sarah wondered how her mother would be feeling about all those shoes on her carpet.

She opened her door a fraction wider. The voices were muted now, further away.

She looked back at the window. If she climbed out, they would see her through the rear windows. She was trapped.

Movement again; the rustling of heavy jackets and footsteps muffled by carpet. Then more voices as the two police officers returned to the hallway.

"We would like to speak to everyone who was at the farm. To get a clear picture of what happened, and who was involved. I assume your injury was sustained there?"

"None of your business," said Ted.

"Of course," said Dawn.

"So when your daughter comes home, you'll be sure to let us know, won't you?"

"How?" Ted's voice.

'I'm sorry?"

"We don't have no phone. How will we contact you?"

"Oh, we'll be around the village for a while yet. House to house. You'll find us."

Ted grunted.

"Mr Evans?"

"Yes," said Ted. "We'll find you."

Sarah heard the door being opened and closed. She leaned back against the wall, her nerves on fire.

CHAPTER THIRTEEN

She waited five minutes — an agonising count to three hundred — then ran down the stairs.

"Sarah!" Her father was in the kitchen. He came towards her.

She turned to Dawn. "Where did he go, Mum? Where is he?"

Dawn cast Ted a worried look. "I don't know what you're talking about, love."

"We need a word," said her father. "The police want to talk to you."

"What's this about a murder?" Dawn asked.

She felt ice run down her back. "A murder?"

"They're making enquiries," said her father. "A murder investigation."

Her hands felt cold, and her feet leaden. "Not the kidnappings?"

"They said nothing about that. Murder, is what they said." He advanced on her. "You should never have brought him here."

She backed into the wall. "No! No, they've got it

wrong. It was Robert. He took us. He got the others to…"

Her parents were staring at her. They were never going to believe what Martin had told her. She wasn't sure if she did herself.

But killing Robert hadn't been murder. It was self-defence. It was mercy.

She pulled open the door. "Mum? Which way? Which way did he go?"

Her mother shook her head at her. Tears rolled down her face. "Forget him, love. He's left."

Sarah shrieked in frustration then hurled herself through the door.

Outside, the blue lights still flashed off the house fronts, providing a contrast to the yellow-green clouds that hung over them. The air felt charged, as if electricity was running through her veins.

Two uniformed policemen stood in front of one of the houses, waiting. Clyde stood outside the JP, gawping. Clyde was the landlord and also the custodian of the village boat. It was he who had brought them all home.

A small crowd had gathered around him, watching.

She glared at them. This was supposed to be a community. They pulled together. They didn't stare at each others' troubles.

The road out of the village was blocked by a police car. Would Martin have gone that way? Would they have seen him?

She caught movement to her left. The door to Ruth and Ben Dyer's house opening. A woman in a grey suit walked out. The woman who'd been in her own living room, minutes before?

Behind her followed Ruth. Her head was bowed and she wore a torn T-shirt over a pair of faded jeans. Her hair was dishevelled and she had no socks on under her thin shoes. A uniformed policewoman followed her, her hand on Ruth's shoulder.

An older man came after them, dressed in a dark suit and coat, and a tie that was far too bright for the circumstances. Ben trailed him, shouting.

Sarah collapsed to the ground. She watched, open mouthed, as they guided Ruth to one of the police cars. A door was opened — a rear door — and Ruth was ushered inside, a hand on her head. The door was closed behind her. Ben ran at it, pounding it with his fists.

The policewoman turned and pulled Ben away. The female detective spoke to him. He let out a groan then his body slumped, like a marionette with its strings cut.

The male detective got into the car. It headed up the Parade, passing Clyde and the shocked group of villagers.

She had to get to Martin. They had to be told the truth.

There were plenty of places to hide. Houses, trees, thickets of heather. He would have seen their lights before they could have seen him.

He *would* be hiding, though. He would have stopped moving.

Which meant she could catch up with him. She could find him.

CHAPTER FOURTEEN

MARTIN CROUCHED BEHIND A WOODEN HUT AT THE EDGE OF what seemed to be an allotment. Wooden and tin structures dotted the space, along with crates full of compost. Rows of perfectly arranged vegetables spread out around him; carrots, leeks, parsnips, cabbages. It reminded him of his childhood, his grandmother's insistence on self sufficiency. As if the 1953 floods, her obsession, hadn't taught her that crops could be wiped out in a heartbeat.

He'd spotted the police lights as he'd left the centre of the village behind. There were plenty of houses that would have sheltered him, but he didn't want to risk being seen by their inhabitants. The allotment was empty.

The village was quiet now, the police cars having passed him, heading towards the coast.

Had they gone to Sarah's house?

He stood up, not caring who saw him now. He picked his way across the rows of vegetables, careful not to trample them.

The Parade, the village's central artery, was two streets away. He sprinted towards it, not stopping to consider what might happen when he got there. He had to keep Sarah out of trouble.

He passed a row of terraced houses and spotted a man watching him out of a downstairs window. The man was balding and wore a greying vest. He looked irritated.

Martin threw him a wave, hoping that might convince the man that he belonged here. He carried on running.

He rounded the houses and crashed into someone coming the other way.

It was a woman, slim and blonde. She was in a heap on the pavement, clutching her foot.

"Sarah?"

She looked up.

"Martin! You haven't left."

"No. Well, yes. But then I saw the police. I was coming back, to make sure they didn't…"

She stood up and brushed off her skirt. She poked her foot then shook it out, seemingly satisfied. "You thought they'd arrest me?" she said.

"No. I didn't know…"

"Why would they arrest me, Martin?"

"I don't know. I wasn't thinking straight. I…"

"They'd only arrest me if they thought I had some connection to you."

"D'you think they know? I mean, d'you think they'd think that?"

She sighed. "I don't know. I don't know anything anymore."

A car approached, heading out of the village. Martin grabbed Sarah's arm to pull her out of sight, then let go. She didn't acknowledge the contact.

They watched round the corner of the house. It felt as if the car was going at one mile per hour, so long did it take to be out of sight. A man and a woman were inside, in the front seats. The back seat was empty.

Martin felt his stomach clench.

"Why have they gone?"

Sarah turned to him. "Didn't you see the last car?"

"No."

"They've arrested Ruth."

He pushed down memories of the encounter in the farmhouse kitchen. Robert holding a knife to Sarah's face. The fear in her eyes…

"Are you alright?" she asked.

He frowned. "Yes. Why?"

"You suddenly went very pale."

He fingered his cheeks. "Sorry. I've got to get back, tell them the truth."

"What truth?"

He eyed her. 'You know what truth. It's me they should be arresting."

"You were protecting me. All of us."

"Ruth doesn't deserve to get the blame."

"Even though she finished him off?"

He stepped back. "Sarah. It wasn't like that. You know that."

She pulled her hands through her hair. Martin wondered if that man would be watching again, from his window.

"I'm not myself," she said. "It's my dad."

"Has he hurt you?"

Her eyes went to his chin. The plaster had fallen off; he had no idea how the wound looked.

"No," she said. "There's been a lot of shouting, though. A lot of posturing."

"He's only trying to protect you."

"He's got a funny way of showing it."

He looked past her, towards the village centre. "Look, I don't think you should come with me."

"No."

"Good. You wait here, and I'll go on ahead. Unless you want to get safely home first?"

"I mean *no*. Don't go back. They'll kill you."

"I have to go to the police, Sarah. I can't be responsible for Ruth."

"That doesn't mean you have to face the village." She paused. "I've got a better idea. I'll talk to them. I'll tell them what he did to me. That Ruth was defending me. Jess will back me up."

"She wasn't there. Not for all of it."

"She'll back me up, Martin. I got the feeling she knew what Robert was like, better than any of us. And she'll want her sister-in-law home."

"And what about me? What will you tell them about me? They'll ask you about the abduction."

"It wasn't you who took me."

"This is dumb. You can't do this."

"I can, Martin. If you're a part of this, it'll make my dad so much worse. Trust me. Carry on walking. Get out of here."

She hesitated for a second, searching his face, then turned and ran. He watched until she was out of sight, hating himself. How could he let her do this?

He retreated into the shadow of the houses, not taking his eyes off the spot where Sarah had disappeared. Was she right? Was it better for everyone if he didn't get involved? Or was she lying, to protect him?

Don't be stupid. Why would she want to protect you?

He sighed and picked his way back across the allotment. At its far end was a wood, and then the road south.

He stopped next to a wooden shed, its door hanging open.

He couldn't leave her. Not like this. But he had to do what she told him.

He slid into the shed, checking no one had seen him. He closed the door and let himself slide to the ground, clutching his knees.

CHAPTER FIFTEEN

SARAH HURRIED BACK TO THE SQUARE. THERE WAS STILL A solitary police car: house to house. She scanned the buildings, trying to spot them. Would they go inside, or stay on doorsteps?

Maybe they were in one of the roads leading off the Parade, somewhere in the warren of streets and buildings.

"Sarah!"

Her father was standing outside their front door. He wore a shirt and thin trousers, and a frown so deep she felt it might eat her alive.

She looked behind him, into the doorway. *Mum?*

"Get in here, now!"

She took another look around the houses in hope of seeing the police officers. But the square was empty, fear having sent everyone indoors. She wondered what it had been like here after she and the others had been taken, how the village had reacted. Shocked, afraid, angry?

Did they blame her? Did they blame her family?

"I said, now!"

She took a deep breath and ran towards him. "No need to shout."

He raised his good arm as if to clip her round the head then thought better of it. She ducked past him into the house.

Inside, Dawn was sitting on the sofa, staring out to sea. The breakfast things had been washed up and cleared away and the kitchen table was as clean and empty as ever. Sarah felt a tug of guilt at not being around to help.

Ted slammed the door. "What the fuck are you thinking, running off like that!"

"Sorry." She cast a look at her mother, who continued staring ahead.

She felt a hand in her hair. She turned, flailing against it. Ted had her long hair by the roots and was pulling her towards the living room.

"Ow! Stop it! I'll come! I'll do what you want!"

Dawn turned, her mouth open. She inhaled but said nothing. Sarah threw her as reassuring a smile as she could manage. She tried not to look at the strands of hair on the carpet.

"Sit down." Ted jabbed his finger into her chest and pushed her onto the sofa, next to Dawn. She let herself fall.

Her mother's hands were clasped in her lap, her fingers twisting around each other. Ted gestured at them.

'Stop it, woman! It's bloody annoying!"

"Sorry." Dawn's voice was no more than a whisper.

Sarah looked up at her father. "You can't treat her like this. She's done nothing wrong."

Ted leaned forwards. He looked into Sarah's face. She stared back into his eyes, forcing herself not to blink.

Then he slapped her across the eyes.

She clapped a hand to her face and held in a shriek.

Dawn stood up. "Leave her!"

Dawn shifted to stand in front of Sarah. Sarah stared at her mother's back, trembling. Her father had never hit her before. He'd threatened to, plenty of times, but this was the first time he'd carried through.

She knew that the first time was like a locked door. Now it was open, she had no idea what to expect. She stood up, pushing Dawn out of the way.

The two women struggled, each vying to place herself between Ted and the other. He stood back and folded his arms across his chest, chuckling.

"What the fuck are you stupid women doing?"

He reached between them and shoved Dawn aside. She tumbled to a chair, her head hitting the wooden armrest. Sarah looked at her, panicked. Dawn raised her head. She wasn't cut, thank God.

Sarah swallowed the bile in her throat. "Please, Dad. I know I shouldn't have gone out. I'm sorry."

"Sorry?" his spit landed in her face and she resisted an ache to wipe it away. "Sorry is as sorry does, girl."

He jabbed at her again and sent her crashing onto the sofa. Then he grabbed her arm and yanked her off it and onto the floor. Her leg twisted beneath her and she landed on it awkwardly.

She fumbled on the floor. Her leg throbbed. She tried to move it, but it was stuck beneath her.

"Stop it!"

Dawn was in front of her again, her hands raised in front of her face. "You promised me you'd never touch her!"

He looked from Dawn to Sarah and back again. "That was before she decided to go gallivanting about with that bloody boy."

"She's not gallivanting, Ted. She went to see Sam."

"Sam?"

"Sam Golder. He's—"

"What the fuck has Sam Golder got to do with any of this?" He turned to Sarah, who was still twisted on the floor. She'd managed to get her leg out from under her and was trying to figure out how to pull herself upright. "And what are you doing seeing boys?"

"It's natural, Ted," pleaded Dawn. 'She deserves better than—"

"Better than what?" His eyes were blazing, bulging like they might explode. "Better than me?"

He balled his fist and struck Dawn across the jaw. She collapsed sideways, into the armchair. There was a crack as her head hit its arm.

"Mum!" Sarah shrieked. She was up on her feet, unaware of her own pain. "Mum!"

She turned to her father. She opened her mouth to speak. He cocked his head, challenging her. She closed her mouth.

Not now. Not yet.

She collapsed to the floor, muttering in her mother's ear. Ted cleared his throat loudly then slammed through the front door, leaving them in an aching silence.

CHAPTER SIXTEEN

Sarah was woken from her trance by someone pounding on the door.

"Is everything alright in there?"

She ushered their visitor inside: Jess.

"I heard shouting, then I saw Ted marching towards the JP. He looked like he'd swallowed a bee's nest. Are you OK?"

Sarah shook her head. She turned towards Dawn, lying crooked against the sofa.

"Oh my God." Jess went to Dawn's side. She lifted her arm and held her wrist, her eyes closed. "She's got a pulse."

Sarah's eyes widened. It hadn't occurred to her that she wouldn't.

Jess held Dawn's head in her lap. "But she's unconscious. What happened, Sarah?"

Sarah looked at her mother. How much should she say? What would Dawn say?

She took in a deep breath. "She fell."

"She fell? Just fell, like that?"

Sarah nodded. If she opened her mouth, she would scream until her lungs burst.

"What about the cut on her eyelid?"

Sarah squinted to look. Sure enough, Dawn had a small cut above her eye. It was starting to bleed. That was a good sign... wasn't it? Blood?

"I, I don't know. She must have got that earlier."

"Look, Sarah. It isn't for me to pry into your family's business. But you can talk to me, you know. You can trust me."

Sarah nodded, her lips clamped shut. The last thing her father would tolerate was for her to tell the steward their secrets.

Jess sighed. "Have it your way. But you might want to think of something to explain away the bruise you're going to have in the morning."

Sarah put her hand up to her face. The flesh to the side of her right eye stung. The pain in her ankle had come back now, but it didn't feel as if anything was broken. Just a twist, or a sprain.

Dawn blinked a few times, then opened her eyes. She looked at Jess, and her eyes widened. Her expression held more horror than when Ted had been attacking her.

"Jess," she murmured. "What are you doing here? Where's Ted?"

"He left. I'm just here to help Sarah get you to bed."

Dawn and Sarah exchanged glances. Dawn's face held remonstration, while Sarah tried to inject a plea into hers.

Jess stood up. "Come on then."

The two of them lifted Dawn to her feet. Her legs were weak and she could barely put weight on them. Sarah bit down on her lip, trying to shut out the pain in her ankle.

They half-dragged, half-carried Dawn to the stairs. Jess shifted Dawn's weight to take most of it.

"No," said Sarah. "Let me."

"She's light as air, and you're limping. I've got her."

Sarah trailed behind, taking Dawn's legs, as Jess hauled her mother up the stairs. Jess puffed out sharp breaths as she ascended, struggling in the confined space until they reached the top.

'Which room?"

"That one."

Jess backed into the door to Dawn and Ted's room. The room was gloomy and bare. They staggered through with Dawn between them. She made an involuntary noise every time she touched the doorframe, or the wall.

At last Dawn was on the bed. Sarah heaved the duvet out from under her and slid it over her. Dawn gave her a weak smile of thanks.

"Is she badly hurt?" asked Jess. "What did he do to her?"

Sarah lowered her eyes. "She isn't bleeding."

"That doesn't tell us anything. We need Ruth."

"Yes."

Jess closed her eyes. She looked tired. Sarah remembered that she'd walked forty miles to find her and the others who'd been taken, just a few days ago.

Jess eyed Sarah. "You know where she's gone?"

Sarah nodded. "I wanted to talk to you about that."

"I can imagine what you've got to say about things, but I don't want to hear it. I need to speak to the police, calm the village. It's not easy, being steward."

"Can I come and find you? I don't want to leave Mum right now, but I think I can help."

"Do you?" Jess replied.

"Yes."

"OK. Give me half an hour. I'll stall the police. If I can. You want to tell them something?"

"Yes."

"Right."

Jess gave Dawn one final worried look then left. Sarah listened as she hurried down the stairs and closed the door behind her.

"Mum? Can you hear me?"

Dawn opened her eyes. "Of course I can. Sit down here. Talk to your old mum."

"You're not so old."

"You know what I mean." She patted the bed next to her.

Sarah sat down, taking her mother's hand. "Does your head hurt?"

"Nothing that won't get better." She tried to smile. "Don't worry, love. I've had worse."

"I'm sorry."

"Don't be." Dawn closed her eyes. Sarah wondered if she was about to lose consciousness. She gripped her hand tighter.

"Ouch."

Sarah let go. Dawn opened her eyes.

"I'm sorry, love."

"It's not your fault."

"He's never hit you before."

Sarah lowered her eyes. He'd hit her mother, plenty of times.

Dawn continued. "I always promised myself that if he touched you…"

"Promised yourself what, Mum?"

Dawn closed her eyes. "Nothing. Things are too complicated, right now." She opened her eyes. "You need to stay out of trouble, love. Keep away from that boy."

"I know."

"And you need to get out of this house. You're a

woman now. You need a place of your own. I'm sure the council would give you and Sam that vacant flat."

Sarah dropped Dawn's hand. "Don't be ridiculous."

"Its not ridiculous, love. Sam's a good boy. Reliable, Even tempered. Safe. He's what you need."

"That's not what Dad thinks."

"He'll come round." Dawn looked into her eyes. "You know why you have to leave us. I can't have him hurting you again."

"Then why do you let him do it to you?"

"I don't have a lot of choice. Besides, your dad isn't as bad as all that."

"Mum."

"When you get to my age, you'll understand that life isn't all black and white." She paused. "I think you've had a bit of a taste of that lately, haven't you?"

Sarah felt herself blush.

"Well. Do the sensible thing. Talk to Sam. He's in love with you. He's got a job, of sorts, and a good family. He's what you need."

"I don't love him, Mum."

"And you do love this Martin boy?"

"That's not what I said."

"Stay away from him, Sarah." She squeezed her eyes shut. "He's a killer."

"No. No, he's not."

"I know his type, love. He's bad news."

"I'm not you."

Dawn's eyes sprang open. "That's not what I said."

Sarah held her gaze for a moment. Both women knew what her father was, but both were scared to give voice to it. But Martin wasn't Ted.

She stood up. She smoothed the duvet over her mother

then turned for the door. Jess had gone. The bedroom was entirely dark now; where had the day gone?

She walked into the hallway and looked at herself in the mirror. Her face was dimly lit from one side, through the window. Her hair was tangled and the skin under her eyes yellowing with a growing bruise. "He really isn't," she said to her reflection.

She closed the bedroom door and stumbled down the stairs. She needed to find Jess.

CHAPTER SEVENTEEN

Jess was standing at the door to Ben and Ruth's house. She reached into her pocket and put a key in the lock. Sarah had never known Ben and Ruth lock their door before.

"Jess! Stop!"

She looked round. Sarah approached her, glad the square was quiet. She could hear the dim roll of thunder behind her, inland.

"Sarah. You had something to tell me."

"Yes. It wasn't Ruth's fault."

"I saw what she did, Sarah. I have no idea how she's going to defend herself. We can't exactly afford a lawyer."

"You didn't see what happened before that. You came bursting in after my dad, when he was on the floor, fighting Robert. Right?"

"You were kneeling over him."

"I hadn't been."

"What do you mean, you hadn't been?"

"When Dad saw me, from the yard. I was sitting at the

table. With Ruth. Robert had a knife against my cheek. He moved it to my forehead. He cut me."

She lifted her hair to show the scar that she knew zagged across her forehead.

"That was you. Not Ruth."

"I was in the cell next to her. I heard him visiting her."

Jess's eyes widened. "He raped her?"

"No. But he was going to. He threatened her with it, all the time. Kept going on about Ben and how he was going to steal her from him. None of it made any sense."

"They knew each other at school. Things happened."

"I gathered that."

"So you think she's got a defence? He was going to rape her?"

"When they brought me and Martin back, she appeared from upstairs. I think he'd forced her up to his room. He wanted her to live with him. It was sick."

Jess looked down at the ground. Sarah watched her, waiting. Was there something she didn't know about the Dyer family, and its history with Robert Cope? Something Jess knew, but wasn't revealing?

"You can try telling the police that," said Jess. "But Ruth's best chance is if they work out who really killed him."

"You think so?"

"Sarah, you know who grabbed that knife and went for him. Ruth only finished it off."

"Right." Jess had still been outside at that point, helping the other women escape. But she had to know...

This wasn't going to work. Martin was already far away, and Ruth was going to prison.

"I didn't see what Ted did," said Jess.

"Sorry?"

"Your dad. He went flying in through that door like he had wings. Did he see Robert hurt you?"

"I guess so. The first I knew, he was on top of him. He wasn't strong enough though."

"How is his shoulder?"

"Strong enough for him to do what he did tonight."

"Yes. Sorry."

"Don't be. You helped us."

Jess looked back at the house. "I need to get back in. I'm sure you can imagine the state Ben's in."

Sarah followed her gaze. Ben, Ruth's husband, was someone she'd never had cause to speak to. This was the first time she'd spoken to his sister Jess at any length. But in the last week his wife had been abducted and then arrested. He had five-year-old twins to think about. He must be breaking down.

"Sorry. I'll leave you to it. Maybe I can track Martin down."

Jess visibly relaxed. "That would be a huge help. For Ruth."

"Yes."

Jess put her hand on Sarah's arm. "He helped you get out, didn't he?"

"Yes."

"Is that why you wanted him to come back with us?"

Sarah blinked back tears. "It was a bad idea."

"Maybe not at the time. But now, maybe yes."

Sarah sniffed. "Go. Go to your brother. He needs you. I'll try to help."

"Thank you." Jess opened the door and went into the house. It flickered with the warm light of a log fire. She thought of her own house after power-down, the single candle allowed in each occupied room.

Jess closed the door behind her. Sarah watched it for a

moment as if it might open again, then turned. She dragged herself across the square.

Ted was outside their house, elbowing the door open. She felt her heart pick up pace. What would he do, when he found Dawn upstairs in bed?

She peered towards the main road – *Martin, where are you?* – then clenched her fists and walked towards home.

She opened the door as quietly as she could. The house was quiet. She slid inside, her eyes on the staircase.

A shadow loomed at the top.

She squared her shoulders as he descended in silence.

"Hello, love."

"Hello." Why was he being so normal?

"Your mum's asleep."

"Yes." *She's not asleep, you bastard, she's half conscious because of what you did to her.*

"Best you go to bed too, eh."

She frowned at him. No apology. No anger. No continuation from where he left off.

Was this what he was like with Dawn, after he hit her?

She looked past him, up the stairs. "I'd like to see Mum."

"No, lass. She's fast asleep. She won't want you disturbing her."

She stared up the stairs. The faint light of a candle glowed from her parents' room. Did she dare stand up to him, barge past and insist on seeing Dawn? Would that make things worse for her mother?

"Right."

He smiled at her, then turned and started climbing. She followed, trying to shut out the sound of his heavy footsteps. His breathing was laboured; his shoulder would be giving him pain. She wanted to hit him, to knock him down the stairs and make him land crookedly against the sofa, like he'd done to Dawn.

But Dawn wouldn't want that. She wouldn't thank her.

She tiptoed up after him, keeping her breathing under control. It was an effort.

He stopped just past her door and turned. He gave her another smile.

"'Night, then."

She put her hand on the doorknob. "'Night."

He watched as she slipped inside. She closed the door behind her and let herself breathe again.

She sat down on the bed. The curtains were open and the moon shone weakly into the room. She stood to see it better, out beyond the clifftop. Maybe she should throw herself off. Maybe that would be better for everyone.

She heard a scratching sound at her door and spun towards it. A key, turning.

She ran to it, turning the handle. It didn't budge. She placed her hands on the wood, imagining him on the other side.

She wouldn't call out. Wouldn't give him the satisfaction.

She retreated to her bed. She'd only slept ten hours in the last five days.

She lay down and let sleep wash over her.

CHAPTER EIGHTEEN

IT HAD BEEN DARK FOR HOURS, AND THERE WAS NO SIGN OF Sarah. Martin had watched the final police car pass along the Parade, empty expect for its driver and a detective in the passenger seat.

Had Sarah gone to them? Had she told them what she'd need to, to release Ruth?

It wouldn't work. The only thing that would lead to Ruth's release was his own arrest.

They would be looking for him. No one from the village had told them he'd come back with them, as far as he knew. So they'd go to the farm.

That was where he needed to be.

He pushed the shed door open. The night was damp, a faint moon shining through scudding clouds. He shivered in his thin shirt. He'd need more than this if he was going to make the walk past Withernsea.

He heard voices beyond the edge of the allotment. Men. He crouched down low and listened. The sky was lightening a little, over the sea. Sunrise, already?

"She's not what you think," said one of the men.

"Not as *old*!" the other joked.

"Don't."

"She was our *teacher*, Zack."

"*Was* being the operative word. That was years ago. We're men now, not boys. She knows that."

"So she likes you too?"

"I think so. There was something between us, when we were off looking for the women. Sorry."

"Don't."

"I didn't mean to—"

"I said it's alright. Tell me more about Jess. What's she like in the sack?"

Martin heard the sound of a fist hitting fabric.

"Oof. You didn't need to do that."

"Don't take the piss, little brother."

"Not so much of the little. I'm bigger than you now. I've been doing weights."

"Ten minutes, Sam. That's all I'm saying. It counts."

Martin held his breath, wishing the sky would stop brightening. He was behind a tiny shed in the middle of a featureless allotment. There was no way he could get away without them seeing him.

"So what about Sarah?"

"What about her?"

"Her mum's keen on you. Is *she*?"

"She will be."

"Don't. I've seen enough of that sort of talk with Robert Cope."

"I didn't mean it like that. But once that Martin geezer is out of the way, she'll come round."

"I hope so, mate. She's pretty."

"I know. That hair."

Martin closed his eyes and pictured Sarah's hair. Even when matted and clogged with mud, it had an ethereal quality, strands of it wafting around her face like she was something out of a painting.

"Hang on. Here's Danny. Craig too."

"Better shut up about women then."

"Oh no, mate. We're getting all the mileage we can about you taking up with the steward."

Again, Martin heard flesh hitting cloth. Then a chuckle, followed by more voices.

He ducked inside the shed. He was going to have to wait it out.

CHAPTER NINETEEN

DAYLIGHT WAS FILTERING THROUGH SARAH'S THIN curtains. She looked at the wind-up clock next to her bed: 9am.

She groaned. She'd slept over twelve hours, and her mother was out there alone.

She went to the door. It was still locked. She rattled the handle.

"Let me out! I need the toilet."

Footsteps hurried up the stairs. She heard breathing behind the door.

"I've brought you some breakfast, love."

"Mum? I need to get out. I'm bursting."

A pause. "You promise you won't try to run out again?"

She crossed her fingers. "Promise."

She stepped back as her mother unlocked the door. She had a bruise across her forehead and the beginnings of a black eye.

Sarah reached a hand towards her but Dawn shrank back.

"Where's Dad?"

"Out."

"Out where?"

"He didn't tell me. Here, take this."

Dawn pushed a bowl of porridge into Sarah's hands. Sarah put it on her bedside table.

"How are you?"

"I thought you needed the toilet."

"That can wait. You were in a bad way, last night."

Dawn looked at the carpet. It was pale blue, with stains where the sun had bleached it. "I'm fine."

"You don't look it."

Dawn looked up to make eye contact. "Do you need the toilet, or not?"

"Yes."

Sarah pushed past her mother to the bathroom. When she returned, Dawn was gazing out of her bedroom window.

"You can't keep me locked up in here."

Dawn nodded towards the porridge. "Eat."

"Where's Snowy? He needs to be let out."

"I've done it." Dawn crossed to the door. "Eat that. You need to regain your strength, after everything that's happened to you."

Everything that's happened to you. Was Dawn ever going to ask her about what happened? The abduction, the attempted rape, the escape? The killing.

"Mum? Can we talk, properly, please?"

There was a sound from downstairs. Dawn flung her head to one side, her nostrils flaring.

Silence. She looked back at Sarah and backed out of the room. "Eat."

Dawn closed the door and locked it. Sarah ran to it, hammering it with her fists.

"Mum! Please! You can't do this!"

"Your dad's orders."

"But he's not here."

Silence. Sarah hoped her mother wasn't leaving.

"You're going to let him imprison me?"

She heard movement against the door. Dawn was sliding down to the floor. Could she hear sobbing?

"I don't want to antagonise him, love. Not after he hit you. We need to keep the peace. Until we can get you out of here. With Sam."

"I'm not interested in Sam, for God's sake!"

"Don't blaspheme. You should be."

"Mum, why is Dad doing this? He's not normally this bad."

"He's scared, love."

"What the hell does *he* have to be scared of?"

Silence again. *Come back. Talk to me.*

The key clattered in the lock and Dawn opened the door. "Mind your language. You don't understand. This village is a place of refuge. It's safe. Or it was. It's not now. And you bringing that boy here hasn't helped."

"He helped me escape, Mum."

"He also took you. Or have you forgotten that?"

Sarah slumped onto her bed. "No." She looked at Dawn. "I'm confused, Mum. I don't know what's going on."

"I know." Dawn sat next to her and slid an arm around her shoulders. Her flesh was cold but the touch was welcome. Sarah leaned in, feeling her mother's breath on her cheek.

"Mum, I know how to help Ruth. I can tell them the truth. Tell them that it was Martin who killed Robert."

Dawn stopped stroking Sarah's hair. "You can?'

"Yes."

"You will?"

"Yes. I just need to find Jess. She must have a way of contacting the police."

Dawn stood up. Sarah stared ahead, her eyes on her mother's hands, red from household chores.

"Are you sure about this, love?"

Sarah looked up. "I'll be quick. I'll come straight back."

"Well…" Dawn glanced at the door. "I don't know when your father will be home. If you're not here…"

Sarah grabbed her hand. "I'll be quick. I'll run straight there and straight back."

"It's a fair way to Jess's house."

"She'll be at Ruth's. With Ben."

"Alright then." Dawn stood back. Her eyes were wide with fear. "But be quick, please."

CHAPTER TWENTY

MARTIN WAS WOKEN BY MOVEMENT OUTSIDE THE SHED. HE sprang to his feet and grabbed the nearest weapon he could find. A trowel. Fat lot of good that would do.

There was a knock at the door. He frowned at it.

"Sarah?"

"It's Sam."

"I thought you'd gone out to work."

"I should have. But then I spotted them."

"Spotted who?"

"Just let me in, will you?"

Martin eyed the door. He'd tied it closed with a length of garden twine he'd found.

Could he trust Sam? He'd want Martin gone, with the way he felt about Sarah. He might have brought Ted with him.

"Are you alone?"

"Yes. Get a move on!"

He untied the twine and shoved it into his pocket. He pushed the door open a crack, gripping its edge tightly so he could slam it into Sam if he needed to.

"What is it?"

"They're after you."

"Who?"

"Ted. Some others."

"How did they find me?"

"They must have spotted you. You need to move."

He leaned out of the shed and looked back towards the road. Sure enough, a small group of men was making its way towards them. Ted was at its head. His coat was draped over his bad shoulder; how did he have such strength, when he'd been stabbed?

"Shit."

"Exactly. Come on, I can get you out of here."

Martin let Sam pull him out of the shed and started running across the allotment. He muttered a silent apology each time his foot fell on something growing, but he didn't have time to be careful.

At the far edge of the allotment was a track. Martin looked back. The men were almost at the shed now, struggling across the heavy soil. Ted yelled something. Behind him was Harry and two other men Martin didn't recognise. They were all looking at Ted as if waiting for orders.

"Get back here, you little shit!"

"Run, now!" hissed Sam.

Martin ducked under a wire fence Sam was holding up and started to run. They sprinted along the track, dodging tree roots and potholes. He heard voices approaching from behind.

He looked round. They were coming under the fence now, Harry holding it up for the others to pass. Ted was yelling at them.

He felt Sam's hand on his sleeve and was pulled sideways into the hedge.

"Ow!"

"Sorry! They won't see us, this way."

Martin stared at Sam, who was shoving brambles and bracken aside. Thorns rebounded behind him, hitting Martin in the face. He held his arms up to shield himself.

"Where are we going?"

"The boat house. It's your only way out of here."

He stopped running. "I can't steal the boat!"

Sam turned. "I'll take you along the coast a couple of miles. That'll give you a head start. Now, run!"

Martin pushed down the questions and did as he was told. At last the undergrowth spat them out into a clearing. Ahead of them was a path leading to the boathouse. He looked at it, guilt eating at his insides.

"I can't…"

"You bloody well can. They'll kill you."

"Is this about Ruth?"

"They don't care about that. Ted doesn't, anyway. It's about Sarah."

He felt his heart drop inside his rib cage. "Is she alright?"

"She's fine. She's in there, getting the boat ready."

"What?" He ran ahead, careering through the door to the boathouse and almost falling into the boat.

Sarah was next to the boat, untying a rope.

"Hello."

"Sarah? What are you doing here?"

She shrugged. "Sam spotted me, when he was coming for you."

He stepped towards her. She took a step back. There was a bruise on her cheek.

"Did he hurt you?"

"Yes. But he won't do it again."

"How can you be sure?"

"Because I'll look after her," said Sam, closing the boathouse doors. Sarah flinched.

"Does she *need* you to look after her?" asked Martin.

"I didn't mean it like that. She just needs to get out of that house."

"Both of you, stop talking about me like I'm a child," said Sarah. "Help me with the boat."

Sam grabbed a rope off Sarah.

"I stole some food," she said. "From home. I thought you might need it."

"But you thought I'd left."

She shrugged. "I wasn't sure."

He smiled at her. She seemed to know his next move before he did. "Thank you."

Another shrug. "It's nothing."

"You know that's not true. You have rations here."

"My mum will cover for me."

"Let's hope so."

They opened the front doors of the boathouse and tugged the trailer onto the beach. Martin scanned the path behind the boathouse. Sure enough, the men were close.

They pulled the boat into the sea, cold water making him wince. Sam was unfastening it from the trailer. At last it was in the water, its hull lightly wedged against the sand.

Martin climbed into the boat. Sam was next to it, pushing it off. Sarah helped him on the other side.

"Good luck," she whispered.

He nodded. "I'll turn myself in. When I get to the farm. Get Ruth released."

She bit her lip; he knew she had to trust him.

There was a crashing sound as the door to the boathouse flew open. Ted stumbled in, followed by Harry. Sam and Sarah started pushing harder.

Ted ran through the boathouse and onto the beach. "What the fuck? Stealing our boat again?"

"I'll bring it back!" Sam called back. "You want him gone, right?"

"Not like this."

Sam nodded at Martin. "We need to get going."

Martin nodded. He jumped out of the boat to help push, the water almost at his hips. Behind him, Sarah bent to push the boat, immersed up to her knees. She gave him a sad smile. He resisted the urge to ask her to come with him. Sam would be better for her.

"And as for you…" Ted ran onto the beach behind them, stumbling across the sand. He splashed into the shallows and made a lunge for Sarah. She shrieked and jumped into the boat. Martin felt it dip and touch the sand. He kept pushing.

Sam's face was red, his muscles straining. He stared at Sarah. "Get out!"

She looked back at Ted. He was level with Martin now, screaming at her. Martin pulled in towards the boat, desperate to avoid Ted's touch.

Ted turned to him and growled. Martin took a deep breath and jumped into the boat.

"You can get out now, Sarah!" he told her.

She took another look at her dad. His face was red with exertion and anger. Harry stood a few feet behind, water lapping at his feet.

Sarah turned to Martin. "I'm coming with you."

"What?" cried Sam. He stumbled against the side of the boat.

"Its fine, Sam," she said. "I'll take him. Drop him off a few miles south then bring the boat back."

"No you bloody won't!" Ted cried. She ignored him.

"Are you sure?" said Sam. "You know how to sail this thing?"

Sarah nodded. "How hard can it be?"

Sam gave the boat a final push. A wave caught it and dragged them back into shore. Martin cursed and grabbed an oar.

"Start rowing!" he told Sarah.

She fumbled for the other oar and they started pulling the boat out to sea. The coastline was steep along here and it wasn't long before they were deep enough to engage the outboard motor. Ted was behind them, screaming obscenities and waving madly despite the sling on his arm.

Martin took a look at Sarah. She was starring out to sea, her jaw set.

"You sure?" he asked.

She nodded, but didn't meet his eye. "Let's get going."

He pulled on the cord and started the motor.

CHAPTER TWENTY-ONE

DAWN STARED OUT OF THE KITCHEN WINDOW. IT LOOKED
out to the side of the house and if she leaned over the sink,
she could see the square, or at least part of it.

Sarah, where are you?

She'd been gone for nearly an hour now. How long did
it take to get to Ruth's house four doors away and speak to
Jess?

She washed her hands under the tap again, knowing
she was wasting water but unable to resist. Her hands, like
her home, were always scrubbed clean. Today they
smarted, raw flakes peeling off between her fingers. She
pulled at one of them then put it in her pocket. Better than
letting it fall to the clean floor.

She heard a key turn in the front door. She rushed to it,
ready to bundle the girl upstairs and back to her room.

The door opened, bringing a blast of fresh air inside.
She pulled her cardigan tighter.

"What are you doing, lying in wait like that? Give a
man a heart attack."

"Ted. Sorry."

"You look startled. Why do you look startled?"

"Sorry, I didn't mean to. The door, your coming back, it just…"

"Hmm. Put the kettle on."

She hurried to the kitchen and pulled the kettle out of a cupboard. She placed it on the stove and lit the gas. The blue flame warmed her hands; she held them close to it, glad of the metal heating up. This was the only time she used gas; it came from a bottle outside and was strictly rationed.

Ted was behind her, watching over her shoulder. "What's the matter?"

She stared at her reflection in the kettle. "Nothing."

"You're jumpy."

"No. No, I'm not."

"You let her out."

"No. I took her breakfast."

"Turn round when I'm talking to you, dammit."

His voice was low, calm. Dawn hated it when he spoke like this.

She turned, twisting her hands together against her apron. The knuckles were bleeding. Her head throbbed.

"Look at me."

She lifted her head and looked into his eyes, then looked quickly over his shoulder. He put a finger on her chin and pulled it down.

"I said, look at me."

She swallowed and did as she was told. Could she distract him, send him out again? Until Sarah came home?

"Why?" he asked.

"I'm sorry, I don't…"

He took a step backwards. She watched him pace into the living room, angsty like a big cat. She stroked her knuckles, feeling blood on her fingertips.

He sat on the sofa, looking out of the window. The sky was white with cloud and the hedgerows at the top of the cliff were a dull, shadowless green.

She shrank back into the kitchen. The kettle whistled behind her, making her jump. She knocked it, spilling hot water onto her hand.

She yelped and thrust the hand into her mouth. She turned to run the tap, to soak it.

"Leave it. Come here."

She shoved her hand back in her mouth. She shuffled towards the living room, feeling her pulse running through her throbbing fingers.

"Sit with me." He patted the sofa next to him.

She shuffled in and lowered herself to sit, keeping to the end of the sofa.

"Closer. You're my wife, dammit."

She shifted a millimetre towards him. He sighed and turned to her.

"Why did you lie to me?"

She stopped sucking her hand. She felt her pulse pick up.

He leaned in. "I said, why did you lie to me?"

"I don't... I don't know what you mean."

He drew up his chest and she shrank back. Then he turned away from her, sinking into the sofa.

"She got away."

Dawn felt her body go heavy. She said nothing.

He turned to her. His face was softer now, less angry. She knew that meant nothing.

"How was she in the boat house, when you had her locked up here?"

Stupid girl. Sarah had promised that all she was going to do was to find Jess, then to hurry back.

Dawn shook her head.

"Well?"

"She told me she could help Ruth. She was going to find Jess."

"Well, she didn't, did she?"

Dawn shook her head. She lifted the tips of her fingers to her lips. The spot on her thumb where she'd spilt the water was throbbing.

"Take your bloody hand out of your mouth, woman."

She plunged her hand into her lap. She clasped the other one over it. It would be raw, later. Like the rest of her skin.

He stood up and crossed to the window. "She's out there somewhere."

"What?"

"She buggered off in the village boat. Took it."

He turned to face her, daring her to remind him of the time he'd stolen the village boat, with Harry's help. She said nothing.

"Is she alone?"

"No, of course she's not bloody alone! She's got Martin with her. Sam Dyer helped them."

"Sam?"

"Yes. Sam." He advanced to stand over her. "This is all your fault. You and your busybody matchmaking. She's nineteen. You've no right to go making some lad think he's got a chance with her."

"Nineteen is old enough to—"

"Are you not listening to a word I've said? She's gone off with that Martin, and Sam's helping them!"

Dawn looked at the window. The village boat was tiny, just a leisure craft with a tiny cabin for the driver and open benches at the back. If they were out on the North Sea…

She stood up and pushed past Ted, not caring now

what he did. She leaned on the glass, cupping her hands around her eyes.

She turned to him. "Why?"

"Why what?"

"Why did they go? Did you threaten her? Did you hurt her again?"

She'd promised herself. If he hit Sarah, she'd leave. But now it had happened, she was too scared.

His face clouded. She hurried past him to the front door, not stopping to grab her coat. She flung the door open and ran for the beach.

CHAPTER TWENTY-TWO

THEY TRAVELLED IN SILENCE, THE ONLY SOUND THE HUM OF the boat's engine and the occasional bird swooping overhead. Sarah took the wheel after a few minutes, determined to accustom herself to this thing. Ahead of them the sky was dark, thick clouds pushing their way up the cliffs.

After perhaps twenty minutes, Martin broke the silence.

"Shall I go into shore now, carry on on foot?"

"What?"

"That was Sam's plan. He was going to let me off a few miles south then take the boat back."

"Oh." She thought of Ted, chasing her down the beach, into the waves. Sam's plan meant her steering the boat back home. Taking it back to him.

"We can push on a little further," she said. "So you don't have to walk as far."

"You sure?"

She nodded, staring ahead of them. The clouds were lowering now, scudding along the horizon like a threatening black army.

Martin shifted towards her. "Maybe we should pull ashore for a bit," he said. "Wait for that storm to pass."

"No."

"This boat is tiny. I know it's seen worse, but there's no point in—"

"I said no. We keep going. If it gets rough, then we head in to shore."

He sighed. "Let me take over for a bit. You'll need your strength for the trip back."

She let him take the wheel and shifted to the seat behind, careful to avoid physical contact. She stared at his back. Was he remembering the first time they'd been together on this boat? She'd been unconscious, but he would have known exactly what was going on.

She pulled her sweater more tightly around her. Spray hissed up from the water, coating the boat. The bottom was swilling with it. Should she bail it out?

She searched around for some sort of receptacle. A bucket, cup, anything.

All she could see in the bottom of the boat were ropes, and the food she'd brought for Martin. Bread and apples. The bread would be soggy.

She pulled it out of its paper bag. It was like a sponge, dripping and blue. She chucked it back to the bottom of the boat.

'What's that?"

"Bread. I brought you food, remember."

"Where did you get it?"

"We've got a bakery."

He watched her for a moment, calculating. She wondered what they ate on the farm. Oat biscuits were all she'd been given when she'd been imprisoned there. Stolen, probably.

"You grow wheat, up here?" he asked.

"We buy the flour. In Filey."

"How?"

She frowned. "Some of the men go out to work. At the reclamation works." She paused. "Sam's one of them."

Sam. She hoped her father wouldn't blame him.

Martin looked towards the shore. "I think you should drop me off now. It's getting choppy. There's a stretch of beach just there."

"It's still safe enough to continue."

He turned the boat. "I want you to go home."

She placed a hand on the wheel. "Not yet."

"Is it Ted? Are you scared of him?"

"Just keep going."

"No." He continued steering them in to shore. "You know how to sail this thing, don't you?"

"Please, carry on round that outcrop. Just a couple more miles."

"I'm worried about you going back in this weather."

They'd caught up with the clouds now and large drops of rain were falling on the boat. There was tarpaulin under Martin's feet; Sarah pulled it over as much of the boat as she could.

"Cover yourself," he said.

"I'll be fine."

"You don't have a coat. Here, have mine." He unzipped his coat.

"I'm fine." She shook her head at him. She was tired of people telling her what to do.

"At least use the tarp."

She shrugged and pulled it over her knees. She looked ahead; the sky was almost night-dark, and the waves were growing.

"We should get to shore," Martin said. She didn't argue this time. He pulled the boat hard to the right. As he did so, she heard a cracking sound.

"What was that?"

He was pale. "I don't know."

She lifted the tarpaulin and searched the bottom of the boat. Had something moved? Was it on the outside of the boat?

The boat lurched to one side. She grabbed the tarpaulin but it slid out of her hands and into the sea. She leaned over the side, her fingers brushing it.

She felt hands on her waist. Martin pulled her upright.

"What are you doing?" he shouted.

"Trying to save the tarp."

"I thought you were jumping in."

"Don't be daft!"

Rain was driving into her face now and she could barely hear her own voice. The boat listed to the left, bringing her dangerously close to the surface of the water. She scooted to the other side, hoping to balance it. It shifted a little but continued to list.

"We need to hurry," Martin shouted. His coat was soaked through and his face wet. He spat water out of his mouth as he tried to see over the boat's low windscreen and find somewhere to moor.

The boat lurched again and Sarah felt something scrape along the bottom.

"Oh my God!"

The boat ground to a halt. They were on the edge of a jagged pile of rocks, marooned.

"Help me push!" Martin leaned past her and over to the rocks. He placed his palms against them and pushed.

Sarah followed suit. The boat made some more ominous sounds and then dipped, as if going down in a lift.

"We need to get off!" she shouted.

"We can't leave it!"

"We have to! We'll drown!"

She eyed the rocks next to the boat. They were dark and slippery. To the other side was a beach, just a short swim away.

She tugged at Martin's arm. "Come on!"

"We need to save the boat!"

"We'll come back after the storm. Hurry!"

She climbed onto the side of the boat, her legs unsteady. It lurched again, almost tipping her into the water. Martin grabbed her round the waist.

"What are you doing?" he panted.

"We need to swim."

"You can't just jump in. You don't know how deep it is."

He was right. She ducked down to lean over the side of the boat, bringing her weight round so her legs dangled over the side. Martin shifted his hands to hold her under the arms.

She looked into his eyes then slithered down into the water. Her feet hit rock.

"It's not deep," she said. "But the rocks are sharp."

"Right." He climbed out after her. She felt her way along the rocks, placing each foot carefully in front of the other and holding her arms high for balance. As she walked, the rocks fell away.

"I'm going to swim." She pushed herself off towards the beach. A wave broke over her head, sending her down into the murky water.

She pushed herself up, spluttering. The water was freezing and she felt like her chest might explode.

Martin was behind her, gasping.

She had to ignore the pain. She had to focus.

She looked ahead of her, picking out a tree on the horizon. Her target.

She started to swim.

CHAPTER TWENTY-THREE

Dawn ran out to the clifftop, her heart racing. She stumbled to a halt at the edge, glad of the scrubby hedge that kept her from falling.

The sea was hazy, shrouded in cloud, but she couldn't see any boats.

Sarah, why?

She ran for the path that led down to the beach, not stopping till the sand slowed her footsteps.

Down here it was cold, and lonely. A group of wading birds shifted in and out of the shallows, making hard, cackling sounds. The waves were low, thrumming into the sand like a bulldozer.

She slumped onto the sand, not caring about the damp through her skirt. She threw her hand over her eyes and scanned the sea. Nothing. Grey waves, birds bobbing on the surface. No boats. To the north, the rocks at Brigg End were white with sea spray, the water splitting dangerously over them.

She hoped they knew what they were doing. Sarah had never been out in the boat – at least not before she was taken... And Martin, well hadn't he fallen in the sea during Jess's misguided rescue, and given himself hypothermia?

She sniffed. *Don't cry*, she told herself. *Keep it together, like you always do*. Her daughter was lost, maybe drowned. *Stop it*, she told herself. *She'll come back, God willing*.

She took a ragged breath and pushed herself upwards. Watching the sea as she went, blindly hoping the boat would suddenly emerge, she picked her way back up the hill. She needed to get back to Ted. To calm him.

CHAPTER TWENTY-FOUR

SARAH DRAGGED HERSELF ONTO THE SAND, SPLUTTERING out sea water. Martin wasn't far behind. He lay next to her, pulling in breaths.

She sat up and turned back to the sea. Waves lapped at her feet. She'd lost a shoe.

Martin sat next to her, not touching. Not speaking.

They stared back at the boat, wedged on the rocks.

"We need to save it," she said.

"It's too dangerous."

"It's not ours to leave. It belongs to the village."

He stood up. "Let's work out where we are first. Come back for it, when the tide's gone out."

She eyed him, wondering if he had any intention of returning. She regretted jumping into the boat with him now, listening to the shrill voice in her head telling her to get away from her father.

She had to go home. Her mother needed her. And this escapade would only make her father more angry.

She shivered.

"You're soaked through," Martin said.

"So are you."

"At least we were close to shore."

She watched the water pushing at the boat. It shifted its weight on the rocks, looking as if it might capsize. Her throat felt tight.

"We can't leave it."

He turned to her. "You need to take it back."

She nodded, her lips trembling with the cold.

"Let's walk a bit, see where we are. If we're close to the farm, I can get them to help us with it."

A dark cloud passed through her mind at the thought of the farm. Even with Robert dead, those men were still there. Including Leroy, the man who'd attacked her.

What the hell had she been thinking? Why was she here?

She stood up. "I'm going out there."

"No. Please, not right now." He looked past her. "Wait, I think that's…"

He ran a short way along the beach, looking back at her from time to time. She watched, puzzled.

After a minute or so, he shouted something she couldn't make out. She shrugged exaggeratedly.

He waved his arms, beckoned her. She looked back at the boat. She shook her head.

Her skirt tugged at her, heavy with water. She lifted the front of it and wrung it out in her raw hands. She was shivering.

He ran back.

"The beach huts," he panted. "They're just out of sight. We came further than I thought."

She looked past him. The beach huts meant shelter. A modicum of warmth, compared to this wind that was clawing at them.

They also meant that the farm was nearby. The farm where she'd been imprisoned. The farm where that man had tried to rape her. And Robert had held a knife to her face.

She put a hand to the wound on her forehead. She traced the thin red line where it had scabbed over. She hadn't noticed the plaster Ruth had given her falling off.

Her breath was catching in her throat and her skin felt tight. Her head span.

"The farm," she said.

His shoulders slumped. "We won't go back there."

She was shivering, her knees trembling. "I can't."

"We won't. I promise. Just the beach huts. We get shelter, then we work something out. I'll help you with the boat." He cocked his head. "Take you home, if it comes to it."

She shook her head. "No. I'll go back alone."

"Very well." He was smiling at her but his eyes looked sad.

She clenched and unclenched her fists, willing the nausea to subside.

"OK," she said. "But I go in one hut, and you have the other."

She needed to be alone, to work through her conflicting fears; returning here, versus the threat of what her father would do when she went home.

"That's fine. Come on."

He turned towards the huts.

She looked back at the boat. It was a little higher in the water now, the waves dropping. How long before the tide was out far enough for her to traverse those rocks?

In the meantime, she could use some shelter. Her feet were numb, and her fingers felt like a thousand needles were jabbing at them. And if she tried to walk any distance, she would pass out.

Martin was almost out of sight. Reluctantly, she followed him.

CHAPTER TWENTY-FIVE

HE WASN'T LYING.

Around the curve of the beach was the spot where they'd taken shelter before, when they'd been running from the farm.

Were they really heading back to it? Was she that stupid?

Her hands felt clammy, her chest tight. She'd let him bring her back here. She had to get away, as soon as she could.

She'd rest here for an hour or so, get as dry as she could. Wait for the tide to drop. Then she'd go back to the boat. It had been damaged but it hadn't taken on water, at least not much. It was seaworthy. Martin would have to go on alone, as he should have all along.

The beach huts were much as they had been before; one without roofs and two of its walls, the other two intact. She pointed at one.

"I'll go in there. Alone."

He hardened his jaw but didn't argue.

She pushed open the door to the hut. In here the air

was cool but still; it smelled of wood, sand and salt. The wind, instead of beating at her, whistled outside in a way that reminded her of childhood summers. It felt calm.

She stripped down to her underwear, wringing out her skirt and blouse. She'd never known just how much water two garments could take on board. She kicked off her remaining shoe and tried to wring it out, but it was too stiff.

This was the hut where they'd spent the night, after fleeing the farm. Martin on the floor and her on a high shelf. It made a perfect drying rack. She arranged her clothes, stretching them out for maximum exposure.

She looked outside. The rain had stopped now; would her clothes dry quicker if she put them outside, took advantage of the wind? Or would they simply blow away?

Either way, she wasn't about to open the door dressed only in her underwear. She patted her clothes, trying to push the water out by sheer force of will.

She lifted herself up to sit next to them, feet dangling over the ledge. Outside, the beach was quiet. The hut next to her, Martin inside, was still.

She leaned against the wall, breathing in the musky scent of wood. Her toe throbbed from her fall last time she was here – was that really only two days ago? – and her back was sore where she'd scraped it on a rock during her swim. Every muscle in her body screamed at her, longing for sleep.

She didn't have time.

She leaned her face on the window, glad of the cool. Her face felt hot; she probably had a temperature. She knew from the warnings Ruth gave them that she shouldn't ignore a fever. It might be the first sign of infection, and with antibiotics so scarce it could be fatal.

She blinked her eyes open, cursing her feebleness. How

long had she been in here? The sky was darkening now and the sun had shifted in the sky. She'd been sleeping.

She pulled herself off the bench. Her clothes weren't much drier, but she had no choice. She dragged them on, wincing at the damp fabric rippling over her tingling flesh.

She padded to the door, abandoning the lone shoe, and pushed it open. She eyed the hut next to her. Would she tell him where she was going, or not?

He'd tell her it was dangerous. Warn her away from the rocks. Maybe try to go himself.

She couldn't go back to the farm.

She'd slip away, like she'd never been here.

She stepped down onto the sand and pushed the door closed. She sniffed the air, glad the wind had dropped.

She stepped away from the hut, turning for the direction they'd come. As she did so, she spotted someone next to the other hut.

Martin. He looked shrivelled and wet, his curly brown hair wild with water, sand and salt. He was talking to someone.

She felt her heart stop.

Run.

She turned and started to sprint across the beach, cursing the sand for dragging her down.

"Sarah?"

She forced herself not to stop, not to turn.

"Sarah! Come back!"

She heard footsteps behind her, heavy and quick. Martin's steps were lighter than that. She ignored the rising pulse in her throat and continued to run.

A hand grabbed her arm. She yanked it away, stumbling.

She righted herself and carried on running.

"Sarah, stop!"

She paused. She knew that voice.

Her chest was on fire now, her legs screaming at her to slow down. She ignored them.

The feet behind her kept coming. She could hear his breath now; short, sharp pants. A hand on her arm again.

She screamed as her legs buckled and she fell to the sand.

"Get off! Leave me alone!"

"I'm not going to hurt you."

She blinked up. Standing over her, blocking half the sky, was a man. He had dark, greasy hair that curled around his ears. He smelled of dirt, overlaid with mint. His face was weather-worn and ruddy and he had a tattoo that snaked up his right arm, under his shirt.

It was Bill. The man who'd taken her.

CHAPTER TWENTY-SIX

DAWN EASED OPEN THE FRONT DOOR, HER SENSES SHARP. The house was quiet, the only sound the ticking of the carriage clock on the mantelpiece. She'd found it in a cupboard upstairs, a week after moving into this house. Two weeks after Ted had been elected to the village council. She wondered who it had belonged to in a previous life and why they'd hidden it away.

She closed the door and leaned against it, trying to control her breathing. Her breaths were shallow and tight and her stomach ached.

She felt like a hole had been ripped out of her. Without Sarah, there was no reason to live.

She stepped from the doormat onto the wooden floor of the hallway, keeping her footsteps light. She glided to the kitchen. Outside, the sky was clearing, clouds shifting towards the south.

Had Sarah gone that way, with him? Had they gone back to that farm?

No. Dawn had been too scared to pry into what had happened to Sarah there. But she knew from the haunted look in her eyes that it was something to which her daughter never wanted to return.

She sat at the kitchen table; a chair was already pulled back so she didn't have to make a sound. She placed her arms on the table and leaned over them.

She caught movement from the corner of her eye. A shadow, shifting in the living room. She stilled her muscles.

He stood up from where he'd been sitting, concealed by the back of the sofa. His face was calm. Dawn pulled back in her chair.

"Where have you been?" His voice was little more than a whisper.

"Looking for Sarah."

"And?"

She shrugged.

He advanced. "And?"

She met his stare. "No sign of her."

He frowned and took the chair opposite her. She looked down at her hands, motionless on the table. She was scared to move.

She raised her head. "What happened? Why did she go off with him?"

"Because she's a stupid girl, that's why."

"But I don't understand. Why would she go off with him, when Sam was—"

"What's this about Sam?"

She swallowed. "Sam's a good boy. He's what she needs."

"Since when was that up to you?"

She blinked. "I—I don't know."

"She's too young. You shouldn't be putting daft ideas in her head."

"No."

He was right; if she hadn't filled Sam's head with hopes of Sarah, he wouldn't have helped them.

"Where is Sam?" she asked. "Is he alright?"

"I went to speak to his parents, while you were out."

She imagined Ted banging on the Golder family's door, demanding to be heard. Mack Golder, Sam's father, barring his way. Refusing to be cowed. Mack was a big man, as were his sons. His bulk had shifted from muscle to fat in middle age but he was still more than a match for Ted.

"What did they say?"

"They said nothing, woman. What do you imagine? They wouldn't let me see him."

"Why was he at the boathouse? What did he do?"

Ted shifted back in his chair. Dawn flinched.

"He got the boat ready, for that boy. Stupid idiot was going to go with him, or at least let him nick it. Typical."

Was Ted thinking of the time when *he'd* stolen the boat, taken it to go and find Sarah? Of the way Jess had been forced to take a rescue party south on foot, because of him?

Probably not.

"So why was she in the boat, and not Sam?"

He leaned in. "Because she's a fool, that's why. When she gets back here…"

"Please, Ted. If she comes back, go easy on her. We need to welcome her. To help her forget."

He stood up. "Welcome, my arse. That girl's going to get beaten to the back of beyond when I get my hands on her. She's made me look like a fool."

Dawn felt herself crumple. Sarah had gone again and all he cared about was how he looked to the village.

There was knock at the door. Ted glared at Dawn as if she'd invited the devil to come visiting. "Who's that?"

"I don't know."

She stood up. He put a hand on her shoulder to push her down.

"I'll go."

He ambled to the door, tensing as it knocked again. "Alright, alright, get some bloody patience."

Dawn rounded the kitchen table, anxious to see who it was. Could Sarah have come back?

"What do you want?" Ted's voice was hard.

"Sorry, Ted. Can I come in?"

"Whatever it is can be done on the doorstep."

Dawn advanced on him, her heart racing. Why was Jess here? Was there news?

"Very well," Jess said. She spotted Dawn over Ted's shoulder and threw her a tight smile. "Evening, Dawn."

"Evening." Ted turned to glare at her and she backed away, towards the kitchen. When he turned back to Jess she took a step forwards.

"What is it then?"

"It's the police. They're back."

"Jesus."

Dawn crossed herself. She hated the way he blasphemed.

"Why?" he asked.

"They still need to talk to people."

"About your sister-in-law?"

A pause. "They didn't tell me. I've got to go to Filey. They're going to talk to other villagers here. People who were there."

"I didn't see anything. I had a bloody knife sticking out of me shoulder."

"I told them that. It doesn't change anything."

"Jesus Christ." Ted leaned back to grab his coat.

"Don't go anywhere while I'm gone," he told Dawn, not looking at her as he slammed the door behind him.

Dawn slid to the floor. This was it. Ted was going to be arrested, and Sarah was gone. She was alone.

She heaved herself up, her limbs heavy. There was a rope in the loft.

She would get it down, and she would wait twenty-four hours. If neither of them returned, she'd use it.

CHAPTER TWENTY-SEVEN

Martin ran towards Bill and Sarah. He could only imagine how Sarah would be feeling, with one of the men chasing her across the sand. The very man who had grabbed her outside her house when she was barely awake, clamped a drug-soaked rag to her mouth and slung her over his shoulder.

Did she know it had been Bill?

He ground to a halt as he reached them. Bill gripped Sarah's arm and she was shouting into his face.

"Let me go, you bastard! I need to go home!"

"Not in that thing, you won't." Bill nodded towards the headland where the beach disappeared. "I saw your boat. It's washed up, further along."

Sarah's eyes widened. She pulled away from his grasp and resumed running.

"Sarah, stop!" Martin cried. "Let me help you!"

She skidded to a halt and looked back at him. Weighing up whether to believe him, no doubt. He hadn't lied to her, not once. Not unless he counted lying by omission.

He jogged to her. "Let's pull the boat in. Get some rest. Bill'll take us back to the farm."

"If you think I'm going back there…"

"When you jumped in the boat with me, you knew where I was going. I offered to get out, to let you go back, but you refused. Where exactly did you think we'd end up?"

"I don't know."

Bill caught up with them. He stopped a few paces away, and exchanged glances with Martin.

"It's alright," he said. "It's just me here now. The rest of them have gone."

"Gone?" said Sarah. "Where? Why?"

"They didn't like the police sniffing around."

"They came here?" asked Martin.

"Please, let's talk about this inside. I'll bring you up to speed. Things are very different around here now."

Sarah looked incredulous. "In two days?"

"A lot's happened."

Bill gave Martin a sideways glance. Martin wasn't sure what that look meant: blame for stabbing Robert, or relief that he'd ended the man's reign of terror.

Martin turned to Sarah. "I believe him, for what it's worth. We only need one night. We can get cleaned up, dried off."

"What about the boat?"

"Let's drag it further up the beach, for now. We can come back for it in the morning. You can. It's getting dark, there's no way you can sail it now."

She looked out to sea, then at Martin, then Bill, then the boat. Martin watched her, his chest tight.

"OK," she said.

"Thanks."

They walked towards the boat. The sand was damp and swallowed their feet.

"What happened to your shoes?"

"I lost one. It's easier with none."

"If you're sure."

She rounded on him, her hair flying out as she turned. "Yes, I'm sure. Stop trying to control me."

He raised his palms. "Sorry."

They reached the boat. He and Sarah grabbed a rope each and Bill pushed it from the back. They managed to get it halfway up the beach, to a spot where the sand was dry.

"It'll be OK here," said Bill. "I know this beach."

Martin looked at him. "You sure?"

"Sure."

Sarah stared at it for a moment then stepped away. Martin resisted the urge to take her hand. She looked cold, tired and dejected.

"Come on," he said. "Let's get you warm."

She scowled at him. *Don't control me.*

"You can't stay long," said Bill.

He felt his chest sink. "Why not?"

"The police, stupid. They're looking for you. You need to get away."

"They arrested Ruth."

"They did *what*?" Bill frowned then shook his head. "Makes sense."

"It wasn't her fault," said Martin.

"She did finish him off. Pushed the knife in harder, watched him die."

"It was me who put it there in the first place."

"Seems you're both as culpable as each other."

"It wasn't Ruth's fault," said Sarah. "I heard him with her, I know what he wanted from her."

A deep purple blush flushed up Bill's neck. How much did he recognise his own responsibility in all this?

How much do I recognise mine, thought Martin.

"I'll be off at first light," said Sarah. She looked at Bill. "Take us to the farm. You'd better be telling the truth."

She started walking along the beach, back to the huts.

"This way's quicker," Bill called after her.

She turned and gave him a wary look, then followed. They found a narrow path through some tall grasses, so dense that they had to fight their way through. The grass was stringy and wet and whipped Martin in the face as he passed.

At last they were spat out onto a road. Martin looked along it; no sign of life.

He pointed to the left. "This way, right?"

Bill nodded. Sarah shuddered. Her face was pale, the faint glow on her cheeks gone. She looked like a creature of the sea, or of the fairies. Martin remembered the stories his mum used to tell of spirit women, the way he'd hung off them as a child then laughed at them as a teenager.

They walked in silence. Martin listened to his and Bill's footsteps on the tarmac, wondering how long this road had been here. How long it would last. Sarah dragged behind, her footsteps slow. Her toe was bleeding and the bruise on her face was darkening. He stared at it and reminded himself not to offer help. *Don't control me.*

At last the farmhouse was ahead, staring out to sea. Bill unlocked the front door and ushered them into the kitchen. Martin's senses pricked for signs of habitation but there was nothing; no footsteps, no voices upstairs. No shouting.

The wooden floor had a dark patch near the back door where Robert's blood had been scrubbed away. He moved quickly to block it from Sarah's view.

The last time they'd been here, Robert had had her at

knifepoint, and Bill had restrained Martin with twine round his wrists. He and two other men had dragged Martin and Sarah back here, and brought them to Robert. So much for his plan to rescue her.

Sarah sat carefully, her eyes ahead, glazed. She looked small, ten years younger than her nineteen years. Martin wanted to walk to her and give her a hug. He wanted to drag the sadness out of her and replace it with love.

He thought of Ben, clutching at Ruth in this kitchen. The way she'd shrugged him off. Was this all Ben's fault?

No. It was Robert's.

Bill filled the kettle from the tap. "There are spare clothes upstairs. Not the best fit, but better than what you're wearing. You need to get dry, both of you. Before you catch hypothermia."

"Thanks," said Martin.

"Have a cup of tea first. It's mint. Can't keep the stuff at bay, but at least it's useful."

"Thanks."

Bill handed him a mug and put one in front of Sarah. She looped her fingers around it and sipped. A hint of colour returned to her cheeks.

"How did they know about Robert?" he asked. "The police."

"They wouldn't tell me. But I've got a good idea." He gave Sarah a nervous look.

"Go on."

"Leroy. I couldn't find him after you left. Hadn't seen him for a few hours. I reckon he saw the whole thing and shopped us." A pause. "Shopped you."

"He never liked me."

Sarah's grip tightened on the mug; she almost spilled it. Leroy had visited her in her cell, he knew. She'd refused to tell Martin what he'd done.

"It makes no sense," he said. "Leroy hated the cops."

Bill looked at Sarah. "Maybe he wanted to avoid getting into trouble himself."

Martin felt his face heat up. He needed to toughen up if he was going to be any help to Sarah.

"Where are the clothes?" asked Sarah.

"Upstairs," said Bill. "They're all men's, but Robert was smallest. And his clothes are clean."

"Right," she said. "Where?"

"Upstairs, big room at the back. There's a wardrobe. You can sleep there too. Both of you."

Sarah's eyes widened.

"No," said Martin. "I'll have my old room."

The room he had shared with Leroy and Mike. Thank God it would only be for one night. One night, and then he would never see Sarah again.

CHAPTER TWENTY-EIGHT

THERE WAS A KEY HANGING ON A PEG OUTSIDE THE bedroom door. Sarah took it and closed the door behind her. She turned it. It worked.

She had no idea if there was another key. If she was safe.

She turned to search the room. It was sparse, just a high, lumpy bed, a wardrobe that looked at least a hundred years old and a wooden chair.

Flowers lay on the floor in front of a cast iron fireplace, dried and purple. She felt a cold shadow pass through her, imagining Ruth in here. She'd been coming down the stairs when Bill had brought them back to the house. She'd either escaped, or she'd never been locked up in the first place.

Escaped. Surely.

Sarah grabbed the chair and wedged it under the door handle, having no idea if this actually worked. It would at least topple if the door was opened, give her a warning.

She opened the wardrobe. Inside was a row of laundered and ironed shirts. She ran her hands over them; they were white and stiff with bleach. She took one out and lay it on the bed.

She felt sick; the sight of Bill, approaching them across the sand, kept flashing in her eyes. Followed by the recollection of turning outside her house and seeing him there, coming at her.

She took a few shaky breaths and tried to focus on the clothes. Next to the shirts hung blue jeans, also well cared-for. She took a pair. She could at least be clean and warm before she got away. And the door was locked.

Beyond the bed was another door. She pushed it open, hesitant, expecting it to lead onto the roof.

It didn't. There was a bathroom. It was clean and spartan, with a bar of soap by the sink and a heavy bathtub with a brown stain running from the tap to the plughole. She leaned over it and ran her finger through the stain; it came away clean.

She turned the taps, biting her lip. A bath. She hadn't taken a bath in years. The water was tepid, though; not hot.

She turned off the cold tap and let the hot tap fill the tub halfway. When the heat started to fade and the water spluttered, she closed the tap and turned towards the door. This one had a bolt; she would be safe in here.

She slid the bolt then peeled off her wet clothes. She left them in a bundle on the floor; she'd deal with them after she'd cleaned herself. She didn't want that bath cooling any more than it had to.

She lowered herself in, eyes closed. It felt good, like silk brushing against her skin. She lay still, her eyes closed, for a few moments.

She opened her eyes, wishing she'd thought to transfer the soap bar from the sink. She couldn't face getting out of this water, heaving herself over the side of the tub and splashing across the cold tiled floor.

She gasped in a breath and dipped under the water. She'd learned to go without soap before, when the village supplies were low. The water was all she needed.

She rubbed herself as clean as she could, trying not to look at the bruises on her arms and the deep gash on her big toe. It stung in the water but at least it had stopped bleeding. She raised her fingers to her forehead; it was swollen next to the eye.

When she was clean, she gripped the sides of the bath and pushed herself up. She stepped out and put her foot down on the tiles, carefully so as not to slip.

There was a thin, greying towel on a hook by the sink. She grabbed it and towelled herself down.

She slid the bolt and eased the door ajar, peering through to check no one was in the bedroom. Her heart pounded against her ribcage. It was empty, the chair still wedged under the doorknob.

She opened the door and headed for the bed. She pulled the clothes on. They were large but not ridiculously so. If she tied a knot in the bottom of the shirt it fitted perfectly, and helped to hold the jeans up at the same time. She'd ask if there was a rope or something she could use to secure them.

In the bottom of the wardrobe were two drawers. She pulled one out, almost pulling it to the floor in her haste. It contained underpants and socks.

There was no way she was wearing Robert Cope's underpants but the socks would be welcome. She sat on the bed and pulled them on, wriggling her toes in reluctant pleasure. The sensation of being clean and dry, of wearing freshly laundered clothes, pulled at her. But her fear was still there. She couldn't let herself get comfortable.

She tried the other drawer. It held a wallet and a belt. She tied the belt around her waist, glad not to have to worry about losing the jeans, and picked up the wallet.

It contained no money, unsurprisingly. Instead, there were a few scraps of paper with indecipherable writing, and a small pile of photos. They depicted a woman and two small boys. The woman was short, with thin brown hair and the drawn expression of someone accustomed to a hard life. The boys were toddlers, one of them little more than a baby. The photo was worn over their faces, where they'd been touched repeatedly.

She wondered if this was Robert Cope's family. Some poor woman, who he'd left behind when the flood hit. Or maybe she'd died, or preferred to stay behind. Sarah shuddered.

Missing this family didn't excuse what he'd done.

There was a knock at the door. She crammed the photos back into the wallet and shoved it under the bedspread.

She tiptoed to the door and put a hand on the handle. Her throat felt tight, her skin cold.

"Who is it?"

"Martin. I wanted to check you were alright."

"I'm fine."

"Can I come in?"

She frowned at the door then pushed the chair to one side. She pulled the door open, blocking the doorway with her body.

"What do you need?"

He looked embarrassed. "I just wanted to talk to you. Find out what your plans are."

"My plans are to get home, if I can."

"Can I come in?"

"I'd rather not."

He glanced towards the stairs and lowered his voice. "Will you come out then?"

She followed him into the hallway. It was chilly out here, and her previously warm skin started to shiver.

"I wish I understood you, Martin."

"Sorry?"

"You're being nice to me now. But you took me. You were one of them."

"I didn't want to."

"You told me that."

"Look," he said. "I don't think you should go back. Not yet. Wait till your dad's calmed down a bit."

"You can't stay here. You're a wanted man, remember. And I'm not staying on my own with Bill."

She felt a shiver run down her back. Bill had been quiet since they'd arrived, as if brooding on his own secrets. She wondered why he'd stayed here, when all the others had fled.

"I'll get the boat going," she said. "And if you know what's good for you, you'll get as far away from here as you can."

"You think I'm a monster."

"It doesn't matter what I think. Only you know what you're really like." She prodded his chest with a finger then quickly withdrew it. "In here."

"I'm not like them. Robert. My dad."

"Your dad?"

A nod. "He was a drunk. Violent. Made my life hell."

"And you think that excuses what you did?"

"That's not what I'm saying. But I'm not like them. I'm not going to be like them."

She was too tired for this. She longed for the soft bed behind her, the heavy bedspread. But she needed to get away.

She retreated and started to push the door closed.

"Good luck, Martin. Whatever you've got planned. Just... be better. Don't fall in with people like Robert again."

"I'll try not to. I was planning—"

She held up a palm. "I don't want to know. If I don't know, I can't tell the police."

His eyes widened. "You don't want to tell them about me?"

"I know what you did. We all do. But Robert had it coming. The world's a better place without him. You shouldn't suffer for that. Nor should Ruth."

"Ruth. I need to go to the police, don't I?"

"You might only make it worse. Jess will vouch for her. You can't know what Ruth went through, why she did what she did."

"I know." He hung his head. "I'm sorry."

She heard sounds from downstairs; Bill, moving around in the kitchen. A door opened and closed. She stared towards the staircase, glad her door had a lock.

"I know." She pushed Martin back, but gently. "Now, goodnight."

CHAPTER TWENTY-NINE

DAWN STOOD AT THE TOP OF THE LADDER. SHE WISHED she'd thought to put shoes on; the rungs dug into her feet. She reached into the loft, feeling for the rope.

Her fingers landed on it and she tugged. There was a moment when she thought it might not budge, but then it came away, almost sending her toppling back.

Falling down the ladder; that would do the job. But she wasn't ready. Not yet.

She pushed the rope past her and watched as it went snaking to the floor below. It was stained and mottled, grey with age. Ted had carried it all the way here from Somerset, believing it to be useful. And he'd been right; they'd often used it to tie a tarpaulin over their belongings and sometimes themselves, glad of the protection from the driving rain.

Since they'd arrived here, it had only come out once, when Harry had asked Ted to help him in the boathouse. Ted had come home disgruntled; it seemed Harry and Clyde had better ropes.

She lowered herself down the ladder, hand over hand,

careful. As she was about to place a foot on the floor, there was a knock at the door.

She flinched, almost falling. She composed herself, then stepped down.

She looked at the ladder; did she have time to push it back up into the loft?

She grabbed the bottom rung and pulled it towards her, ducking out of the way as the ladder folded into itself.

The door knocked again; two short raps.

She gave a final heave and pushed the ladder up into the dark space of the loft. Brushing her hands together, she descended the stairs, wishing she'd stopped to look out of the upstairs window first.

As she reached the door the thought came to her that it might be Sarah. She flung the door open, her face bright.

"Oh."

"Hi Dawn." It was Jess.

"What can I do for you?"

"I just wanted a chat."

"A chat?" Chatting wasn't something Dawn did.

"While Ted's talking to the police."

Dawn put a hand on the doorframe. "They haven't taken him?"

"No. They just want to find out what happened, at the farm."

"Can't you tell them?"

"I didn't see it all. I burst in right at the end."

"Oh."

"And they'll want as many witnesses as they can get, I guess."

"Yes."

So Ted hadn't been arrested; that was a relief.

"Can I come in?"

Dawn squinted at Jess. Her thick red hair was unkempt. She looked flushed and harried.

"Go on. Be quick though."

As Jess slipped past her into the house, Dawn peered outside. Hopefully no one would see. Hopefully she would be gone before Ted returned.

Jess shrugged her shoulders a few times then peeled off her coat. Dawn watched her, alarmed. The hall felt cramped with a stranger in it.

"What can I do for you?"

"Like I said, just a chat. Can we sit down?"

Dawn ushered her through to the living room. Jess surveyed the twin sofas then chose one, perching as if she didn't want to crease it.

"Can I offer you a drink?"

"No. But thank you; that's kind."

Dawn never normally offered outsiders food and drink; they were strictly rationed and she had none to spare. She wondered if the other members of the village entertained each other, if they pooled their rations. She shuddered.

"So, what do you need to talk about?"

Jess sniffed. "I'm sorry about Sarah."

"Oh."

"I heard what happened, in the boat house."

"Yes."

Jess turned to her. "I also saw her, before that. She had a bruise." Jess raised a hand to her face. "Right here."

"Yes. She slipped."

"Really?"

"Would I be lying?"

Jess shuffled in her seat. Dawn perched on the edge of her own, her skin taut.

"Dawn, you can trust me."

"I know I can. You're the steward."

"That's not what I mean."

"Is this all you've come for?"

Jess put out a hand then stopped it in mid-air. "We can help you, you know. You and Sarah. This village doesn't exactly have a women's refuge but we can rehouse you, somewhere on the other edge. If needed, we can send Ted away."

"Why would you do that?"

"Because he hurts you."

Dawn stood up. "You have no evidence of that."

Jess looked uncomfortable. "I thought you trusted me, Dawn. After I left you those notes, when Sarah was taken?"

Dawn nodded. It was true that Jess had been the only member of the village with whom she'd had any communication at that time. Jess had left updates for her under her dustbin.

"I appreciate that. But if you don't mind, I've got jobs to be getting on with."

Jess heaved herself up and made for the door. As Dawn opened it, a man walked past the front of the house and Dawn felt her heart skip a beat. She closed the door again.

"I understand," said Jess. "But you can talk to me, if you need help. If he hurts Sarah again."

Dawn pushed her shoulders back; how dare Jess prod at her Achilles heel like that?

"I owe my life to my husband."

"Really?"

"He risked his neck for me and Sarah many times, on our way here. Without him, I'd be lying in a bush somewhere. And Sarah... well, the less said about that the better."

"I'm sorry. I didn't know."

Dawn remembered their journey to the village, the

long walk north. Jess had no idea. She didn't have a daughter who'd been almost raped. A husband who had stopped it in the most forceful of ways.

Then she remembered. "We all had it hard. You had to bring your poor mother."

Jess's face darkened. Her mother, Sonia, had been ill on her journey here and had died not long after arriving at the village.

"I'm sorry," said Dawn. "I didn't mean to…"

Jess sniffed. "It's OK. I don't mind talking about her. But I mean it about Ted. We're here to protect you."

"As is my husband."

"Well." Jess sighed. "That's not how it always looks."

Dawn took a step forward, making Jess step back. "Don't talk about him like that. Don't come into his house, reject hospitality which would be impossible without his efforts, and then make insinuations about him. Please."

"That's not what I meant to—"

"My marriage is none of your concern. Now leave."

They met each others' gaze for a moment then Jess turned to the door. Her gaze caught on the wall next to it.

"Does that give you strength?"

Dawn looked past her at her crucifix. Wrapped in tissue paper, it had made its way here from Somerset. And before that, it had been her mother's and her grandmother's before her. It had survived two world wars; it would survive more.

As would she.

"It does. Strength to know my daughter will be coming back to me."

Jess stared at it. "I hope so."

"I know so." Dawn stepped past Jess and opened the door. She stared at her visitor, urging her to leave with her eyes.

Jess gave her a sad smile. "It's been good to talk to you."

Dawn said nothing. She watched as Jess walked along the path that led to the village centre. She should be in her schoolroom, teaching those poor children. But instead here she was, throwing her weight around and poking her nose where it wasn't wanted.

Dawn pushed the door shut and closed her eyes. She leaned her forehead against the wood and trembled as tears ran down her face.

CHAPTER THIRTY

THE MOON WAS THREE-QUARTERS FULL, CLOUDS DRIFTING across it like slow fingers of mist. Sarah picked her way through the long grass, heading back the way she'd arrived. Around her were the sounds of night; animals shooting through the grasses, an owl somewhere behind her, the sea ahead.

She reached the beach. It looked dirty and littered in the dark, piles of seaweed easily mistaken for washed-up debris.

The tide was on its way out and the sand was damp. She picked her way across it, glad not to be sinking into dry powder but troubled by the cold. She'd found a pair of trainers under Robert's bed; two sizes too big but she'd laced them tightly and stuffed a balled up sock in the toes of each one. They hung on, for now.

She sniffed the salty air and surveyed the shore, looking for the boat. Nothing. She walked closer to the shore, careful not to let the water touch her feet. The rocks where they had come to shore were to her left, dark and moody in the dim light. If the boat had been wrecked, the pieces would be there.

She withdrew from the shore, finding a firm patch of sand to make her way across. When she reached the rocks, she headed back out towards the water. She considered clambering across the rocks, but then remembered how slippery and encrusted with barnacles they were, dips and troughs catching the water and glinting every time the moon came out from behind a cloud.

Then she saw it at the edge of the water, lapped by the waves. A dark shape, listing heavily but still distinctly boat-shaped. She clenched her fists, hopeful. And angry; Bill had been wrong about leaving it on the beach.

She hurried to it and bent to put a hand on the hull. It was dirty but intact. She couldn't see what the underside was like.

She grabbed an edge and heaved. It wouldn't budge. She placed her feet up against the keel, leaning into it. It moved slightly then shuddered to a halt.

"Need a hand?"

She spun round to see Bill watching her. He wore a heavy black coat that made him look larger, and his outline against the pale sand was eerie. She felt her heart flutter.

"No thanks."

He approached her. She had nowhere to go; behind her, the sea, and to her side, the rocks.

"I said no thanks."

"I just want to help." He was closer now; she could smell tobacco on him and heard his coat rustle as he walked. He had a purple scar on the side of his neck; she wondered how he'd got it.

"I don't need any help."

"I can help you move it. Check it over. You want to take the boat home, yes?"

"Yes."

"Right, then. The quicker we get it fixed up, the quicker you can be back with your family."

She glared at him. What right did he have to talk about her family like that?

She turned to the boat and gave it another tug. He snorted.

"You'll never do it like that. It's wedged against that rock, see?"

She looked at the other side of the boat. Sure enough, it was wedged under an overhanging rock.

"We'll need to bring it out at an angle," Bill said.

She couldn't do this alone. "Go on then."

He chuckled. "That's better. Now, you take that end. Pull it upwards, just a little bit, and then angle it out. Like this."

She followed his lead. The boat shifted upwards on the side closest to them and downwards on the other, freeing itself from the rock.

"Now we pull it onto the beach," he said.

"I can take it from here."

He eyed her. "Maybe you can. But it's easier with two of us."

He was right. She said nothing but let him help her. They pulled the boat away from the rocks until there was space for him to slip around the other side. Then they each took one side and heaved it across the damp sand, stopping when it was a few feet over the high water line.

He leaned over and took some deep breaths. "Not as fit as I was. That thing's heavy."

"You told us it was safe before."

"Sorry. Tide's unpredictable, these days."

"Right."

He straightened. "I just want to help you. And Martin. I owe you that at least."

She felt her stomach hollow out and her head lighten. Here she was, miles from home, alone on a beach with the man who'd drugged her, slung her over his shoulder and abducted her.

"I'm sorry," he said.

"Huh?"

"For what I did to you. There's no excuse. Robert didn't coerce me. I just spotted you and thought you'd tell them about Ruth."

She pulled back. She shouldn't have let him help her. It was a mistake.

"I'd like you to leave."

He stared at her for a moment then nodded. "I don't blame you. But you can't take that thing out on your own. Not now."

"Why not?'

"Because you'll drown, out there in the dark."

"I didn't drown on the way here."

"The boat's damaged. I can tell by the way it leans on the sand. Even a slow leak is enough to sink a little thing like this. And you don't know what you're doing."

She turned to him. "How can you know that?"

"Do you have experience at sea?"

She thought of the times she'd sat on the beach in Somerset as a child, watching the other families with their inflatable dinghies and lilos. She'd always been alone, sitting at the spot where the sand began, an observer of these incomers on her territory. In winter they'd be gone and she'd have the beach to herself.

But she'd never gone out on the water. And she'd only been in the village boat three times.

"It's just a day boat," she said. "I can manage it."

He was crouching next to the boat, peering under it. It would be too dark to see properly.

"Please," he said. "Wait till daylight. Then I'll come down here with you, help you get it ready."

"I'd rather go now."

"Shall I tell you what it's like to think you're drowning?"

She shrugged.

"First there's the cold. Your limbs, legs first, drop a degree or two. Then there's the claustrophobia. You're out in the big wide ocean but you feel like you're being hemmed in to the tiniest room. Then there's the panic. You flail wildly, despite the fact that your brain's screaming at you to be still. You know how to be safe, but your body refuses to do it."

"Then?"

"Then you drown. I don't know what that bit feels like. But Martin came pretty close once."

"To drowning?"

"I watched him fall in. Ruth treated him for hypothermia."

"And then he repaid her by bringing her here, with you."

"Sarah, please come back to the farm. A good night's sleep will give you the energy you need for tomorrow. I'll help you get this thing fixed up."

"I don't believe you."

"Why would I lie? I could just walk away now and I'd be no worse off."

"Do you know boats? Can you help me?"

"I've got some experience with carpentry."

She pulled Robert's jacket tighter around her. The sky was lightening very slightly, dawn approaching. She could be back here in just a couple of hours.

"Alright."

"Good."

He turned and headed back for the farm. The darkness swallowed him up, making her wonder if he'd really gone or was just a few paces away.

"Bill?"

No response. Suddenly she didn't want to follow him, didn't want him jumping out at her from the grasses.

She turned back to the boat. It was safe now. This would have to wait until morning.

She looked back the way she had come. Was he there still, or had he left her behind?

Only one way to find out.

She pushed through the grasses, taking a different path, trying not to lose her bearings. When at last the grass let go of her, she was on the road a short way from the farm. She crept towards it, hoping the men were asleep.

She pushed the front door open. Silence. She eased off the damp trainers and crept upstairs, wondering if Bill was a man of his word.

CHAPTER THIRTY-ONE

MARTIN SHOULD HAVE BEEN ON THE MOVE BY NOW, heading as far away from here as he could get, but he'd stayed to help Sarah.

Early that morning they'd dragged the boat to the edge of the beach, where it met the grass. The hull was just scratched; no hole. But the propeller had been torn apart on the rocks, one of its blades flopping loosely onto the sand.

Even if they could get the thing started, Sarah would never be able to control it.

Bill had his arms crossed and his face contorted into a frown. "It's not good."

"Yes, but we can fix it, right?" Sarah asked.

"Not easily. If we had a welding torch, maybe... Anyone got a welding torch?"

Sarah looked at Martin.

"Course not," he muttered.

"What about at the farm? Is there one up there?" Sarah asked.

"Not that I know of," said Bill. He eyed Martin.

"Shouldn't you be gone by now?"

"I'm not leaving Sarah here." He didn't add *with you*.

Bill shrugged. "The longer you stay here, the riskier for all of us."

Martin bristled. He didn't much care about putting Bill at risk. But Sarah…

"You're right," he said.

"No," said Sarah. She looked at Bill, then at Martin. "I'd rather you stayed. Just till we get this thing working."

"But what if the police turn up?"

"We'll hide you," said Bill.

"We'll lie," added Sarah. Her mouth turned up at the corners; he doubted she'd contemplated lying to the police before.

"Thanks. So, what about this boat?"

"I don't know," said Bill.

"Maybe you should come with me," said Martin. "You can't stay here."

She shook her head. "I want to go home."

He understood that. During the early weeks of his flight from the floodwater, he'd thought time and again about turning back for home, seeing his mum again. Not his dad. He'd promised her he'd return with help, that he'd get her rescued. He'd carried through on his promise; at the nearest town, he'd spoken to the guy co-ordinating the boats heading out across the flood-stricken Norfolk Broads and given them directions. But he'd been too scared of his dad to go back himself.

He'd spent six years haunted by the guilt at leaving his mum. He wasn't sure what was worse; leaving her to the floods, or leaving her to his dad.

"Well, you're not getting there in that," he said, gesturing at the boat.

"I could walk."

"You're not walking. It's forty miles."

"I could walk with you," said Bill.

"No," said Sarah. She shifted away from him, her eyes on the boat. "You sure you haven't got anything at the farm you can use to fix it?"

Bill fingered his chin. "We might have. Martin, do you know your way around a tractor engine?"

"I grew up on a farm."

"That doesn't answer my question."

"My dad's tractor was older than *he* was. We were constantly fixing it."

"Maybe you can work out some way to use the parts from one we've got in the barn."

"A tractor engine?"

"A whole bloody tractor. Hasn't moved for years. Pitted with rust, and the floor's gone. But there's an engine in there. It might have usable parts."

"What about fuel?"

"Robert was prepared on that score. He stole gallons of the stuff from a petrol station not long after we first got here. Enough to drive the farm's generator. And besides, there's still fuel in the boat. Isn't there?"

"Yes. Of course."

Sarah's face had brightened and she was looking from one man to the other. Martin thought she might burst with excitement. "I'll help," she said. "Fetching and carrying. Anything."

Martin smiled at her. "Come on. We've got work to do."

CHAPTER THIRTY-TWO

MARTIN WAS AT THE BEACH, FIDDLING WITH THE PARTS HE'D extracted from the tractor. Sarah had been struck by its bulk, the way it loomed at them in the empty barn. There'd been a family of mice nesting under the front seat and the bitter smell of droppings. There was also an acrid, nose-piercing smell that reminded her of her cat Snowy when he sprayed his territory.

She felt her chest tighten. Was Snowy being looked after? Would her mother remember him?

"We'll get this thing fixed soon, don't you worry," said Bill. He'd had a swing in his step since they'd started working on the engine, a lightness in his voice. He was enjoying it. She wondered what he'd do when they were gone. Then she remembered she didn't care. As long as he stayed away from her.

"I hope so," she said.

She was carrying a jagged piece of metal that looked like nothing useful to her, but it was one of the things Martin needed brought to him. He'd gone quiet since starting on the boat, not wanting to be disturbed.

Bill carried a toolbox he'd fished out from under the kitchen cupboard. The tools in it were rusted together, but they were all he had.

"I need to tell you something," he said. She shook her head; she didn't need his confession.

"You've already said sorry."

"It's not that."

They reached the edge of the grass. Martin was a few feet away, lying on his back next to the boat. He and Bill had overturned it so its keel was upwards. It looked vulnerable, like a pale marine creature stranded on land.

They handed him their prizes.

"Thanks." He yanked open the toolbox and picked out a spanner. "Is there a wire brush or something? I need to clean this stuff up."

"Maybe," said Bill. He looked at Sarah. "Come on."

She frowned at him but followed nonetheless, keeping her distance.

When they were in the middle of the tall grass, Bill called back to her.

"In the kitchen, when I had hold of Martin."

"You'd tied him up. With twine."

"I feel bad about that. But he seems to have forgiven me, so I hope you can too."

She continued walking.

He put a hand on her arm and she yanked it away.

"I let him go deliberately," he said.

She turned to face him. "He pulled himself away. He caught you unawares."

"I saw him looking at the knives. I knew what he was thinking. I loosened my grip, in all the confusion when your dad burst in."

She felt a weight descend onto her shoulders at the mention of her father.

"You thought he was going to hurt you. You were saving yourself," she said.

"No. I saw the look on his face. The hatred. The love."

"Don't."

"Sorry. But it's true. The boy adores you."

"That's irrelevant."

"He'd do anything for you. Look at him, fixing up that boat so you can go home. The longer he stays here, the greater the chance of the police finding him. He knows that, but he's still here."

Her face felt hot. "He doesn't want to leave me alone with you."

"Maybe. But that's not why he's doing it. If that was his only motive, then surely he'd make you go with him."

"He can't make me do anything."

"He won't. He knows you've had enough of that. What with your dad, and what we did to you. He knows you need to make your own decisions."

"Good for him." She didn't see why Bill was so interested in this.

"All I'm saying is cut him some slack."

"Whatever."

They were at the road now. Dusk was descending; they weren't going to get the damn boat running tonight. And even if they did, maybe Bill was right about going out there on her own, at night.

"He loves you, Sarah," Bill said as he pushed open the farmhouse door. "And I think you love him too."

CHAPTER THIRTY-THREE

MARTIN'S HANDS ACHED. HIS FINGERS WERE NUMB FROM fiddling with the boat engine in the cold. Luckily the rain had held off, but the damp air meant that his hands were red and swollen.

He stuffed them between his knees as he sat at the kitchen table. It was almost dark now and the night outside was still. No animals stirring, or at least none he could hear. And no police.

Bill put a plate of food in front of him; potatoes and carrots, steaming.

"Is this it?"

"Don't grumble. Without young Sammy, we've lost our hunter."

"Hunter?" asked Sarah. She was tucking into her potatoes, blowing on each and then placing it in her mouth as if it was a delicacy.

"Yeah," said Bill. He wiped his hands on his trousers and sat at the head of the table, between them. Martin wished he hadn't picked a chair opposite Sarah; she refused to meet his eye, and it made him nervous.

"He hunted rabbits for us," Bill continued. "Brought back a sheep once, God knows how he got that home. Only way of getting meat."

"And he disappeared with the others?" Sarah asked. She sounded casual, as if at a suburban dinner party discussing share prices, not the means of getting food when you were half-starved.

"Yep," said Bill. "They all buggered off at the same time. You not eating your veg, Martin?"

Martin pushed his plate away. "Not hungry."

"You need your strength, if you're planning on walking any distance."

Martin shrugged. He heard Sarah breathe out, a long whistling breath that spoke of irritation. That was all he was to her now. An irritation.

Well, if that was how she felt about him, she could sort the boat out herself.

"I'm heading out in the morning," he said.

Sarah dropped her knife. Bill placed his on his plate.

"You're what?" he asked.

Martin met his gaze. "You heard. You both keep telling me I need to get moving. Well, maybe you're right."

Sarah opened her mouth but then said nothing. Bill picked up his fork and shovelled a heap of potatoes into his mouth.

Martin stared at his plate, wishing now that he hadn't pushed it away. He couldn't pull it back now; he was too proud.

"You don't want this?" Bill asked. Martin shook his head.

Bill pulled the plate towards him. He shovelled half of its contents onto his plate and the other half onto Sarah's. It wouldn't be long before she was back at home, eating proper meals. He wandered what Dawn managed to cook with their rations. Better than carrots and potatoes.

Bill cleared his plate and pushed his chair back. He wiped his mouth with the back of his hand and looked between Martin and Sarah. Sarah was staring at her empty plate. So was Martin.

Bill picked up the plates and clattered to the sink.

Sarah stood up. "I'll do that."

"No," said Bill. "That's not right, after last time."

Sarah and the other women had been forced to do chores, when they were locked up here. Martin had supervised Ruth planting potatoes.

She pushed him to one side. Since when had she and Bill got so friendly?

"I know you're not forcing me to," she said. "And it doesn't matter what happened before. You cooked, I'm washing up."

Bill stepped back and gave her a tight smile. "Thanks." He looked at Martin. "In that case, I'm turning in. I want to be up at first light, try and get the boat running before you have to leave us, Martin."

Martin shrugged. It wasn't right that he was behaving like this. Bill had been good to him. And Sarah... well, Sarah was Sarah. He shouldn't abandon her.

"Night," he muttered.

He listened to Bill climbing the stairs. Sarah swilled water around the sink, intent on her task. It was taking longer than it should.

"I'd best be off to bed too," he said.

She turned round. "It can't be past eight. Don't be ridiculous."

"But Bill—"

"Bill nothing. I need to ask you something."

He sat down again. "Go on." He felt his stomach quiver.

She stacked the plates to dry and wiped her hands on her jeans – Robert's jeans. They were stained with rust and dried sand.

"Why can't you get the boat to work?" she said.

He frowned. "I told you. The engine…"

"You've been fiddling with it for hours. And it's just the propeller. I don't see why it won't run."

"I'm sorry, Sarah. I'm trying my best.'

"Are you?"

"What? Of course I am. Why wouldn't I?"

She didn't answer his question. Instead, she turned back to the dishes. She drained the sink and fished around in its depths, pulling out scraps and tossing them onto the newspaper that held food for the pigs. It seemed they, unlike the men, had stuck around.

He approached her. "Sarah, do you think I'm deliberately sabotaging the boat?"

"I didn't say that."

He stood behind her, close enough to smell the mustiness of Robert's aftershave on her shirt. It made him gag.

"I'm trying my best," he whispered. "I don't know anything about boats, that's all. It doesn't help."

She turned, making him back away. He almost toppled onto the table behind him then had a moment's light-headedness as he remembered when he'd last thrown himself onto that table, lunging at Robert, knife in hand.

"You don't want me to go," she said.

He swallowed down the dryness in his throat. "No. But that doesn't mean I'll stop you."

"Really?"

"We're not all like Ted."

She slapped him on the cheek. He threw his fingers up to it, suddenly delirious.

"You hit me!"

"I'll do it again, if you don't help me get that boat working."

"I heard about your dad, you know. When I was on the road. I didn't know it was him then, but I worked it out."

"You're lying."

He shook his head, remembering the long walk north. He'd encountered plenty of people on his way here, some friendly, others not so much. Robert had saved him from two lads who'd beaten him up and stolen his rucksack.

"I'm not," he said. "There were stories of a man with his wife and daughter, around the time I met Robert. What he did to people who crossed them."

She paled. "You told me that was near Lincoln."

He frowned. "Yeah."

"We passed that way too."

"I know. That's what I was saying. Your dad…"

"You don't know what you're talking about."

He was right, he could tell. They'd been near each other, on the road. He wondered what would have happened if they'd met.

She clenched her fists. "I need you to help me with the boat. In the morning."

"But you told me yourself. I need to get away from here. The police…"

"It's been two days. They're not coming."

She did have a point. He'd been wondering the same thing himself; it had been two days now since Ruth's arrest. This farm was less than an hour from Filey by car. Where were they?

Was he, maybe, safe?

"Don't talk like that about my dad," she snapped. Her voice was high, shaking. "You don't know him."

"I know he hit you." He struggled to keep his own voice steady. "I know the fear I saw on your face when you jumped into the boat. I understand, Sarah. My dad used to beat me."

A shadow crossed her face. "That's not— it's not— it's not what you think!"

She pushed past him towards the door. He wondered if Bill had heard them. Bill's room was at the far end of a corridor, possibly too far away.

"I'm sorry," he said. "I just wanted to help you."

"Well don't," she snapped as she threw the door closed behind her.

CHAPTER THIRTY-FOUR

SARAH STARED UP AT THE CEILING OF ROBERT'S BEDROOM. Her body felt numb, and her mind full of concrete.

Had she been too hard on Martin? He wasn't really trying to sabotage the boat, surely. Everything he'd done since leaving this farm last time, he'd been acting in her best interests.

And had he been right, about them being close to each other on the road? Could they have met? Could he have been one of the men who…?

No. He wasn't like that.

But he'd taken her from the village. He'd let Robert bring him along on his mission, taken advantage of Ruth's kindness.

Ruth, who was probably lying awake in a police cell.

She heaved her sore legs out of bed. Her feet throbbed from walking between the farm and the boat in ill-fitting shoes. She felt that if she did manage to sleep, she might never wake up. Her neck ached and her hands were raw and pink.

But maybe he was right about her father, when he'd

said that Ted was no better than him; worse in fact. No better than Robert.

She thought back to the look on Ted's face when he'd chased her down the beach, into the sea. The look when he'd hit her.

How was she going to face going home?

The thin blue curtains were torn and a draft made them shiver from time to time. She pulled them to one side to stare into the yard behind the farm. The outhouses, beyond it, were where they'd held her. Where she'd first encountered Martin. He'd been brought to her, shoved in by Robert, and told to *get on with it*.

But he hadn't. Instead, he'd told her where she was. He'd helped her escape.

She went to the bedroom door and turned the key. Outside, the house was still. She strained to hear Martin and Bill's breathing, but there was nothing, just the rhythmic tap tap of a tree hitting the window at the end of the corridor.

She turned towards the window, peering into each room in turn. They were dishevelled, clearly abandoned. Mattresses upended, curtains torn off their rails. No clothes, no valuables. The men had had time to pack up their belongings, then. If they had any.

She came to a door that was almost closed. She leaned towards it, listening. She could hear breathing.

Was it Martin, or Bill?

She pushed the door very slightly, holding her breath. It creaked. She stopped pushing, and counted to ten. There was no sound.

She gave the door another push, more gently this time. It gave way in silence.

The room was dark. She squinted to adjust her vision and a mattress came into focus, a pale rectangular shape in the centre of a dark floor. On it was a single figure. Tall, thin.

Martin.

The figure moved. He was sitting up, reaching for something.

A weapon?

"It's me," she whispered.

"Sarah?"

CHAPTER THIRTY-FIVE

"ARE YOU ALRIGHT?" HE ASKED. "WHAT'S HAPPENED?"

"Nothing's happened. I just wanted to talk to you." She could feel the blood pulsing through her temples.

"In the middle of the night?"

"Sorry. I'll go." She backed away.

"No." He stood up, filling the room with his height. She could barely see where he ended and the shadows began.

"It's too dark," she said. "And it stinks."

"You want to go downstairs?"

She thought of the route they would have to take to get to the kitchen. Past Bill, no doubt.

"No. Come to my room." She had a bedside lamp. It worked, amazingly; the first time she'd used an electric lamp in years. She'd been so astounded by it that she'd only allowed herself to keep it on for a minute at a time, and then waited half an hour before lighting it again.

"Sure."

She turned into the hallway, half expecting to find Bill out there eavesdropping. But the corridor was quiet. The wind had picked up and the branch scraped more vigorously against the window pane. It needed pruning, she thought. In her village, such things were looked after, tended. If not by the inhabitants of the closest house, then by the gang that looked after the trees and shrubs that had been planted years ago, for the holidaymakers who'd once occupied the houses. Before they'd been allocated to refugees.

At her door she stopped to look back. Martin was padding silently behind her, his breathing regular.

She eased the door open then waited for him to follow her inside. She closed it again. She went to the bed and lit the lamp. She didn't sit down, but stayed upright, watching Martin scratch his neck. He stayed by the door.

"So this was Robert's room," he said.

"You never came in here?"

"No. What's that door?"

"A bathroom."

He whistled under his breath. "Lucky bastard." He reddened. "Sorry."

"Don't worry. I know I'm a lucky bastard. Hot water and electric light."

"I didn't mean…"

"I know you didn't."

"What did you want to talk about?"

She sat down on the bed. It bowed under her weight then rebounded a little. "About tonight. I shouldn't have said those things."

"It's alright."

"It's not. I'm scared. I'm—I'm confused. But that's no excuse."

"I don't blame you Sarah, really I don't. After all the things I've done…"

She patted the bed next to her, feeling her heart thud against her rib cage. "Sit down."

"Next to you?"

She nodded, feeling ice run down her back.

He walked slowly to the bed, his eyes not leaving hers for a second. He looked wary, as if expecting her to change her mind. To lash out at him.

He sat a foot or so away from her. The bed dipped further.

He bounced up and down. "Nice. Better than a mattress on the floor."

"Did you know he lived like this?"

A shrug. "I guessed as much. Never talked about it though. No point."

Her mouth was dry. "You didn't deserve it."

He looked at his fingers, which were twisting in his lap. "Oh, I think I did." He looked up. "I've done things. Bad things."

"We all had to, after the floods."

"Even you?"

"Well. Not me. But my dad did. To protect me and my mum."

"Hmm."

She could only imagine the thoughts going through his head, wild fictionalisations of Ted's behaviour on the road. She didn't feel like contradicting him.

She leaned towards him and put her hand over his. He stopped moving, holding it very still.

"Thank you," she said.

"You don't need to thank me."

"I do. You've looked after me. You're helping me get home."

He shrugged. His hand shifted and he stilled it quickly. His skin was warm.

She twisted her hand to hold his. He moved his own so that they were holding hands in his lap. He placed his free hand over hers.

"I love you," he said.

She pushed down the fear that threatened to spill out of her. "I know."

He was looking at her. She stared ahead, at the window. The torn curtains. She counted the rips in them. Twenty-seven. He watched her in silence.

She turned to him. "Kiss me."

His eyes widened. "Sorry?"

"You heard." She gave him a nervous smile.

He licked his lips, then leaned towards her. She closed her eyes. His lips brushed hers then withdrew.

She found herself leaning forwards, holding onto the kiss. The only time she'd been kissed before was by Zack Golder, at the age of fourteen. It had been dry and horrible and neither of them had mentioned it again.

His eyes widened further then closed, and she felt him leaning in. The bed shifted as he moved to sit closer. He put a hand on the back of her neck and she felt her skin shiver.

His tongue was in her mouth now, exploring. But not pushing, like Zack had.

She thought of Jess and Zack; did he kiss her like that? She laughed into Martin's mouth.

He pulled back. "Have I done something wrong?"

She clapped her hand to her mouth. "I'm sorry! No, no you haven't. I was just thinking of… never mind." She swallowed. *Don't laugh.*

She grabbed his arm and pulled him to her. They kissed again, faster this time, deeper. She squeezed her eyes shut.

She carried on pulling, feeling his weight fall on her as

she toppled back onto the bed. She was lying down now, his weight half on her and half over the side of the bed.

She opened her eyes. He stopped kissing her to pull back, looking down at her.

"Are you sure about this?" he asked.

She nodded.

She shifted her weight, moving to the other side of the bed. He stroked her hair. She lay there, blinking up at him. So this was what bound her mother to her father. She'd heard them at night; his grunts and her moans.

She felt full and empty inside, both at the same time. She wanted him now, more than she'd ever wanted anything.

She grabbed the hand that was in her hair and brought it to her mouth. She kissed it. She smiled at him.

She reached up for his shoulder and pulled him down on top of her. He cupped her head in his hand and kissed her deeply. She pushed back with her tongue, losing herself.

His hand was on her arm, creeping towards her breast. She didn't stop it. She stiffened as she felt his hand rest there, and tried her hardest to keep breathing.

She reached down between them and unbuttoned her shirt. She squeezed her eyes shut, blocking out thoughts of Robert wearing this shirt.

For a second she thought she'd ruined the moment, that the memory of that bastard would get in the way. But she managed to push him away and now Martin's hand was inside the shirt, stroking her nipple.

She moaned.

His face was in her hair now, his mouth at her ear. "When you want me to stop, just say," he said.

She let out a long, shaky breath.

"Don't stop," she told him.

CHAPTER THIRTY-SIX

THE ROOM WAS DIM WHEN SARAH WOKE, SUNLIGHT JUST beginning to filter through the curtains.

She lay perfectly still, her eyes closed. Her fingers tingled and her body felt as if it had been filled with liquid fire.

And today, they were both leaving.

She blinked her eyes open, focusing on the wall next to the bed. There was a damp patch halfway up the wall, and the wallpaper was peeling at the edge. It was textured, painted in a shade of white that had yellowed with time.

She took a few slow breaths, not wanting to wake up. Not wanting the day to start.

At home, she'd have to face her father. Her mother— her mother would know, surely. She'd see it in Sarah's eyes. In the way her skin glowed. And Sam. Would she have to settle for Sam now? The safety, the dependability of Sam?

No, she wouldn't. Not if she convinced Martin to come with her.

She turned in the bed, ready to wake him, to tell him

her plan. The bed shifted under her weight, springs squeaking.

Had they squeaked like that last night? Would Bill have been listening?

The bed next to her was empty.

She pushed herself up, clutching her arms around her chest. She was still naked, and suddenly cold.

She looked at the bathroom door. It was open, with no sound coming from beyond.

She turned towards the door to the corridor; it was closed.

She sat up to check the floor. His clothes would be there; she'd peeled them off him last night, letting them slide to the floor. He'd pulled her shirt off with his teeth.

The floor was empty.

She slumped back.

How could she be so stupid? So naive, and trusting, and *stupid*? He'd lied to her, had got what he wanted from her, and now he'd left. He was no better than Robert Cope.

How would she ever look her mother in the eye again? She should have listened to her. Should have chosen Sam.

Bill would be down there, pottering around the kitchen as he always did. He'd have seen Martin leave. It would be humiliating.

She couldn't face him. She would creep down the stairs and let herself out. If she couldn't get the boat to start, she'd walk home. She'd run. She'd swim if that was what it took.

She wanted her mother.

She crept to the wardrobe, aware that the kitchen was directly below, and took out another clean shirt. Her own skirt and blouse, the soaked clothes she'd arrived in, were nowhere to be seen.

Not to matter. Robert's clothes would be more practical anyway.

She flung on a shirt, then another one on top. It was cold out there, and the coats were by the back door. She grabbed another and pulled it over the first two. It was tight now, but that was good. Tight meant no drafts.

She pulled on a pair of jeans then three pairs of socks. She picked up yesterday's jeans from the floor, blushing to think of how they'd been removed, and slid out the belt. She belted her clean jeans.

Shoes.

The sodden trainers were by the door. She'd lost one of her own, and the other was downstairs somewhere. With all these socks the trainers would fit better.

She slid them on and tied the laces tightly. It hurt, but she knew they mustn't move, mustn't rub. Tight was good.

She grabbed the door handle and turned it slowly. The door opened silently. She crept along the corridor to the stairs. There was a bend – she paused to listen before rounding it, afraid of bumping into Bill – but at last she was at the top of the stairs.

She held the bannister, trying to control her breathing. Her stomach felt as if it would expel its contents at any moment, and she couldn't be sure how. She swallowed. *Keep it down.*

The kitchen door, towards the back of the house, was closed. Thank God. She crossed herself, imagining how pleased Dawn would be to see her.

She placed a foot on the top step, gritting her teeth. It creaked slightly, but nothing that could be heard through a closed door. She took another step, and another, wishing she could tumble down and run through the front door.

As she neared the bottom of the stairs, she heard

voices. She stopped, one foot hovering over the next step. She lowered it carefully, then turned to listen.

Bill; she knew his voice. The other was deeper, as if it belonged to someone tall and broad. Not Martin. And was that a *woman*?

She felt her heart pick up pace. They couldn't hear her. But then—

What if they'd taken more women? What if the other men had come back, with more captives? What if they were women from her village?

She slid to the bottom of the stairs, wishing she'd thought to wait before putting the shoes on. She stood next to the kitchen door, her chest rising and falling, her stomach growling. Her thighs smarted from last night. She hated them.

"So you're saying you haven't seen him since the incident?" The man, the one with the deep voice. Robert?

No. He's dead. One of the other men. There'd been another older man, like Bill. Robert's lieutenants.

"Sorry, but the last time I saw him was when he left here with the people from the village up the coast."

"The village you visited."

A pause. "We got into difficulties at sea. They came out for us. They were very kind."

"And you brought some of them back here with you?"

"There aren't a lot of people like us around here. Refugees. We wanted to make links with them."

Liar, she thought.

People like us. If he wasn't talking to his own men, who was he talking to? Newcomers? The owner of the farm?

"We need to speak to him in connection with a murder investigation."

Sarah held her breath. It was the police. Did they still have Ruth? And why hadn't Ruth or Jess told them about the abductions? Surely the villagers weren't that mistrustful of the authorities.

Then she remembered the time the village had been invaded by kids from the nearby estate. Their parents too, on the second night. The police had taken the side of the locals.

"Very well. We may have to take you in for questioning."

"Are you arresting me?"

"No."

"Then I don't have to go anywhere with you."

"Very well, Mr Peterson. I expect you to tell us if you see him or the girl."

Sarah clapped her hand to her mouth. The girl?

She backed away from the door. She looked at the front door. They could be out there, blue lights flashing. Waiting for her. For Martin.

She lifted a foot behind her, to the bottom step. She retreated backwards up the stairs, not taking her eyes off the kitchen door.

CHAPTER THIRTY-SEVEN

DAWN WAS ASLEEP WHEN TED RETURNED. SHE'D HIDDEN the rope under Sarah's bed, crossing herself and asking God for forgiveness as she did so. When she heard Ted slam the front door, felt the bed dip under his weight, she hadn't moved.

Now it was morning and she was in the kitchen, making breakfast. Fried eggs from the village hens, his favourite.

She knew he'd been awake when she got out of bed, but hadn't had the courage to turn and make eye contact. *Go easy on her*, she'd told him, referring to their daughter. But would he go easy on *her*?

He stumbled down the stairs, muttering under his breath, and slumped into a chair. He smelled of sweat, and teeth that hadn't been brushed. She pursed her lips, determined to put on a smile. But first, the eggs. She pushed them around the pan, focusing on their spitting, on the way they gradually changed colour as they solidified in the heat.

At last the eggs were cooked. Ted, behind her, was silent. Watching her, no doubt.

She scooped them onto a plate and added a hunk of bread. The bread was rough but satisfying, and always fresh. Although this was yesterday's; today, she couldn't face going to the village shop for her ration. The eyes, the questions. *Where is your daughter? Does your husband hit you?*

She pushed her shoulders back and took a shallow breath. She forced a smile onto her lips; she should be pleased, at least he hadn't been arrested.

She turned, holding the plate. Trying to still her hand.

"Morning love," she said, holding her voice steady.

He was looking past her, out of the window. It faced the side of their house, looking at Sanjeev's wall.

He said nothing.

She placed the plate in front of him and turned back to the bread. She sawed off a piece for herself, cursing her own clumsiness.

"What's this?"

She stopped cutting. "Eggs."

"Where's the bacon?"

She turned. He was holding the plate up at an angle, like it was something detestable. The eggs would slip to the floor if he wasn't careful.

"I haven't had a chance to go to the shop. We ran out—"

He dropped the plate. It clattered to the floor but didn't smash. She couldn't see if the eggs had stayed in place.

"I want bacon."

She hurried towards the hall, to fetch her coat. She would have to face them.

He put out a foot. She tripped over it, landing next to the eggs. Her fingers were in them. The yolks felt thick and viscous. She retched.

"Get up!"

She pulled her fingers out of the eggs and grabbed the plate. She stood, placing it on the table.

He pushed it to one side, sending it to the floor. This time, it smashed. She kept herself from crying out.

"I didn't tell you to leave."

"You wanted bacon."

He grabbed the fingers on her right hand, which were resting on the table, where the plate had been. He twisted a fingernail into her ring finger.

"You're not going out there."

"Right."

He stood up. "Clean up this mess. I'm going to find her."

She looked up from the floor where she was trying to collect pieces of egg white in her shaking fingers. "What?"

"You heard. I'll get some men together. We'll go after them."

"But it's been two days."

"So?"

"She'll be miles away."

He bent over her. She clasped her lips shut, trying not to gag at the smell of his breath combined with the egg.

"How would you know that, woman?"

She pulled away from him, her bottom landing on the cold floor. "The boat. It's fast. Isn't it?"

"How do you know she hasn't stopped somewhere? How do you know he hasn't taken her to that wretched farm?"

"I don't. But you tried this before and—"

He kicked the plate out of her hands. She yelped and shrank back. "Don't you remind me of that! This is different."

"Yes. This time she went willingly." She could hear

herself contradicting him. She never did this. But Sarah's disappearance had banished Dawn's desire for self-preservation.

He froze, eyes boring into her. "You're right."

She chewed her lip, waiting for him to kick her again. Should she stand up, put the table between them? Or would movement provoke him?

"Don't do that, woman. Disgusting."

She stopped chewing. Slowly, she pulled herself up, using the table for support. He didn't stop her but instead stared out of the back window towards the sea.

When the table was safely between them she cleared her throat. "How do you mean, I'm right?"

He turned. His eyes bulged and his cheeks were inflamed. "She went willingly. That's what you said."

"Yes."

"She's going to let him do what he wants to her. Just like she did with those two lads back in Lincoln."

"She didn't and you know it! They would have—" she lowered her voice. "They would have raped her."

His eyebrows were knotted together and his mouth twisted. He sniffed at her.

"Yeah. Well, they won't be doing anything like that again. And nor will she, the little slag."

"Ted! That's our daughter you're—"

He leaned over the table. "She's my daughter and I'll say as I see it. I'll kill her for this."

"Don't say that…"

He spat at the floor. She stared at the globule of spit, anticipating cleaning it. That, and the remains of his breakfast. That left only one egg for the next two days.

"I'll say what I want. Just shut the fuck up and clean up that mess. You disgust me."

He yanked the kitchen door open and flew into the hallway, slamming the front door behind him. Dawn ran up the stairs to watch him through the upstairs window. He sped towards the beach, shoulders hunched.

She slid down the wall, trembling. *Sarah, where are you?*

CHAPTER THIRTY-EIGHT

SARAH STARED AT HER BEDROOM DOOR, WAITING FOR IT TO open. For the police to come for her too.

She pulled the shirt tighter around her, tugging at the sleeve. She was hot, in all these layers.

At last there was a knock. She swallowed down the lump in her throat. She still didn't know what she was going to say to them.

"Come in."

"It's locked."

She crossed to the door and unlocked it. She pulled back to the bed again.

The door opened. It was Bill, alone.

She ran out and peered along the corridor. "Where are they?"

"So you heard."

"Yes. What did they want?"

"Martin." He gave her a look. He knew.

"I don't want you in here," she said. "Wait downstairs for me."

He shrugged. "You won't run off?"

She felt her cheeks redden. "No."

He nodded then left her. She watched him amble towards the stairs as if this was any other day. What would he do, now they were alone?

She felt a shiver run down her body.

She went back into the bedroom. On her first night, she'd cleared away the shards of pottery that lay on the floor, along with those blue flowers. Cornflowers. The flowers were a deep purple now, but the pottery remained. She picked up a sharp piece and wrapped it in between the layers of shirt. Then she took it out and wedged it in the back of her jeans.

She cast a last look around the room, trying not to stare at the bed, then headed downstairs.

Bill was sitting at the kitchen table, waiting for her. It was the stillest she'd seen him. He looked up. There were two mugs in front of him. He gestured to one of them.

She lifted her chin, determined not to let him humiliate her. "Did they take him?"

"No."

"Where is he then?"

"He went out the back. They were at the front."

"They didn't have people at the back, waiting for him?"

"Seems not. There were only two of them."

She grasped the mug and laced her fingers around it. She wanted to ask if Martin had said he was coming back.

"I think I should go home," she said.

"He had flowers."

She looked up. "Who?"

"Martin. He'd been out picking them. Soft lad. He was grabbing some breakfast for you both. An apple each. Crappy breakfast, but there you go."

On the table were two green apples. She glanced at

them then sipped at her drink, glad of the mug hiding her face. It tasted bitter.

"What's this?"

"Herbal tea. Not sure what herbs."

"It's vile."

"You get used to it."

She pushed the mug away. "What sort of flowers?"

"Yellow ones. I don't know much about flowers."

"Where are they now?"

"He took them. He had them in his hand, when the police arrived."

She looked towards the back door. Maybe he'd dropped them out there. Maybe he was still holding them, running with them.

It didn't matter now.

She stood up. "I'm going to the boat."

She turned towards the hallway and the front door. She turned back and grabbed a coat. Robert's. Martin's was still there, on its peg.

There was knock at the door. She stared at Bill, her heart racing.

Another knock, louder this time. Two more.

"Hide," Bill said.

CHAPTER THIRTY-NINE

SARAH WAS SURE THEY WOULD HEAR HER BREATH ECHOING in the cramped confines of the cupboard. She shifted her weight, cramp already developing in one foot, then instantly regretted it as a tin shifted next to her, scraping on the floor. Her eyes darted to the door, but no one came.

She'd wanted to run up the stairs when Bill had gone to the door, but knew that they would hear her. That they would search the bedrooms. They might not think of this walk-in cupboard.

She heard movement upstairs, footsteps moving from room to room. She tried to remember how she'd left the bedroom. Was there evidence that a woman was here?

More noises upstairs, thuds and thumps. Drawers being opened, the smash of a lamp falling to the floor. The one in her room?

She held her breath, staring at the door. It smelt musty in here, and stale. There was the tang of pickled onions and the strong odour of feet. The air was dry. She wanted to cough.

Feet came down the stairs and she heard voices getting closer.

"You can't do this," said Bill. "Not without a warrant."

"You want us to arrest you too? Aiding and abetting? Obstruction? Not to mention squatting."

"No."

"Then let us do our job."

"Squatting doesn't really count, not any more."

"I'm sure the owner of this farm would see it differently."

"They haven't been back here in nearly five years. I doubt that they care."

"Are you always like this, Mr Peterson?"

"Like what?"

"Difficult."

Shut up, thought Sarah. *Don't wind them up.*

They were in the kitchen now. A shadow passed under the door. She clenched her fists, counting.

"We need to look in your outbuildings."

"Fine."

She heard keys being gathered, the back door opening. Was Martin hiding out there? Could he be in the very cell she'd been kept in, in the outhouse behind the farm?

She felt as if her insides might dissolve at any moment.

The voices receded but there was still someone in the room, moving around. A more junior officer maybe, prowling the kitchen. She shuffled further back in the vain hope she might be disguised by the empty boxes and tins.

Then the back door slammed. She held her breath and listened but there was no one in the kitchen, she was sure of it.

Unless they were sitting in silence, tempting her out.

No. If they were that clever, they'd have found her hiding place.

She took a hesitant step towards the door and gave it a tiny push. Light streamed in, illuminating the dust that danced in the confined space.

She waited. Nothing.

She pushed it a little more, to see the table. There was no one there. The only place for a person to hide would be right behind this door. And if they were there, it was too late anyway.

She eased the door open and lowered herself to a crouch, almost crawling along the floor. She looked at the door to the hall. It was open, but there were no shadows, no movement.

She crept to the back door, which was closed. She crouched behind it. Its lower half was solid but the top half had a pane of glass.

She glanced back at the other door then slid upwards, her hands on the wood. She had to see.

There were five people out in the yard, including Bill. A tall, broad-shouldered man in an ill-fitting suit and a younger woman wearing a bright blue jacket. The man talked to Bill while the woman watched the outhouse.

With them were two uniformed officers, both women. They prodded the piles of junk around the yard as if Martin might spring out from under them.

She could see shadows in the corridor at the front of the outhouse, that led to the four cells where she and the other women had been kept. She put her ear to the glass and heard the cell doors being opened and closed. She wondered again how much the police knew about what had happened to her, Ruth and the others. Why hadn't Ruth told them? Why wasn't Bill being arrested for taking her?

The shadows shifted and a shape appeared in the

doorway to the outhouse. Sarah ducked down, almost toppling in her haste.

"No sign of him."

She felt her breathing still. He'd be far away by now, running across fields. Maybe crawling through the muddy ditch they'd taken together, when he'd helped her run.

How many police would be looking for him? She knew police resources were stretched, had been since the floods and the economic collapse, so Filey would only have a handful of officers. They were probably all here.

"What's this?"

She peered over the doorframe to see one of the uniformed women standing at the side of the outhouse. There was a door there, behind which was the most unbe-lievable stink. Sarah had never had cause to open it, thankfully.

The detective turned to Bill. "Give us the key."

Bill took the keys from his pocket then stared at them. The detective snatched them from his hand.

"I suggest you help us. Better for you."

The detective tossed the keys to his colleague and she approached the uniformed officer, arm outstretched. They both disappeared round the corner of the outhouse.

Sarah held her breath. Her eyes prickled.

"Got him!"

She clutched her stomach, fighting nausea.

The two women emerged around the side of the outhouse. Between them, his head low and his jeans stained dark brown, was Martin.

Sarah bit her lip, ignoring the blood. She reached out for the door handle.

The male detective squared his shoulders. He turned to Bill. "Did you know he was there?"

"No idea." Bill had his head up, defiant.

"Hmm."

Martin was shoved in front of him. His face was streaked with dirt and he looked younger, like a boy being reprimanded by his parents. Sarah wanted to run out and grab him.

"Martin Walker?" the detective said. Sarah bit down on her lip, realising she'd never asked the surname of the man she'd slept with last night.

"Yes."

"Good. I'm arresting you for the murder of Jacob Cripps and Zahir Ali."

CHAPTER FORTY

MARTIN STARED UP AT THE WINDOWS OF THE FARMHOUSE AS they bundled him into the back of the unmarked police car. This wasn't his first time; he'd been arrested for shoplifting as a teenager, had spent a night in the cells. His mum had arrived the next morning to collect him and he'd been released with a caution. His dad had been apoplectic when he arrived home; not at the crime, but at the fact he'd been caught. Martin had stood in front of his dad's faded armchair, head hung low, and taken the bollocking. He'd only moved when his dad had told him to stop blocking his view of the TV.

The door closed with a thud and the car dipped as two people got in the front. A uniformed woman in the driver's seat, and the man who'd arrested him next to her. He had a flat face with a scar that ran from his nose to his upper lip. Martin wondered how he'd got it, and hoped it was nasty.

The car started. They waited for the marked car to go ahead of them then sped off down the lane as if released from a catapult. He couldn't remember the last time he'd travelled at such speed; it had been six years since he'd been in a car.

He clung to the seat, muttering under his breath, hardly daring to look out of the window.

The detective turned in his seat. "Stop that."

Martin stared at him. He stopped muttering, but tightened his grip on the seat and dug his nails in.

His horror at being found had been almost matched by his relief at getting out of the toilet where he'd hidden. It was little more than a cesspit, a receptacle that the men who weren't privileged to live in the farmhouse had slung their slops into every morning. The smell had been solid, like an object hovering in the air. He could still taste it.

As they dragged him out he'd stared up at the back windows of the farmhouse, wondering if Sarah was awake. If she'd woken to find him gone. She would hate him for that. She would think he'd taken what he wanted, and then run.

Would Bill tell her he'd been arrested?

He screwed up his eyes, battling tears. But the thought of Sarah's pale face on the pillow was too much for him. She'd responded to his touch, her body quick and lithe. He'd gone slowly, waiting for her to say no at any moment. But she hadn't.

Now she would wish she had.

The detective was staring ahead, talking to his colleague in a low voice. Martin wondered if Ruth would still be at the police station, if he could help her. He would tell them that he killed Robert, that she bore no part of the blame.

But Robert's hadn't been the name they'd given him. *Jacob Cripps and Zahir Ali.*

Who were they?

No one he knew, that was for sure. Was this a red

herring, a pretext for getting him to the station, where they could poke and prod him, extract information about Robert's death?

If it was, he would tell them everything. Everything up to the point where Ruth stood over Robert and ground her foot into his chest. Martin had lunged for Robert, plunging a knife into his throat. That was what killed him.

Yes. That was what he would do. He would tell them he'd killed Robert, that he had no idea who the other two people were, and that Ruth was innocent. He would co-operate.

Maybe they'd be lenient. They didn't have the resources to hold him for long. Maybe they'd let him out after a couple of years. Sarah's family might accept him as the man that had saved Ruth.

But the thought kept nagging him, pushing its way above the surface. Who were Cripps and Ali? And how was he supposed to have killed them?

CHAPTER FORTY-ONE

SARAH THREW HERSELF OUT OF THE KITCHEN DOOR. BILL
was gone.

She ran around the side of the house, not caring who
saw her now. Bill was standing at the front corner of the
building, looking along the lane to the north. He turned
towards her, his hands in his pockets. Casual.

When he saw her, his eyes widened.

"Why didn't you tell me?" she screamed. "Why?"

"Tell you what?"

"That he's a murderer!"

"Martin isn't a murderer. He was provoked. He was
defending you."

"I'm not talking about Robert! Who the hell are Jacob
Cripps and Zahir Ali?"

Bill's face darkened. "You heard."

"Yes, I heard."

"He didn't kill them. Look, Sarah—"

"That's not what the police say. You should have
told me!"

She lurched at him, her hand whipping out to hit him.

He caught it, the two of them locked together. She glared at him.

"Let me go."

"You need to calm down. Martin didn't—"

"No. I just learned that the man I let into my bed last night is a double murderer."

Bill let go of her wrist, flinging it away. She brought it back up, but his look stopped her.

He turned to the back of the house. "Come inside."

She clattered into the kitchen and stood with her back to the door. He sat at the table. Their two mugs sat on it, cold. She wondered what the police would have made of them. Bill's and Martin's, they would have assumed.

"You're all as bad as each other," she said. Her voice was hoarse and her throat ached. She wanted to slide to the floor and let it swallow her up.

"No," said Bill. "They've got it wrong."

"I'm sick of your lies. I'm going home. Help me with the boat or don't. I can walk anyway."

She pushed the door open and stormed into the yard. Bill followed.

"Sarah, stop!"

"I'm not staying here with you."

"You'll never get that boat working. I don't know how to do it."

"Then I'll walk."

"It's forty miles."

"I don't care!"

There was a clap of thunder. She looked up, expecting to see lightning coming straight for her. Instead a faint flash echoed off the walls.

She was going to get wet. She might die of exposure.

She didn't care.

"At least wait till the storm's gone," said Bill. Rain was

lashing down now, hammering into the corners of the yard and bouncing back at her. Her hair was already wet.

"No."

"You really want to go home?"

"I need to face my dad." She shuddered.

"He's not the monster you think he is, you know."

"He killed two people."

"Not Martin. Your dad."

"My dad is none of your business."

Her hair was stuck to her face, but she refused to push it away.

"I saw his face, when he found you. When he saw what Robert was doing to you. He was scared, Sarah. Terrified."

"So was I!"

"He saw his little girl with a knife to her face. He wanted blood. He loves you."

"He hits my mum."

A pause. "I didn't know that."

She stared at him. He stood in the doorway, only his chest wet. She ignored the water seeping into her shoes and through the layers of socks.

"There's a lot you don't know," she said.

He stepped down from the doorstep, squinting against the rain. "I'm sorry."

"Don't be. My mum's right."

"Right about what?"

"About Sam. He's safe, dependable. He hasn't killed anyone."

"Who's Sam?"

"Just a boy, at the village. A man. He loves me."

"Martin loves you."

The rain had worked its way through all her layers now. It felt like it might permeate her skin. She shook the strands of wet hair out of her eyes. "Martin lied to me."

Bill stepped forwards. "He loves you. And you love him."

"No I don't."

He arched an eyebrow.

"I don't! How can you know how I feel?"

He stared at her, not speaking. She wanted to hit him.

"I don't care what you think. I'm going."

She turned away. She hoped there would be road all the way home, no muddy fields to traverse.

"Stop."

She carried on walking.

"I said stop. I have a better idea. For you to get home."

CHAPTER FORTY-TWO

THE LANES WERE NARROW AND WINDING UNTIL THEY reached the main road to Filey. Martin gazed out of the window, trying to imagine what it would have been like to walk this route, as Jess and her friends had done to find Sarah.

The car slowed as they reached a turning to the right, in the direction of the sea. He pulled himself up, his hand on the window.

They passed through a gateway and along a road that held no other cars. On either side, small houses stared out at them, their facades giving nothing away. The rain bounced off the car windows and no one was outside for a soaking.

They proceeded to an open area then took a right turn. Martin felt his stomach flip.

He knew this place. This wasn't Filey; it was Sarah's village.

He sank down in his seat, glad of the rain obscuring the windows. He wondered if they'd come here to arrest someone else, to take them to Filey too. Or maybe they would let him out here, give the villagers a chance to mete out whatever justice they deemed fit.

He felt a small noise leave his lips. For the first time in almost five years, he was scared.

The car pulled to a halt outside Ben and Ruth's house. The uniformed woman got out and knocked on the door, adjusting her cap to keep out the rain. Martin looked behind him; had the other car followed them? Yes. It was parked a few feet away, a marked police car like a beacon in this quiet, reclusive place.

The door opened to reveal a man in the doorway. The policewoman spoke to him and he leaned out to peer at the car.

Martin felt his chest stiffen: Ben. But where was Ruth?

Ben pointed along the road in the direction they'd come. The policewoman said something then returned to the car. Ben frowned after her and closed his door.

The policewoman brought cold and damp in with her. "She's at her house, guv."

"Where's that?"

"Back by the road."

"Shit. Turn round."

The woman swung the car around the open square, ignoring the ruts in the tarmac. They glided back towards the entrance to the village, the detective counting under his breath as they passed houses. Martin imagined the people inside, staring out, wondering what was happening. He sank further in his seat.

They turned left, then quickly right, and stopped in a cul-de-sac. It was neat and homely, and reminded Martin of the kinds of places his school friends had once lived. He'd envied them their narrow lives of TV and football at weekends, the fact they weren't expected to fix tractors and scrub concrete floors covered in pig shit.

The detective got out this time, leaving the uniformed woman with Martin. Once again, the other car stopped a short distance behind. Martin wondered who they were looking for. He still hadn't seen Ruth.

The door to a house opened and Jess emerged. He clenched his teeth, waiting for her to spot him.

The detective exchanged a few words with her. She stepped out into the rain and held her arm over her face, sheltering her eyes. She peered towards the car. The rain was easing now, sunlight making an effort to break through the clouds. He had nowhere to hide.

She said something to the detective. She looked animated, shocked. He put a hand on her arm and she shook it off. She raised her voice.

Martin stared at her, confused. Had they sought her out in her capacity as steward, or as a witness?

The detective shook his head and Jess closed the door in his face. Martin smiled, admiring her courage. He'd never dare do that, despite the attitude to the authorities he'd witnessed in his father. Maybe because of it.

The detective opened the car door and slid in. He wore a pinched expression.

"None of them are talking," he said. He turned to face Martin. "You should be pleased."

CHAPTER FORTY-THREE

Sarah paused for a moment, then carried on walking. He was stalling her. She had to leave, now.

"Wait!" he called after her. "There's a bike."

She turned. "A bike?"

"Ben brought it. When he came for Ruth."

"A *bike*?"

He nodded. "Easiest way for you to get home."

She approached him. "You had a bike here all along, and you didn't tell me about it?"

"You were intent on the boat…"

"You let me spend days fixing up that boat. You let Martin stay here, knowing the police might catch up with him, knowing that he could leave here on a bike?"

"Sorry."

"Why?" She raised a palm. "Don't tell me. Same reason you drugged me and dragged me onto that boat, I imagine."

"No. I saw you and Martin working together. I thought maybe you had a future."

"Martin's a murderer."

"No, he isn't. Sarah—"

"So where is this bloody bike?" She wondered what her mother would make of her language; it felt liberating, to swear.

He sighed. "Come with me."

She followed him to a door around the side of the house. It led to a shed of sorts, full of rusting tools and piled up junk. At the front, balancing precariously, was a blue mountain bike. It was scratched, and one of the tyres was low, but it would get her home.

"You bastard."

"I thought I was doing the right thing."

She pushed past him and grabbed the bike, hauling it out of the tangle. She lifted it up and heaved it out of the shed, not caring if she hit him.

"You weren't," she said.

"I'm sorry. Look, if you find Martin, I'd be grateful if you could—"

"I have no intention of going looking for Martin. I'm going to go back to my village to tell the police that it was him who killed Robert. Then they'll release Ruth."

"You know he did it for you."

She shook the bike at him, feeling stronger than she ever had. The clouds had cleared; she needed to get on the road while it remained light.

She realised she had no idea how to get home.

"Are there any maps here?"

"Sorry?"

"Maps. Of the area. I don't know the roads."

"Oh. Yes."

He dashed into the back of the house. She propped the bike against a wall and followed him inside. She stayed in the kitchen, suddenly uncomfortable being alone here with this man.

He was in a room deep inside the house, one she hadn't ventured into. She listened to him banging around and cursing under his breath. Eventually he emerged, brandishing a torn Ordnance Survey map. "Here."

She grabbed it, not stopping to examine it. She stuffed it inside her shirt and went outside.

He followed her out. "Don't you want to check it first?"

"I know which way the police went. I can start that way. I'll check the map when I'm safely away from here."

"Sarah, it's not like that. You know that."

"I don't know what I know anymore." She wiped a tear away. *Don't cry. Don't show your vulnerability*. "I just want to go home. Put all this behind me."

He nodded. "Good luck."

She sniffed at him. Another man was being kind to her one moment, then lying to her the next. It was worse than being at home.

She threw her leg over the bike and cycled away, ignoring the chill that pierced her clothes.

CHAPTER FORTY-FOUR

TED THREW THE FRONT DOOR OPEN AND SHOT OUT OF THE house. Dawn hurried after him, wiping her hands on her apron. She'd almost dropped the plate she'd been washing in her shock at his sudden movement.

He ran towards the Parade. He was waving his arms, shouting. She watched, not daring to call after him. She scanned the surrounding houses; who would be watching?

He turned, his fist still clenched in the air. She slipped back inside, into the kitchen. She picked up the plate and began to scrub it, conscious of her heart pounding so hard she thought he'd hear it.

He slammed the front door and threw himself into a chair behind her. She flinched.

"What the fuck are they doing here?" he shouted.

She placed the plate on the draining board and inhaled.

"Who, love?"

She heard him shift in the chair. She could imagine him scowling at her back. Had she injected enough lightness into her voice?

"The police."

She felt her chest lift. She turned.

"Have they found her?" she asked.

"What? No. Of course they haven't."

"I thought…"

He stood up. "We didn't ask them to look for her, so why should they?"

"Oh." She hated that no one trusted the police anymore. But she couldn't go against Ted. Even if she dared to, how would she get to Filey on her own?

"They had someone," he said. "In the back seat."

"Oh."

He looked at her like she was an idiot. "You don't know what that means, do you?"

She shook her head. "Sorry."

"It means they've arrested someone. Put him in the back."

Maybe one of those men, she thought. But no one in the village would have trusted the police with enough information for them to come to any conclusions.

Perhaps Ruth had? It was her best defence.

"Could it be one of those men?"

He grunted. "Hopefully that little bastard Martin. I'd like to see him fester in a police cell."

"If they have him, they'll have found Sarah."

"Not necessarily." He balled his fists on his hips. "You haven't got a clue, have you?"

There was a knock at the door. Ted strode to it. Dawn watched, her hands shaking.

"Is everything alright?"

It was Sam.

Ted stepped forward, almost touching Sam. Dawn followed her husband into the hallway and looked past him at the boy. She gave him a weak smile.

"Are you alright, Mrs Evans?"

Ted stepped forward again, out of the house. Sam took a step back, his eyes still on Dawn.

"Why wouldn't she be?"

Sam looked back at Ted. "Sorry, that's not what I meant. It's just, I saw the police car. I thought they might have found Sarah?"

Ted drilled a finger into Sam's chest. "And what damn business is it of yours?"

"I was just concerned."

"She'd be fine and dandy if you hadn't stuck your oar in."

Sam's broad face paled. He was staring into Ted's eyes, his mouth wide. "I'm sorry. I shouldn't have done that."

Dawn stepped forward. "You were only trying to help."

"Trying to meddle, you mean!" Ted turned to glare at her. She shrank back.

"He wanted Martin out of the way as much as you did, love," she said. "He was trying to help Martin leave."

Ted turned back to Sam. "Fat lot of good he did."

"I'm sorry, Mr Evans. I just wanted the best for Sa—"

Ted raised an open hand. Sam clamped his lips shut. He lifted his chest. "You can't threaten me."

"Can't I?"

"I've done nothing wrong. I care about your daughter, that's all." He peered round Ted. "Mrs Evans, please can you tell me if she comes back?"

Ted's face turned from red to violet.

"Yes, Sam," Dawn said. "Now I think you should leave."

"Right." Sam gave Ted a last wary glance then hurried towards his own home.

Ted slammed the door shut. "What the fuck was he doing?"

"He was just concerned, that's all."

"Why would he be concerned?"

"He cares about Sarah."

Ted careered into the kitchen, pushing Dawn with him. She came to a stop against the stove, glad she'd turned the gas off.

"He's what she needs," she said. "Keep her away from that Martin."

"She needs to be with her family." He looked back towards the door. "Maybe that little runt knows more than he's letting on."

"Sam?'

"He helped her get away. He'll know where they were heading."

He pulled back. Her hips were sore where they'd been pressed into the stove.

"Don't follow me," he said, and grabbed his coat.

CHAPTER FORTY-FIVE

DAWN SAT AT THE TOP OF THE STAIRS, WATCHING THE ROAD through the small window. She'd been up and down the stairs for the last hour, alternating between watching for Ted's return and busying herself downstairs, distracting herself with polishing Ted's old golfing trophies that lived in a wooden cupboard. Trophies that he'd insisted on carrying all the way here, despite forcing Dawn to leave family photos behind.

She'd never been to Sam's house, but Ted had. He knew this village better than she did.

Sam's parents were good people who kept themselves to themselves and did more than their fair share of work to support the community. They'd sent their two oldest sons, Sam and Zack, out to work as soon as they were old enough, knowing the risks. Sam had told her that his mum liked Sarah, that she thought he'd be a good match for her son. And now she'd be punished for that by having Ted bowl up at her door.

It wasn't right. Sarah was nineteen; she needed to live her own life. She needed a boyfriend, a husband one day.

She couldn't stay here forever, picking her way through the tense atmospheres and stony silences.

Dawn's legs were numb. She stood up and stretched, her eyes on the road outside. A small team of men was working on the shrubs outside her house, pruning them. She wondered if they could hear through her front door; if they ever listened in.

She felt her chest cave in with the shame. Everyone knew about her, the quiet mouse who let her husband terrorise her.

She slid into Sarah's room. Like the rest of the house it was tidy, the bed made. A small cuddly toy sat against the pillow; a panda Sarah had brought north with her. Snuggled up next to it was her beloved cat Snowy. He'd been a stray who'd taken a liking to Sarah, refusing to leave and eventually being accepted as a member of the family, albeit one Ted wanted nothing to do with. Only the childhood toy was a link with home. Would they ever return home? She doubted it. This was home now, for all its failings.

She sat on the bed, stroking the cat between the ears. He purred in his sleep. It was warmer in here than in her own room, with the low sun slanting through the window. She stared out towards the sea, watching the distant waves.

She thought of the rope, hidden under Sarah's bed where Ted would never think to look. But Sarah might be coming home now. She would take it back up to the loft.

She couldn't stay here like this. She needed to be ready, when he came home. She returned to the top of the stairs and hesitated, her hand on the banister. More cleaning, to keep her busy? Once the trophies were gleaming she'd scrubbed the kitchen floor and swept under the cabinets, piling chairs onto the table to give it a proper job. Everything was back in its place now; neat, ordered, pristine. The Lord looked down at her from his crucifix next to the door. She crossed herself and muttered a prayer for her family.

Her limbs tingled with nervous energy. She'd lost count of the days she'd spent like this, shut up in this house, hardly daring to emerge for fear of their stares. Waiting. Cleaning and tidying to distract herself. Cooking. She could make the rations stretch further than anyone else here, she was sure of it.

But today, she'd had enough.

She pursed her lips and stepped into the hall. She took her coat from its peg, questioning herself. He would be angry if she wasn't here when he returned. But she had to go after him, to still the waters.

She took a few breaths, her hand on the doorknob. What if he was outside already, coming home? She would pretend to have seen him from upstairs, to be welcoming him home.

She clenched and unclenched her free fist then pulled the door open.

The men pruning the shrubs looked up and nodded in greeting. She offered up a tight smile in return and they dipped their heads back to their work.

She looked past them, towards the Parade. Sam's family lived near the edge of the village, in a house that would barely contain two hulking sons and three younger siblings, as well as the parents. She thought of her own house, too big for the three of them. Maybe it would be the perfect size for a more lively family.

She caught movement from the corner of her eye and looked up. Something was rounding the bed, ahead of her. A bike?

She stepped onto the path, pulling the door behind her. Nobody had bikes here. They were too bulky for people to have carried them, and too expensive - too unnecessary to buy. Was it those boys again, from the estate? The ones who'd threatened those poor children?

She stood her ground, ready to tell them to leave, wondering where her strength had come from.

Then she realised it was a woman riding the bike, long white-blonde hair flying out behind her.

Sarah?

CHAPTER FORTY-SIX

HER MOTHER WAS AT THE FRONT DOOR, HER ARMS WIDE, her jaw dropped.

"Sarah!"

Sarah brought the bike to a halt and threw it to the ground. Almost tripping over the wheel, she ran to her mother who gathered her up in a tight hug.

"You're safe! Oh dear Lord, I'm so glad to see you." Dawn drew back to push a stray hair out of Sarah's eyes. "Did he hurt you?"

"It wasn't like that."

Dawn frowned then looked towards a group of men who were tending the plants four houses along. "Come inside."

She pulled Sarah in, slamming the door behind her.

"The bike?" Sarah asked, her voice frail.

"We can worry about that later. Oh, come here. Let me hold you."

Sarah let her mother gobble her up again, feeling like a lost child. She felt tears run down her cheeks.

Dawn held her at arms length again and stroked her cheek. "You poor love. Here, you need warming up."

Sarah let her mother drag her into the kitchen and guide her to a chair. She was shivering, her layers of clothing soaked through.

"Can I get changed?"

"Of course! You go and clean yourself up while I warm you up some soup."

Sarah smiled in thanks and slid upstairs, listening for her father. He seemed to be out; causing trouble no doubt.

Her room had been tidied, her panda propped up on her bed like she was six. Snowy was on the windowsill, staring out at the sea. She gathered him up in her arms, sinking her face into his soft fur. He struggled against her and she put him gently back down, ruffling the fur behind his ears. He jumped off and slid downstairs. She watched him then crashed to the bed, exhausted.

Her mind felt full and empty at the same time. She couldn't quite believe she was home. Could things get back to normal now? Did she want them to?

She pushed herself up and went to her chest of draw-ers. One drawer held skirts, neatly folded. Another held blouses. She took one of each and some clean underwear. It felt good to have her own clothes next to her skin.

She sat heavily on the bed, thinking of the last time her clothes had been removed. Of Martin's touch on her. He'd been gentle, tender. How could a murderer be so considerate?

A deep longing to lie down was pulling her back to the bed. But she was hungry, and she'd promised her mother. She could smell pea soup. Her favourite.

She sat at the kitchen table and wrapped her chilled fingers around the mug. Next to it was a misshapen granary roll. She tore into it and dunked it into the soup, only now realising just how hungry she was.

"Thanks, Mum." She swallowed the soup in great, hungry gulps, smacking her lips when it was finished. She looked at the pan on the stove, hoping for more. But it was empty.

Dawn sat opposite her. Her face was pained, her forehead deeply lined. She smelt of the soap she made from seaweed and lavender.

Sarah looked down at her empty mug, hoping Dawn couldn't read the changes on her face. No one needed to know what had happened last night. The sooner she put it out of her own mind, the better.

"What happened?" her mother asked, her voice gentle. "Did he force you to go with him?"

Sarah shot her head up. "He's not like that." She felt her cheeks flush. "He's not."

Why was she lying? Martin was a murderer who had tricked her into bed.

She felt her stomach clench. What if she was pregnant?

"What is it, love? You look like you've got the cares of the world on your shoulders."

"I'm just tired."

"No surprise there. But you're home now, thank the Lord. We'll look after you. We'll help you recover."

"We?"

Dawn stiffened. "Your dad was worried about you."

"I bet he was."

"Now, Sarah. Don't go talking about him like that. He loves you, in his own way."

So does Martin, thought Sarah, then shook her head. "He's got a funny way of showing it." She pointed to the bruise on her forehead.

"I'm sorry about that, sweetheart. It won't happen again."

"How can you know?"

"Because I won't let it."

Sarah eyed her mother. Was she finding some courage at last? Was the sight of her daughter being hit by the man who'd dished out the same punishment to her time and time again enough to turn her?

"How?"

Dawn smiled. "Your dad's had a hard time, love. What with his injury, and that Martin causing trouble. He just needs a rest from all that."

"You don't think other people have had a hard time too?"

"He's different. I know how to look after him. I neglected him, for a while. I won't let it happen again."

Sarah slumped back in her chair. Dawn had it all wrong. It was she who needed to be treated better, not her husband.

She heard a key turning in the lock, and turned in her chair. Dawn pulled her hand off Sarah's. She stood up and put Sarah's mug and plate in the sink.

Ted pushed the door closed behind him, his face dark. Sarah held her breath.

"Hello Dad."

He spun round. "Sarah?"

She tried to smile. "I'm home."

He advanced on her. "Oh!" For a moment she thought he might hug her. Then his face fell. "What the hell were you doing, jumping into that boat?"

"I'm sorry, Dad. I was stupid."

"Fucking impetuous more like!"

"Ted," Dawn whispered. She was prepared to put up

with violence but not with swearing. Sarah had never understood it.

Ted loomed over Sarah. She pulled herself up but he placed a hand on her shoulder, pushing her gently down.

"You shagged him, didn't you?"

Her eyes widened.

"Ted!" Dawn hissed. "Please don't talk like—"

Sarah recovered herself. "No," she said. "You've got no idea what you're talking about."

He grunted. "Well, you're grounded. No going running after him – and no seeing Sam Golder." At this his gaze flicked up to Dawn, who made an involuntary sound.

Sarah shrugged. "Fine with me."

"Good." He grabbed her shoulder and hauled her up. His own shoulder was free of its sling. "Get upstairs."

"Dad, I'm nineteen. You can't—"

"I said *go upstairs!*"

She looked at her mother, who nodded assent. She raised herself from the chair, leaning back to avoid making contact with him. She rounded him and made for the stairs.

"This is stupid," she said. "You can't lock me up."

"That's what you think," said Ted.

"You're no better than them."

He took a step towards her, his arm raised. Dawn's face crumpled. "No, Ted, please! She's been through enough!"

He lowered his hand, glaring at Sarah. His chin was trembling, his pupils dilated. She stared back at him.

She looked at her mother. She was close to tears.

"Like I say, you can't lock me up forever."

She ran upstairs and threw herself on the bed.

CHAPTER FORTY-SEVEN

SARAH WOKE TO A GREY ROOM, SUN SEEPING ROUND THE curtains. She yawned and sat up in bed, her limbs heavy.

For a moment she forgot everything that had happened over the last ten days; she was at home the way she'd been before Martin first came to the village. Before they'd taken her. But then the thought of it fell onto her, like lead cloaking her shoulders. She sighed and leaned back against the wall.

She was hungry. When was the last time she ate; twelve, fourteen hours ago? Her stomach growled as if in answer.

She flung her feet out of bed and found her slippers. She padded to the door.

It was locked. She rattled the handle, annoyed.

"Mum!" she called. "My door's stuck."

"No it isn't."

Her mother's voice was directly outside the door.

"Have you been sitting out there?"

"I wanted to make sure you were alright, when you woke."

"I'm fine. But I'm hungry, and I need the loo. Let me out."

"I can't."

She rattled the door again. "Of course you can. I need to eat."

"Look on your chest of drawers."

She looked at the chest of drawers. There was a plate on it, with some goats cheese, a hunk of bread and sliced up apple. The apple was starting to brown at the edges.

"You came in here? You left it?"

"I wanted to check on you. You were asleep."

"I still need to use the bathroom."

"You'll have to hold on. Wait till your dad gets home."

"I can't."

"I'm sorry, love."

She heard creaking and rustling outside as her mother stood up. There was a moment's silence; was she out there, looking at the door, coming to a decision?

"Let me out."

"You have to wait."

Sarah threw herself back onto the bed. Her stomach grumbled again. She went to the chest and picked up the plate. There was a glass of water next to it. She munched on the food. Maybe she shouldn't have come home after all.

She heard voices outside, below her window. She pulled the curtains aside and opened the window. Jess was on the grass below, running across the back of the houses that overlooked the cliffs.

"Jess?"

Jess stopped. "Sarah? Since when have you been back?"

"Yesterday afternoon. They've locked me in."

Jess looked towards the glass doors below Sarah's

window. Was Dawn down there, discouraging her? Shooing her away?

"Sorry, I've got bigger things to deal with. I'm sure they'll let you out soon. Your mum's downstairs."

"It's her who's got me locked in. What is it you've got to deal with?"

Jess frowned. "Bill. From the farm."

"What about him?"

"He's turned up with the boat."

"What?"

"Sorry, Sarah. Got to dash."

Sarah ran to the door and hammered on it. "Let me out! I need to go out!"

The door handle turned.

"Stand back," her mother said through the wood. Sarah did as she was told.

Dawn pushed the door ajar. "Sit on the bed. Don't move."

Sarah sat on the bed, arranging her feet beneath her. She'd never seen her mother behave like this.

She watched as Dawn crossed the room, heading for the window. She reached into the pocket of her skirt and brought out a small key. She pulled the window shut then locked it.

"What are you doing?"

"I know you get out that way. When your dad grounds you."

"Why are you doing this?"

"It's for your own good. You need to see sense. Realise that I only want what's best for you."

"But I need the loo."

"Use the glass."

Sarah stared at Dawn. Her mother was the cleanest, most meticulous person she had ever known. The thought of peeing in a mug would be as unwelcome to her as peeling her own skin off.

"Mum? Are you alright?"

"I'm fine." Dawn looked tired, but there was colour in her cheeks and a determination in her eyes. "I'm going out. You stay quiet, and don't try talking to anyone again."

CHAPTER FORTY-EIGHT

DAWN STOOD WATCHING FROM THE SHADOW OF THE HOUSE.

A hundred yards in front of her, Jess and some other council members were talking to a man. The man who'd come to the village with Martin. The man they called Bill.

He was solidly-built with greying hair that was thin on top, and he stood with a stoop. He wore a heavy black coat that stretched almost to his fingertips, with a pale stain running from collar to hem. He had a scar on his neck that made Dawn shudder. Apart from that he looked harmless enough, but that meant nothing. Martin had looked harmless too, with his open face and thick mousy hair.

She wished she could get closer. There was an open space ahead, with nothing to shield her. There were four of them other than the newcomer. Jess, her brother Ben, his friend Sanjeev, and Ted. She wondered what Bill wanted. Why he'd come here.

Ted looked angry. He was shouting at Jess, his arms waving. Ben was tense next to her, looking like he might throw himself at Ted any moment. He'd done it before, a couple of years ago. But Ted was stronger than he looked. As Dawn well knew.

Jess put a hand on Ted's shoulder and he jerked it away, shouting at her. Dawn winced; that would hurt. His words echoed off the buildings but were too muddled to make out. Bill watched them, his frown deepening. *You'll regret coming here now*, she thought. *As you should.*

She stared at him, horrified by his nerve. That he should cart her daughter off like that, imprison her on his farm, then come back here like he'd done nothing wrong. She had no idea why he'd chosen today to come here, but she could guess. He'd found the boat, washed up somewhere, and thought he could use it to inveigle his way into their trust again.

This time she wasn't going to stand by and watch.

She pulled back as Jess turned to glance in her direction. She was gesturing towards Dawn, towards the houses. Dawn crouched down, torn between running away and staying to hear more.

Then it hit her. If he had the boat, that meant he'd taken it from Sarah. He and Martin had worked together to convince her to leave with it, then attacked her and stolen it from her.

Good for her, escaping them. But where had she got that bike? She must have taken it from somewhere.

That wasn't good. *Thou shalt not steal.* But that was only one commandment that had been broken recently. The ones broken by the man she was watching, not to mention his friend who was where he belonged in a police cell; well, they were far worse.

The group turned to walk in Dawn's direction. She slipped through the shadows and darted to the side of Sanjeev's house next to her own, hoping he wouldn't spot her. She crouched behind a side wall and peered out. Jess unlocked the door to the village hall and gestured for Bill to go in. Ted shouted something at her. She looked him in the eye and snapped something back. He growled but didn't reply.

Once Bill was inside, Jess locked the door. She spoke to Ted again then walked off towards the beach. Maybe she was going to check on the boat, talk to Clyde. She was friendly enough with him. Dawn disapproved; it wasn't right, a white woman and a black man. She'd never be as vociferous about it as her husband, but it still made her uncomfortable. It was enough that Sanjeev there had such a hold over Ben. Especially when it was Ben who had saved his life after the floods, so it should be the other way around.

She scurried across the square, stopping at the back of the JP. She leaned against the pub wall, looking around her. A woman passed with two small children; they looked sidelong at Dawn but didn't say anything. She gave them a nervous smile in return and hid behind the bins at the back of the pub.

She waited for footsteps. She heard three sets heading towards her: Ben and Sanjeev, followed by Ted's uneven gait a few paces behind. Ben and Sanjeev muttered as they passed her, but didn't spot her. She drew further back before Ted passed. She needed to be quick.

She slipped around to the other side of the pub, through the archway that linked it to the village hall. She went to the door of the hall and knocked gently.

"Who is it?"

"Let me in."

Bill came to the door. It was half-glazed and she could see him staring out at her. His eyes were small and dark, pig-like.

"Who are you?"

"My name's Dawn. Let me in."

"The door's locked."

"They're keeping you prisoner?"

"Jess said it was for my protection. But yeah, I guess they are. D'you know where to find a key?"

"Even if I did, I wouldn't bring it."

He frowned. "Who are you? What have I done to you?"

"What did you do to my daughter?"

Recognition broke out on his face. "You're Sarah's mum."

"What did you do to her?"

"I'm so sorry."

"I don't want your apologies. I want to know what you did. Did you rape her?"

"What? No. Why would you think that?"

"Why else would you take her?"

He blew out a breath. "I don't know. Robert wanted Ruth. But he told us to take more women. I guess he thought it would give him bargaining power."

"Why is my daughter bargaining power?"

"I didn't say she was. Look, I'm really sorry. She's a good girl. She's forgiven me."

"Don't talk rubbish."

"We got to know each other. At the farm."

"After you captured her, and held her prisoner? I doubt it."

"No, I mean— you don't know, do you?"

"What don't I know? Enlighten me, please."

She looked behind her, towards the village square. Towards her house. If Ted got home and found her missing, would he come back here?

"I came here to tell you to leave," she said. "You and your friends are no good for this village."

"You mean Martin."

"I mean all of you. Don't entertain any notions of becoming part of this community."

"The other men left the farm, you know. I'm the only one there."

"Why should I care?"

He shrugged. "I'd rather be here."

She leaned on the glass, bringing her face close to it. Her fist was clenched, and she feared she might smash through it. "You get back to your farm. God wants us to be left alone, without any outside interference."

He cocked his head. He regarded her for a moment. "She's in love with Martin."

She felt her fist tighten. Was he not listening? "No she isn't. She's got Sam."

"Who's Sam?"

"It's none of your business!" she cried. She looked behind her; best to keep her voice down. "I have to go. If I hear you're still here this evening, I'll send my husband after you. And his friends."

"He doesn't scare me."

"He should. You and your friend Martin."

"He isn't a murderer. Martin. Tell Sarah that."

"What are you on about?"

"He was arrested. For murdering two boys. Young men. But he didn't do it."

"If she thinks he did it, she'll stay away from him."

"She deserves to know the truth."

"And why would you know the truth?"

"Because I was there. I know what happened."

CHAPTER FORTY-NINE

Sarah heard the front door slam. Feet stamped up the stairs.

Those weren't Dawn's footsteps.

She pulled away from her door and sat on the bed, pushed up against the wall. If Bill was here, Ted might have got to him. Pounding up the stairs like that meant he was angry. Had Bill told him about her and Martin?

Her heart was pumping, her flesh shivering, as he threw the door open.

"Why is that man here?"

She wrapped her arms around herself. "What man?"

"You know what man. Bill Peterson. He brought the boat back. Did he take it from you? Was he working with Martin?"

"No!" She flung her arms aside, pushing up on the bed. "Martin's not what you think."

Ted stepped inside the room. It felt claustrophobic with him in here, his head inches away from the sloping ceiling. "So what is he? Your precious Martin?"

"He's not my precious anything."

Ted loomed over her, his face pale and his eyes bulging. She shrank back, folding her arms around herself in protection.

"I know men like that, girl. They're bad news."

She gritted her teeth.

"Are you listening to me?" he demanded, the colour returning to his cheeks.

She nodded.

"He left you, didn't he? He abandoned you. That's why you came back."

"It didn't happen like that."

"So why wasn't he with the other bastard?"

Her mouth felt dry, her tongue swollen. "He was arrested."

Ted blew out a long breath. "See? Bad news. Thank God you got away from him when you did."

She nodded, sniffing back a tear.

Ted went to the door. "So how come Ruth isn't back yet?"

"It wasn't Robert's death they arrested him for. Two others, names I didn't recognise."

Ted raised his hands to his temples, his fists clenched. "I'll kill him, the little shit. If he laid a hand on you—" He turned to her, his eyes questioning.

"No." She fought to keep her face under control. "No, Dad. He did nothing. He was arrested, and I came home. On Ben's bike."

"Ben doesn't have a bike. What are you on about?"

"I don't know. But Bill said he'd brought it to the farm."

Ted shook his head. "Fuck."

She stood up. "Can I come out now? I need the loo."

"No. I don't trust you."

"Please. I'm desperate."

He spun to face her. "I said no! Why doesn't anyone give me any fucking respect around here?"

He reached out and grabbed her hair. She screamed. He stared at her, nostrils flaring. She met his gaze. *Stop*, she thought. *Let go.*

He pushed her to the floor, spitting on the carpet.

"He's a killer. Stay away from him."

She said nothing but pulled herself up to sitting.

He took a step towards her. "You hear me?"

She nodded. "I heard you."

"And?"

She could feel her lungs tightening, her breath coming out in gasps. "You'd know about that though, wouldn't you?"

He let out a yell and hit her across the cheek with the back of his hand. She fell backwards, slamming into the bed.

"Respect, girl! You don't talk to me like that."

He turned and clattered down the stairs, his footsteps echoing in the empty house. She watched him, blinking away tears. Her cheek throbbed and her shoulder ached from where she'd hit the bed.

But he'd left the door open.

She ran down the stairs. She had no idea where he'd gone. He could be in the hall, waiting for her.

She had to risk it.

She stopped at the bottom of the stairs. Ted was in the living room, slumped on the sofa. Staring out at the growing dusk. His shoulders rose and fell heavily.

She grabbed the door handle, her eyes on him. He stood up. He rounded the sofa and sped to her, slamming the door shut, almost shutting her hand in it.

She grasped the door handle, pulling as hard as she could. He stared at her.

"Come into the living room," he said. "Talk to me."

His voice was low now, his cheeks had lost their colour. But she'd heard this tone of voice before.

He turned the key in the front door lock and pocketed it. "Living room. Now."

She bowed her head and hurried into the room, anxious to keep ahead of him, out of his reach. She perched on the arm of the sofa.

He sat in the armchair opposite her.

"Where's your mother?" he asked.

Sarah shrugged.

"Tell me."

She thought of Dawn, arriving home to this. "She told me she wouldn't be long. Maybe she had to go to the shop."

"It'll be closing soon."

"That means she'll be back soon."

He turned towards the window.

"It's beautiful, isn't it?" he said. "The sky. The sea."

She said nothing.

"Nearly losing you has made me appreciate what I should be grateful for." He leaned forward and grabbed her hand. She pulled on it but his grip was tight. Her heart rate picked up.

"Don't be scared, girl," he said. "I won't hurt you."

She stared out of the window, not making eye contact.

"I'm glad you're home," he said.

Yeah, she thought. *So you can lock me up. So you can hit me.* It wasn't much better than what they did to her at the farm.

She looked at him. She'd seen him do this before, with her mother. Go from ninety miles an hour to nothing in the blink of an eye. He wouldn't hit her again. Not tonight. "Can I ask you something?"

"You can ask."

She stared ahead. "After I left, in the boat. With Martin. You were worried about me."

"Of course I was."

"Did you tell the police I was gone?"

"The police?"

"Yes."

"That's not what I'd do. Not what any of us here would do."

"I don't mind, Dad. I understand you were concerned. You wanted me back. You'd do anything you thought might bring me home."

He tightened his grip on her fingers. "I never called the police, Sarah. How would I? We don't exactly have a phone."

"I just thought, maybe Jess…"

"Jess doesn't have a phone either."

"But they came here."

"They did."

"Did you speak to them?"

"Not about you."

"Are you sure, Dad?" She gathered her courage. "Did you tell them where to find Martin? So they could arrest him?"

He'd been grinding his teeth; she didn't notice until he stopped, plunging them into silence. "No."

"But somebody did."

"They did you a favour."

She didn't respond to that. "But if you didn't, then who did?"

"I did."

She spun round to see Dawn standing in the doorway.

Her face was flushed with cold and she was peeling off a headscarf. Her lips were pinched together and her face had a tightness, a smooth hardness, that Sarah had never seen before. Sam was standing behind her, looking sheepish.

"I did, Sarah," she repeated. "I told them where to find him."

CHAPTER FIFTY

THE POLICE CELL WAS CLEANER THAN MARTIN HAD expected. Instead of being lined with filth, it smelt strongly of disinfectant. He wondered who had been here last, and if the disinfectant had been necessary for some reason.

He'd been in here for hours and still they hadn't told him why. When he'd arrived, there'd been a repetition of the charge – murder of Jacob Cripps and Zahir Ali – but when he asked when, or who they were, the detective had looked at him with irritation.

He counted the rows of bricks lining the walls, desperate to occupy his mind. When that was done, he counted the pockmarks on the tiled floor. Sixty-three. Just under twice as many as there were rows of bricks.

There was a high window in the corner, with obscured glass. He thought of Sarah in her cell back at the farm, the moss-hazed glass of the outhouse windows. He'd done that to her, played his part.

Whether he'd committed the crime he'd been arrested for or not, he deserved punishment.

He tried to push out the thought of her waking to find

him gone, the deep sense of betrayal she would feel. She'd trusted him and he'd left her. Never mind that it hadn't been voluntary. He thought of the flowers he'd picked, tossed to the floor in his desperation to hide.

He heard footsteps outside his door and rushed to it, placing his mouth close to the cold metal.

"Hello?"

The footsteps stopped.

"Please, I need to speak to someone! I don't know why I'm here."

The footsteps grew closer. "Pull the other one, mate. I've heard 'em all." A female voice, edged with the harsh tones of a smoker.

"No, really. I've been arrested for murder, but I don't know who the people are I'm supposed to have killed."

"People? You're happy to shout around these cells that you're a serial killer, are you?"

"I'm not a serial killer. I'm not a killer at all."

He thought of Robert and felt his stomach churn.

"Is Ruth Dyer here?"

"Shut up."

"I need to know. She's a – a friend of mine. I need to know if she's OK."

The hatch slid open to reveal a pair of brown eyes. "Will you shut the bugger up?"

"What about Ruth Dyer?"

The eyes narrowed. They wore heavy mascara and blue eyeshadow that reminded him of his mum when she was going to the farmers' dances.

"She was released. This morning. I'm not telling you anything else."

The hatch slammed shut.

Martin slumped onto the bench at the back of the cell, wondering why Ruth had been released. Had she told them she'd been acting in self-defence, or something different?

He heard the rattling of keys and then the bang of the door opening. He sat straight.

The policewoman stood in the door, her head cocked to one side. "Come on then."

He stood up. "Where are you taking me?"

"To see your solicitor. That's what you want, isn't it?"

"I don't have a solicitor."

She shook her head: *another idiot.* "You've been allocated one. Lucky you: it normally takes longer than this. Come with me."

CHAPTER FIFTY-ONE

SARAH ROSE TO FACE HER MOTHER. SAM STOOD BEHIND Dawn, his mouth agape.

"Why?" she asked.

"For Ruth, of course. They needed someone else to arrest. He was the best choice."

Sarah had told Dawn nothing about what had happened in the farmhouse kitchen, about Martin throwing himself on Robert. Ted had arrived right at the end, and couldn't have seen it all.

"Why him?"

"It couldn't be anyone from the village. They needed someone to blame. Two birds with one stone."

Ted was trembling. "How could you?"

Dawn looked at him, puzzled. "I thought you'd be pleased with me."

"We don't talk to police. Not after the way they've betrayed us in the past."

Dawn's face dropped. "I don't see it like that." She drew herself up. "What would you rather I did, let Ruth go to prison?"

"Co-operating with them… it's not what we do."

"Well, it worked."

"Did it?" asked Sarah. "Have you seen Ruth come back?"

"Give it time."

Sarah stared at her mother. "Did they tell you anything about why they were looking for him?"

"They didn't say anything like that. It was my idea."

"But they didn't…?"

Ted grabbed Sarah's wrist. "You're hiding something."

She looked at Sam. *Help me.* "No. I'm not."

Sam squinted at her. "You've got a bruise. On your cheek." He reached his hand out and Sarah shrank back.

Sarah looked at her father. He was glaring at her mother, his eyes full of warning.

"She fell," said Dawn. "I brought you here because it'll do her good." She gave Sarah a look that brooked no defiance.

Sam shrugged. "OK." He gave Sarah a nervous smile.

"Right," said Dawn, her voice sharper than Sarah had ever heard it. "Sarah, I think you and Sam should take a walk together."

"A walk?" cried Sarah. "A promenade, like an Edwardian lady and gentleman? I hardly think this is the time." She caught Sam's sigh. "Sorry, Sam. Nothing personal."

"You're not going anywhere," said Ted. "Sam, go home lad. Don't come back till I say you can. Alright?"

Sam nodded vigorously and turned for the door. Dawn reached round and grabbed his fingers. He was too polite to pull out of her grasp.

"No," she said. "I think Sarah needs some air. We can't trust her on her own. But we can trust young Samuel here."

Sam hunched his shoulders. Sarah felt for him; this was

probably the most excruciating thing he'd ever experienced.

"Ted," said Dawn, "let her go. Just for half an hour. He'll take care of her, won't you Sam?"

"You know how I feel about all this," said Ted. "You got no business, leading young Sam on."

Dawn let go of Sam's fingers and took a step towards Ted. "If they go, you can deal with me."

Ted twisted his lips but said nothing.

"You're angry with me," said Dawn. "I'd rather you didn't tell me just how angry, not with the young people here."

Sarah felt like her mind was going to tear itself apart. "Mum, why are you doing this?"

Dawn smiled at her. "Like I say, a walk would do you good. And Sam here will keep you out of trouble. Go."

Sarah looked at her father. He looked from her to Dawn and back again. "Go," he muttered.

CHAPTER FIFTY-TWO

SARAH HURRIED OUT OF THE HOUSE, SAM ALONGSIDE HER. The door closed behind them and she looked back at it, confused. Scared.

What would her father do to her mother, after she'd stood up to him like that?

"Let's be quick," she told Sam. "Maybe down to the edge of the beach and back. Quick as we can."

She sped off, leaving him trailing in her wake.

"Sarah!" he called. "Stop. I don't need to walk. We can just talk."

She stopped. "Where?" It was cold out, and almost completely dark. The sky was clear, stars visible in the blackness of the night sky. She could barely make out the shapes of the houses, and was going more by memory than sight. Racing to the beach wouldn't be a wise idea.

"There's a bench, by the JP."

"That's a bit public."

"It's dark."

"Even worse. Someone could listen to us."

"OK. Where do you suggest?"

"Come with me."

She grabbed his sleeve and pulled him to the back of her own house. There were two garden chairs out there, to the side of the sliding doors. The doors were heavy and the curtains closed. Her parents would never think to look out here.

She lifted a chair from its position against the wall and unfolded it as quietly as she could. Sam followed suit with the other one. He sat down and blew on his hands.

"We could always go to my house," he said. "Mum's got a fire going."

She thought of his cosy home, full of people who loved each other. "No," she said. "This is better."

"Fair enough." He tugged on his coat sleeves, dragging them over his knuckles. The coat was a grey fleece, a size too small for him.

"What d'you want to talk about?" she asked.

"I don't know. Whatever you want. Martin?"

"Why would you want to talk about Martin?"

"Dunno. Understand the enemy, and all that." He grinned.

"He's not the enemy."

"I don't mean it like that. Just that he's my rival." He paused. "For you."

She leaned back, wanting to laugh. One man was a double murderer and the other was dull enough to satisfy her mother. He was kind though. Trustworthy. And he looked at her like she was some kind of minor deity.

"Did he really kill Robert Cope?" Sam asked.

She huddled into herself. "It's complicated."

"Well if he didn't, then who did? Not Ruth, surely."

"Like I say, it's complicated."

"Bill?"

She sat up. "What do you know about Bill?"

"Just that he's in the village hall. Jess locked him in there."

"Really?"

"Yup."

"Why would Jess do that?"

"Buys her time, I guess. Your dad's mad at her."

"My dad's mad at everyone." She paused. "Sam, tell me about your family."

"What about them?"

"Anything. The ordinary stuff. What irritates you about them. What you love about them."

He chuckled. "Zack's a nightmare since he got together with Jess."

"He did?"

"Yeah. While they were out looking for you."

"I thought she was with Clyde? Well, sort of."

"Nah. He fancies her, but she just laughs it off. Her and Zack are the real deal."

"Good for them."

"That's alright for you to say. Try having a brother who's going out with the steward."

She laughed. "You're pleased for him though, right?"

"Course."

She paused, listening to the sea beyond the headland. It was calm tonight, beating the drumroll of the waves. "What's it like, having brothers and sisters?"

"Difficult to say. I've never known any different. What's it like being an only child?"

"I've never known any different either. But sometimes I'd love a brother, to stand up to my dad. Or a sister, to share things with."

"Ain't as easy as that. Most of the time, they hate you."

"Yeah." She heard a door open and close somewhere. She stood up. "What was that?"

"Nothing."

"You didn't hear it?'

"Hear what?"

"Someone's around. They could be listening."

"We're just chatting about our siblings."

"Sam, d'you think Zack might be able to talk Jess into letting us into the village hall?"

"Why would he do that?"

"I want to talk to Bill."

Sam's voice dropped. "Why?"

"I just need to ask him some questions is all. Can you help me?"

"Alright," said Sam. "But you won't need to ask Jess."

"Why not?"

"Because Zack's got a key."

She almost cheered. "Brilliant!"

"He might not let us have it though."

"You can ask him though, can't you. Please?'

CHAPTER FIFTY-THREE

A WOMAN SAT ALONE AT THE TABLE IN THE CENTRE OF THE room, her loose skin and makeup-smudged eyes not flattered by the fluorescent light. She stood up as Martin entered.

He took the proffered hand and shook it limply. She was a woman of around fifty, with a tight-fitting blue suit and grey roots showing under her yellow-blonde hair. She looked tired, and eager to be done with this meeting.

"Evening, Mr…" she opened a file on the desk, stooping over it and placing a hand on her back. She looked up. "Mr Walker. My name's Judith Ramsay. I'm your solicitor."

"I don't have a solicitor."

"I've been appointed. Duty solicitor." She sat down, muttering *for my sins*. Martin wondered if he was supposed to hear.

She gestured at the seat opposite her. "Sit down."

Martin did as he was told. The seat was hard and cold but better than the bench in his cell.

"So," she said. She sat back, her eyes brightening. "It's not often I get a murder."

He frowned at her. He wasn't some sideshow, entertainment to brighten up her dull job. He shrugged. "They've got it wrong."

She huffed out a laugh. "If I had a pound for everyone who said that."

"I mean it. I don't even know who Jacob Cripps and Zahir Ali are."

She coughed and opened her file again. She looked up at the policewoman, who was still standing behind Martin. "I'll let you know when we're done."

Martin heard the door close behind him.

"Maybe this will jog your memory," Judith said. She pulled some photographs from her file and slid them in front of Martin.

The first one depicted a young Asian man. He was lying on a rutted tarmac surface in a skewed position. His eyes were closed and his skin pale. His clothes were covered in blood.

Martin felt his throat tighten. He pulled the other photo out from beneath the first. It depicted a white man, also young, with a shaved head. He was lying on his front, a pool of blood at his side.

Sweat broke out on his forehead. Was this what Robert's men had done to those two boys?

He hadn't actually seen the boys, not properly. They'd jumped him from behind, and they were wearing hoodies. But this had to be them.

His solicitor withdrew the photos and placed them back in the file. She took out a typed sheet and held it up to her face, squinting.

"Sorry," she said. "Don't carry my glasses in the evenings. I was out for a curry with my husband."

She didn't sound resentful of being dragged away from her night out; despite the bags under her eyes and the dullness of her skin, she sounded excited, intrigued.

This was a game to her.

"I know who they are," he said.

"You do?"

"Yes. They attacked me. After the floods, when I was heading north. They beat me up and took my stuff."

"When exactly was this?"

"I can't be sure exactly. But it was February. March maybe."

"That tallies. What sort of stuff?"

He shrugged. "A rucksack. Food, and a tent I'd managed to—" he licked his lips. "I'd managed to steal. From a camping shop. Abandoned."

He twisted his hands in his lap. He was being accused of murder, but still wanted to account for stealing a tent from an abandoned store.

"They beat you up?"

"Yes. Left me for dead."

"So how did you do this?"

"I didn't."

She leaned back so far he thought her chair would tip. Her forehead caught the light as she did so, reflecting yellow off her skin. "The police think you did. They have your fingerprints on a knife that was found next to them."

"Fingerprints?"

"Mmm."

"But it was six years ago."

"Seems like they had it on file. But it's only now that they've caught up with you."

He nodded. Ruth would have given them his name.

"Is there a Ruth Dyer being held here?"

Her eyes darted up from the pad she'd been writing on. "Who?"

"Ruth Dyer. She's from the refugee village just south of here."

"I've got no idea. Why?"

"She's been arrested for killing the man who did this."

"Sorry?"

Martin sniffed. "His name's – was – Robert Cope. He was the leader of a group of men I was part of. They took me in after those kids attacked me. They retaliated."

"And what's that got to do with Ruth Dyer?"

"They abducted her, and some other women. A few days ago. Ruth was arrested for killing him."

"Whoah. You've been busy up here."

"It's not funny."

"Look, Martin, I'm not sure about your story or about this Robert Cope, but the police have got a pretty good case against you. How did your fingerprints get on that knife?"

"It was my knife."

"Your knife?"

"Yes. I took it with me when I left home. I used a boat, an inflatable dinghy. I lived with my parents in Norfolk. It was pretty bad there."

"But you're telling me that someone else used it to kill the men. Despite it being yours."

"It might have the killer's prints on it too."

"Robert Cope's."

"No."

She lifted her head to the ceiling, stretching her neck. She sighed. "You're making no sense, Martin. It's late. Just tell me what happened."

"Robert found me, unconscious. After they'd beaten

me. He and his men had captured the boys that did it. Then they killed them, and asked me to join their group."

"*They* killed them. Exactly who did it?"

He closed his eyes, trying to remember. He'd been woozy, delirious. It had happened out of his sight. He could remember their screams, though. "One of Robert's men. Maybe two. I don't know."

"You don't know."

"Sorry."

"That won't be good enough. Not in court."

"But—"

She stood up. "Look, Martin. It's late, and my husband's waiting for me. You say it was this Robert bloke, or his cronies, that killed the boys. But you don't know which one and you've got no evidence. And there's the prints."

Martin swallowed the lump in his throat.

"I'll talk to the CPS. But I doubt that it'll wash. Your best bet will be to plead guilty. Then I can get you a lower sentence."

She offered her hand again. Martin took it, his chest sinking. He'd planned on taking responsibility for Robert's death. At least that was something he'd done. But this... this was the last thing he'd expected.

CHAPTER FIFTY-FOUR

Dawn stared at Ted as the door closed behind their daughter, feeling her stomach flutter. She'd never commanded him before, never told him what to do.

It felt good, and dreadful at the same time.

She clamped her teeth down on her bottom lip, waiting for him to start shouting. She wasn't sure which transgression he'd be most angry about; the police or the defiance.

"Stop that," he snapped.

"Sorry?"

"Biting your lip like that. It's ugly. Makes your lips swollen."

She released her lip and held her mouth as still as she could. It felt sore.

She stood by the door, watching him. He stared back at her, his nostrils flaring. She looked towards the kitchen. Could she put the table between them? Would that help?

He strode towards her. She shrank back but he didn't touch her. Instead he yanked his coat from the hook, sending Sarah's tumbling to the floor. She frowned; Sarah would be cold out there.

"I'm going to find Bill," he said.

"You're doing what?"

He pushed his face into hers. "You heard me. He's leaving. Tonight. I don't care what it takes."

"That might not be such a good idea."

"I'm sorry?" His tone was sarcastic.

"Maybe he knows something. About Robert Cope's death. About them taking Sarah. About what Martin really did. If he leaves here, you'll never know."

He pushed a hard breath out through gritted teeth. "Don't you get it, woman?"

She shrank back, waiting for him to raise his hand.

"I don't care what he really did," he breathed into her face. "It's irrelevant. He took our daughter. He raped her."

Dawn opened her eyes. "She told you that?"

"It's what men like him do."

"How would you know?"

He shook his head. "Don't you remember how I protected you on the road? Kept you and her safe? Those men, the ones who pretended to be her friends. The ones you so enjoyed sharing food with. I caught them slashing her tent with a knife. Grabbing her skirt. I stopped them."

"They were going to rape her?"

"Yes, they were going to rape her. But they didn't."

She felt hollow. How old had Sarah been then: twelve, thirteen?

She shivered. It was too much.

"Did you kill them?" she asked.

"Worse."

"What's worse than that?"

He grinned. "I sliced their dicks off with their own knife."

She felt faint. "Oh, sweet Jesus." She crossed herself.

"Yes. I imagine he was watching."

She slapped him. "Don't talk about the Lord like that!" She pulled back, horrified. "I'm sorry. I'm so sorry. I didn't mean—"

He rubbed his chin, where she had caught him. The slap had been a clumsy one, and only glanced off him. He looked pleased about it, vindicated.

"See?" he said. "We're all the same. Violent animals, when we need to be. Me, you. Martin. He'll have raped her, I'm sure of it. And if I can find him, I'll kill him."

"She'd have told me if—"

"You think that, do you? Had a lot of heart-to-hearts with her lately?"

"No."

"She hates you just as much as she hates me. Trying to force Sam on her. Ridiculous."

"He's what she needs."

He pulled back. "What she needs is her family! What she needs is her mother to stop meddling where she doesn't belong!"

She said nothing, but stared at him, feeling numb. She shouldn't have sent Sarah out there, without her mother to protect her.

"Did you hit her again?" she asked, her voice shaking.

He stared at her. He blinked. "Stop snivelling," Ted snapped. "I'm going to sort this once and for all."

"Ted, please—"

"Don't beg, woman. It's disgusting. You stay here. Send her to her room when she gets back. I'm going to break in the village hall and give that Bill bloke what for."

CHAPTER FIFTY-FIVE

SARAH WASN'T USED TO BEING OUT AT NIGHT. THE shadows shifted every time the clouds moved, and it was as if there were living things here, things that only appeared once the human beings were safely in bed.

"What's that?" she whispered, grabbing Sam's arm.

"Ow. Just a fox or something. We're not the only things that call this home, you know."

She nodded as if to signal that she was reassured, but kept hold of his arm anyway.

They reached Sam's home. It was a squat semi-detached house, on the corner of the Parade. He turned to her.

"You wait out here. I'll get the keys."

She felt her eyes widen. "No. I'm coming with you."

"I can sneak in and get them. If you're with me, they'll want to know why."

"Can't I hide somewhere, in the house?"

"Stay here. I promise I'll be quick."

She clenched her teeth and pulled her arms around

her. It was freezing out here, the kind of damp cold that permeated the skin. She wished she'd taken a coat.

He threw her an encouraging smile then eased the front door open with the assurance of someone who regularly let himself in unnoticed. She wondered what hours he worked, and whether everyone would be asleep when he came home from the gangs with his brother.

She approached the house to watch him but the curtains were drawn. Instead she shifted from foot to foot, blowing on her hands as quietly as she could.

When he re-emerged, he was patting his pocket.

"What took you so long?"

"I was only gone a minute. You OK?"

"I'm fine. Come on then."

They made their way towards the village hall, keeping to the shadow of the buildings along the Parade. When they reached the open space that had once been a traffic island, they darted across, hunched low.

The dark was like a blanket, a thick layer surrounding them and smothering the village in quiet. She heard scurrying in the bushes next to the road and stiffened, then forced herself to relax. Probably mice. Her cat Snowy had caught enough of them.

At the village hall, they hunched against the door, peering through the glass. It was black inside, no way of telling if Bill was in there. If he could see them, he wasn't showing it.

"Should we knock first?" asked Sam.

"Best to, I think."

She tapped gently on the door. There were noises from within, the sound of someone moving around. Bill's face appeared at the window, soft with sleep.

"What do you want?"

"Sorry," said Sarah. "Can we come in?"

"They locked me in."

"We've got a key."

"Then I haven't got much choice, have I?"

Sarah stifled an urge to apologise. She stood to one side as Sam unlocked the door and replaced the key in his inside pocket. She wondered how long it would be before Zack found it missing, and how much trouble Sam would be in.

They slipped inside and pulled the door closed. It was black in here, the only light the faint glow coming in at the front window. This had been a restaurant once, or a coffee shop, Sarah wasn't sure. Tables and chairs were piled in the corner; no longer used for serving coffee, they were put into service at village meetings.

"You got home OK then," Bill whispered.

"Yes. Thanks."

"Did they punish you?"

She didn't want to talk about it. "Why are you here?" she asked.

"I got the boat working. Thought I should bring it back."

"It would have been useful to you."

"I know that. But I felt bad, alright?" He coughed. "Wishing I hadn't bothered now."

"Why didn't you just dump it on the beach?"

"Because I've got no way of getting back to the farm now. Other than walking forty-odd miles. And I thought maybe I could live here."

"*Here*?"

"Fat chance, pal," said Sam. "After everything you've done."

"I know." Bill looked at Sarah. "But things have changed now, with Robert dead."

Sarah turned to Sam. "Bill helped me. Us. He helped me get the boat working, so I could come home."

"But you came back on a bike, your mum told me."

"Long story."

She turned to Bill. "I need your help again. I want to know why Martin was arrested."

Bill dragged a hand through his stubble. "I thought you knew."

"Yes. But who are Jacob Cripps and Zahir Ali?"

A shadow drifted across the back wall of the hall. They all shuffled to one side, afraid of being illuminated.

"What the—?" exclaimed Sam. A car passed outside, its headlights by far the brightest thing in the village.

"It's the police," Sarah said. She felt her heart quicken. "It has to be."

CHAPTER FIFTY-SIX

THEY SHRANK BACK TO A SIDE WALL, HOPING THEY HADN'T been caught in the glare of the lights. Sarah stared at Bill.

"Are they here for you?"

He shrugged.

There was hammering at the door. It opened. Sarah cursed herself for not asking Sam to lock it again. Outside the lights had stilled, shining along the road towards the beach. Everything else was plunged into darkness, including the doorway.

"What the fuck are you doing here?" It was Ted.

Sam stepped forwards. "It was my idea, Mr Evans."

Sarah pulled him back. "Don't be stupid. It was me, Dad. I wanted to talk to Bill."

"You said you were going for a walk."

"I know."

She felt the air shift as he approached. She stood her ground, watching as his face materialised.

"Get home."

"No, Dad. I need to——"

He grabbed her chin in his fingers and pinched the skin. She lifted herself up, trying to move with him.

"I said get home. I'll deal with you later."

"It's me you want," said Bill. "Don't be so hard on the girl."

Ted dropped Sarah. She stumbled, catching her arm on the corner of a table. She raised a hand to it; it throbbed, but there was no blood.

Ted rubbed his shoulder. "Bloody girl, you made me hurt myself."

"It wasn't my fault," she said.

"Let her go," said Bill. "Deal with me instead."

"Oh I'll do that, mate. I will." He turned to Sarah and Sam. "Now – *go!*"

Sam pulled Sarah upright. He stepped towards Ted. Sarah slid in front of him.

"No, Dad. I came here to find out the truth."

"Oh, fucking Christ. The truth about what, exactly?"

"About Martin."

She felt his fingers brush her cheek as he made to slap her. Had it been a warning, or had he genuinely missed?

"Come on," said Sam. "I'll take you to my place."

"No. I need to find out if Martin really killed those people. I think Bill knows."

She felt another bite at her cheek, harder this time. Her father had caught her with the back of his hand. She resisted an urge to put her fingers to it.

"Forget your obsession with that snivelling turd. Get home."

Sam stepped between them. "You shouldn't have hit her, Mr Evans."

"*You shouldn't have hit her, Mr Evans.* Oh, listen to yourself. No wonder my wife loves you."

"He's right," said Bill. "You need to calm down."

"And who's going to stop me?"

"We are."

Sarah looked past her father to see Zack standing in the doorway. Jess was behind him.

"When I found my key missing, I guessed you were up to something, little brother."

"Not so much of the little."

"Ten minutes. It counts."

Sarah felt Sam slump beside her. All the fight had gone out of him. She wondered what Martin would do in this situation.

She knew what he'd do.

"You can't treat people like this, Dad. Bill's right."

"And how the fuck should you know?"

"Ted, please." Jess stepped around Zack. "Ruth's back. I need to deal with the police. Can all this wait until morning?"

The room went dark as the headlights outside were extinguished. Sarah felt hands at her side, grabbing her. She couldn't be sure who it was, but she dipped and side-stepped out of the way.

Then there was a voice in her ear. Bill.

"Come with me. I'll tell you everything."

He grabbed her hand. Together they ploughed through the confused bodies and ran out into the road.

CHAPTER FIFTY-SEVEN

MARTIN LAY ON THE BENCH IN HIS CELL, STARING AT THE ceiling. He would appear before the magistrates tomorrow, first thing, pleading Not Guilty. He didn't care what his solicitor said.

He ran through the months after the floods in his mind, trying to remember exactly when he'd met Robert. When he'd come across those boys. He hadn't killed them, but he wished he'd had the courage to do so.

He'd been walking for six weeks, maybe more. Winter was starting to turn into spring. He remembered snow-drops flowering alongside the road, a few daffodils emerging. The rain beat down on his shoulders some days, tiring him out. But it was better than the storms two months earlier. He'd spent days sheltering in old farm buildings, hiding out. He knew there were others on the road, people like him. But he heard shouts some nights, and screams. He kept himself to himself.

The last date he remembered was February 16th, when he'd broken into an empty supermarket, water up to his ankles, and stolen some food. There'd been a clock on the wall, one of the old-fashioned kind. It showed the time and the date, and had been ticking away unseen for weeks. 16th February. Two days before he'd been beaten up, and met Robert.

It fitted with what the solicitor told him.

His prints were on the knife. He'd been in the area at the time of the boys' deaths. Hell, that supermarket may even have had cameras.

And he didn't know which of Robert's men had killed the boys.

He had no chance.

It wasn't him who'd killed them, and it wasn't Robert. Robert had been in front of him the whole time, watching his face for a reaction as the boys had screamed.

But *who*?

There was only one person who knew, and Martin had a feeling he should be here in his place.

CHAPTER FIFTY-EIGHT

SARAH STUMBLED OUT OF THE DOOR, BILL DRAGGING HER along.

"Sam!" she cried.

"Here!"

"Come with us!"

She heard movement behind her; Sam pushing his way through the crowd.

"Oi, stop it."

She stopped, pulling Bill back with her. Sam was squaring up to his brother.

"No, Sam. This isn't your business."

"It isn't yours either."

Zack shrugged.

"Sarah needs me."

Zack shook his head as if marvelling at his brother's naivety. "Go on then."

She turned and jiggled Bill's arm, willing him to run. As she started to move, a foot flew out in front of her, sending her crashing to the ground.

"No, girl."

"Dad, please."

"He's right," said Jess. She pushed past Sam and Zack, Zack's eyes on her. "Bill needs to talk to the police. For Ruth's sake. If he knows something…"

"The bastard's gone," said Ted.

Sarah realised that her hand was empty. Bill, already out of the door when they'd stopped, had taken the opportunity to slip away.

"Bill!" she called. "Come back!"

He didn't know his way around the village and could have run towards the cliff edge. She turned back to Jess.

"We'll have to look for him in the morning," Jess said. "No point in this dark."

"We can get torches," said Ted.

"You have a bright enough torch to search the entire village?" said Jess.

"No."

"Exactly. And we don't want everyone waking up wondering what the hell's going on. I need to see Ruth."

"Is she alright?" asked Sarah.

Jess eyed her. Despite her air of command, she had dark circles under her eyes, and her thick hair was matted.

"She will be. No thanks to Martin."

"He was protecting me."

"I don't care what he was doing. He brought trouble to this village, and we shouldn't have let him come back with us."

"But you said—"

"I don't care what I said. I was wrong."

Ted was smiling, vindicated. "Go home, lass. I'll deal with you in the morning."

"I want to know what's going on."

"It's alright," said Jess. "I suggest you go home. Your

mum will be worrying about you." She turned to Sam. "Sam, can you walk her home?"

Sam nodded and smiled at Sarah. She felt herself slump. Everyone was against her. Ted was glaring at her, anger dancing on his face, and Jess clearly thought she was an idiot. Only Sam was on her side now.

"Alright," she said, and stepped outside with Sam.

The police car was still parked in the road, between the village hall and her house. Candles were lit in Ruth and Ben's house, flickering in a window. She wondered what sort of reconciliation they'd have; she'd seen the look on Ruth's face when she'd learned the truth about Ben and Robert. It had been all for Ben that this had happened; Robert's desire for revenge after Ben betrayed him so many years ago. Robert had killed a man, but he'd managed to convince himself it was all Ben's fault, just because he'd talked to the police. Now Robert was dead, and Ruth, of all people, was facing prison.

"Come on," said Sam. He laid a hand on her shoulder and she didn't shrug it away. Sam was a good man, like her mother said. He'd stood up to Ted.

They arrived at her house. Dawn would be inside, waiting. Was she sitting in the upstairs window as she often did, watching for her family?

"Thanks, Sam." She gave him a hug.

Clumsily, he pushed his face into hers and kissed her lips. It was a dry kiss, a cold one. She kissed him back. They stood there for a moment, kissing with closed mouths. She could feel his arousal.

She waited for her own heart rate to rise, for her skin to tingle. It didn't. She slid her face to one side, letting him kiss her neck, and looked up at the window.

Is this what you wanted, Mum?

She pulled away. "Thanks Sam." She smiled at him, feeling guilty.

He grinned. His face was flushed and his breathing heavy. She hated herself.

She turned and put her key in the lock, preparing to creep inside.

She closed the door behind her.

"So you've seen sense."

She started. "Mum?" She searched the dark rooms, her heart racing at last.

"In here." Her mother was in the kitchen, leaning against the cupboards.

"You saw us."

"You've made that boy very happy."

"I don't love him, Mum."

"Who said anything about love?"

"I did. That was the chastest, most unsatisfying kiss I've ever had."

Her mother pushed herself forward so she was standing straight. Sarah approached her, hoping she would understand.

"And you've had plenty of unchaste kisses, have you?"

She felt her skin flush, her fingers tingle. She could almost feel Martin's breath on her, his skin brushing hers. She closed her eyes.

Her mother was right in front of her when she opened them. "You little whore!" she screamed. "Get to your room!" Dawn crossed herself. "Dear God forgive me for raising such a sinful child."

"Mum, it's not sinful. Don't be ridiculous."

"You can shut up!" Dawn pushed her. Sarah stood her ground.

"Up! Now!"

She stared back at her mother. "Fair enough."

She backed away, reaching behind her in the darkness. She stopped at the bottom of the stairs, the coats hanging behind her. She had to be quick.

Dawn stayed where she was, a dark shadow in the dimly lit kitchen. "I said go! I can't look at you, you slut."

She moved her hands across the coats. Her own was woollen, and rough. Dawn's was made of a smooth manmade fabric. Her hand landed on it and she fumbled for the pocket. The key to her bedroom window might still be inside.

There.

But she'd had enough of stealth, of sneaking out of her room.

She turned for the door. She opened it, not stopping to look at her mother.

"What are you doing?"

She slammed the door behind her and ran out into the night.

CHAPTER FIFTY-NINE

SHE LEANED AGAINST THE HOUSE WALL, HER CHEST RISING and falling. Where to? The adrenaline was pumping through her veins, clogging her thoughts.

She could see shapes moving around in the dark ahead of her, hear voices. She squinted. People never came out at night here. It was too dark. What was happening.

She heard someone knocking at a door, followed by voices. She took a few steps forward, straining to hear.

"One of the men is here. The men what did the kidnappings. We're going to get 'im."

She put a hand to her chest. Her father. He was waking the villagers, assembling a mob.

She heard a door close and heard footsteps on the square. She shrank into the wall, her mind racing.

More knocks, more voices. She heard Harry's voice; her father had help.

She felt a hand on her arm, and almost screamed. She turned, expecting her father.

"Sam! What are you doing here?"

"I could ask the same of you. Why are you creeping around your own house?"

"I had to get away from my mum. And my dad. He's waking everyone up."

"I know."

She nodded. "Why are you here?"

"I came to tell you. I know where he is."

"Martin?"

His brow creased. "No. Bill."

"Where?"

"Come with me."

Sam pulled Sarah round the back of the house.

"Your mum's in there?" he asked her.

She thought of her mother, glaring at her. *Little whore.*

"Yes."

"Run, then!"

They ran across the grass at the back of the house. Sarah's chest felt tight and her skin tingled. She expected her mother to open the back doors at any moment, to call her in.

No one appeared.

They carried on running, past Sanjeev's house, Colin and Sheila's, then Ben and Ruth's, until they reached the end of the row of houses. Beyond it was a high fence, and a field. Beyond it the sky was lightening a little; was it almost morning already?

She stared at it. "We can't climb that."

"I'll give you a leg up." He pushed her towards the fence and bent down, his fingers entwined.

"Why are you doing this?" she asked.

"I want to help you."

She placed a foot in his hands. They gave but then stiffened.

"I don't get it," she said. He was helping her to find out

the truth about Martin, so she could decide whether she trusted him or not.

Of course. Sam expected that the truth would pull her towards him.

She looked at the top of his head, stabbed by sympathy. He didn't deserve this. She pushed down and let him haul her up. She grabbed the fence and scrambled over, tumbling to the ground on the other side.

"Grab my hands," he said. His fingers appeared, gripping the fence. She grabbed them.

He lifted himself up so his face was visible. He was grinning and his eyes were sparkling. He shifted his weight forwards and onto the fence. She leaned back and pulled.

"Careful!" he cried. She kept hold but stopped leaning, letting him shift his weight himself. He was soon over and standing next to her, brushing down his already mud-crusted trousers and smiling triumphantly.

"He's in the shed. On the allotments."

"The same place that…"

"Yeah. I hid him there."

"Wow." Was there no end to what Sam would do to end all this? "Is he alright in there? Is he angry with you?"

"Why would he be angry with me?"

"Because you locked him in. Didn't you?"

"No. He didn't want to go anywhere. He wants to stay here, Sarah. He doesn't know that we won't let him, but he's not going anywhere, not yet."

She heard a commotion to her right. Behind the field, back in the village, there was shouting. Two men. Was that her father?

"Quick," she said.

They ran across the field, keeping low, until they came to the edge of the allotments. They sank to the ground and surveyed the area. There was no one around, but people arrived early here. They would have to take care.

She heard voices to the left. Men shouting. She grabbed Sam's wrist.

"My dad. He's been knocking on doors. He's on the warpath."

"I know."

Two shapes approached across the rutted ground, their breathing heavy. Sarah and Sam shrank to the ground, their faces turned away.

The men passed, running towards the centre of the village. Sarah lifted her face from the soil and stared at Sam.

"Quick," she said. She lifted herself up to a crouch and made her way across the open space, glancing towards the village as she moved. It was difficult to run and stay low but at last she was at the shed.

She knocked on the wall of the shed. No answer.

"Bill!" she hissed. "Bill, its me! Sarah."

"And Sam." Sam fell to the ground next to her, breathing heavily. His bulk landing against the shed made it rattle.

Still no reply. She stared at Sam. "Are you sure he's still here?"

Sam shrugged.

She looked towards the village again and went to the shed door, which faced the village. She was vulnerable here but she had no choice.

She tugged on the handle. It didn't budge.

"Bill! Let us in. We're alone."

"There's no one watching you?"

She felt her chest empty at the relief of hearing him.

"Positive. Let us in, before someone comes."

He opened the door. His face was streaked with dirt

and his hair stood up in clumps. He'd cleared a space amongst the tools and junk, and looked like he'd tried to sleep.

"Sam says you can tell me the truth," she said.

Sam pulled the door closed and sat next to it, his hand on the doorknob.

Bill looked sheepish. "Yeah."

"Go on then."

"You're not going to like it."

"I just want to know. Who are Cripps and Ali? And did Martin kill them?"

"No." He frowned and looked into her eyes. "I did."

CHAPTER SIXTY

"Martin. Hello again."

He shifted his feet. He was due to appear before the Magistrate this morning, to give his plea. Not Guilty, despite his solicitor's advice.

"Sit down, will you," she said. She took a file from a shopping bag and placed it on the table between them. "Now, let me see…"

She bent to the file, yawning as she read. Martin stared at the ceiling, unconvinced that this woman would be able to help him.

"Right," she said. She slapped the file shut and leaned back in her chair. She smelled of a heavy musk perfume mixed with garlic. "So, I've spoken to the CPS lawyer."

"The who?"

"Sorry. Crown Prosecution Service. They're keen on plea bargaining these days."

He swallowed. "What does that mean?"

"It means you've got a chance to avoid a long prison sentence." She smiled at him, her brightly lipsticked lips crooked.

"How?"

"If you plead guilty when you go before the magistrates, then they'll give you – hang on." She licked her thumb and leafed through her file. "Twelve months inside then another year under curfew. Ankle bracelet, the usual."

"Sorry. If I plead guilty to what?"

"To killing those boys."

"You mean, they'll give me a year if I plead guilty to murder?"

"Well, no. It's been commuted to manslaughter. On the grounds that they supposedly attacked you first."

"Even so…"

"I know, I know. This would never have happened in the old days. But they've only got half as many prisons now, and twice as many people to lock up. They're keen to get rid of as many of you as they can." She put a hand on her chest. "And thanks to Judith here, you hit the jackpot."

She grinned at him. He felt sick.

"But I didn't kill them."

She waved a hand. "Whether you did it or not is pretty irrelevant."

"That makes no sense."

"Look, Martin. Can you produce any witnesses?"

"There's Bill."

She opened her file again. "Bill?"

"Bill Peterson. He was there. I think."

"And he'll vouch for you."

Martin let his limbs go numb. "No."

She raised an eyebrow. "You sure about that?"

"Yeah."

"So. Anyone else?"

He thought of the deserted farm, the disappeared men. At first he'd thought Bill was lying, that they'd gone off on a foraging sortie. But all their gear was gone.

"No," he said.

"So you don't have a very strong case, do you?"

Stop talking to me like I'm a child, he thought. "No."

She stood up. "I'll let you think about it."

He looked up at her. She had at least two chins and a bead of sweat hanging at the end of her nose. "How long have I got?"

She checked her watch. "Half an hour. There'll be a copper in here, keeping an eye on you. I'll be back."

"Right."

"Seriously, Martin. I suggest you take the deal."

CHAPTER SIXTY-ONE

"YOU DID WHAT?" SARAH PULLED AWAY FROM BILL.

"Well, I didn't actually kill them. But it was me who gave the order."

"What the hell does that mean?" asked Sam. "This isn't the military."

Bill raised an eyebrow. "I think Robert had ambitions in that direction, at one time. He ran things on strict lines of authority. He would tell me to do things, and I would pass them on to one or more of the more junior men."

"Even murder?"

Bill lowered his eyes. "You have to understand. Those were hard times. We were all scared. Those lads were trouble."

Sarah thought of Martin, alone in a police cell. "The lads who attacked Martin?"

"What?"

"When he met you. He told me he'd been attacked, that Robert told your men to kill them."

Bill's brow was creased. "No. It's not them. I've no idea who those little fuckers were."

"Who were they then?"

Jacob and Zahir were part of our group."

She felt her jaw drop. "What?"

"Yeah. They attacked some girls. We told them to get packing."

"You didn't kill them?"

"We roughed them up a bit. Well, the lads did. I wasn't there. They told me it got nasty. Quite a lot of blood."

"They died?"

Bill shrugged. How could he be so calm about this?

"I guess so," he said. "Never thought about it till the police showed up."

"But why have they arrested Martin?"

"Ah."

"Ah what?"

"Yeah. Our lads. They nicked Martin's knife. I guess that's what they used on them."

Sam shifted his weight. Sarah felt as if the shed walls were pushing in on her. The dead men weren't even the ones she'd thought they were.

"Was Martin with you, when this happened? Was he a part of the group?"

"He'd been with us a couple days. Robert commented that it was fate, losing two bad 'uns and picking up a good 'un."

She stared at him, gathering her thoughts.

"We didn't mean to kill them," Bill said.

"Rubbish," she replied.

Bill's forehead creased. "What?"

"Surely you know if you've hurt someone badly enough to kill them."

"You wouldn't understand, you're— well, you're you. But you walked here too, with your parents. You know what it was like. You're telling me your dad didn't use violence at any point?"

She sensed Sam avoiding her eye. "He protected us," she said.

"He defended you, right?"

"Yes."

"He hurt people?"

She felt her head fill with clouds. "There were some men. They broke into my tent, tried to…" She swallowed. "They ran off."

Bill stared at her evenly. "Did you see them again?"

"No. I assumed they'd…" She straightened up. "This has nothing to do with it."

Bill arched an eyebrow.

"No," she said. "It doesn't. You killed those men. If you didn't do it, you told someone else to do it. Isn't that conspiracy?"

"Yes," said Sam. "Conspiracy to commit murder."

"What if we were defending ourselves?" said Bill.

The cramped shed seemed to shrink in on her, as if it would squeeze them in place. "Were you?"

"No. Not at that moment, no."

"So you murdered them."

A pause. She heard an animal scurry up the outside of the shed and land on the roof, its legs beating against the wood. Her breathing was heavy.

"Yes," said Bill. "We did. But Martin had nothing to do with it."

She stared at him. Why hadn't he told the police this, when they came to the farm? Did Martin know?

"You have to tell the police," she said.

Bill shook his head. "I can't do that. Those lads, the ones who did it, they're long gone. It's no use."

"Who was it?"

He eyed her, chewing his lip. He sniffed and lifted his head. "Leroy and Mike."

Leroy. She felt a shiver crawl down her back.

"But what about Martin?"

He eyed her. "He killed Robert, didn't he?"

"He was defending me."

"Was he? As I recall it, your dad had just dragged Robert off you when Martin pounced."

She clenched her fists. Her palms were clammy.

"I suggest you leave," said Sam.

Bill nodded at him. "Fair enough."

Sarah shrank back, almost leaning on Sam, as Bill clambered over the tools to the door of the shed. He hesitated, listening for anyone outside.

"Go," she said. He looked back at her then pushed the door open.

"Now," she said. She felt hot, her body steaming with anger. He stepped outside and let the door swung shut behind them, plunging her and Sam into the mist of the early morning.

She closed her eyes, listening. If there were people out there, they would stop him. What would they do to him? Would they know who he was? Would they take him to Jess?

Not if her father got to him first.

"Come on," she said to Sam. "I need to find my dad."

CHAPTER SIXTY-TWO

MARTIN ALLOWED HIMSELF TO BE LED UP THE NARROW stairs into the dock. He could hear echoing voices above his head and smell disinfectant.

At the top, he turned to see his solicitor with two men beyond a panel of glass. Beyond them was a desk with a woman sitting at it. Another desk, to one side, held two more women. None of them looked at him.

Judith turned and gave him an encouraging smile. He didn't return it.

One of the women at the table to the side started speaking. The woman in the centre, the one he thought was the magistrate, stared at him with dark eyes. She was dressed in a neat grey suit and had hair pulled back in a severe bun. Her eyes weren't friendly.

"Can you state your name please?"

Martin turned to the woman who had spoken. She was almost his mother's age, with a thin face and greying hair. "Martin Walker," he said.

"And your address."

He looked at his solicitor. She cleared her throat. "Er, my client currently has no fixed address."

He looked down at his hands, ashamed. He'd tried so hard to find a home for himself, in the village. But it had been futile from the outset.

"Mr Walker, you are here today because you've been charged with the murder of Jacob Cripps and Zahir Ali on the first of March two thousand and—"

He leaned forwards. "What?"

His solicitor gave him a look. He wasn't supposed to speak.

"March?" he said. "March?"

The woman checked a sheet of paper on the desk in front of her and repeated the date. "March the first, two thousand and eighteen."

He shook his head. "No! No, it was the middle of February. I know that, because of the supermarket."

The magistrate raised a hand. "Mr Walker, you need to calm down please. We will tell you when it's your chance to speak."

"But you've got it wrong! It was February when it happened. Not March. How can you—"

Judith was leafing through her file, looking panicked. Martin heard footsteps behind him. He turned to see a policeman standing a foot away from him.

"You've got it wrong!" he shouted. "It's not me. The dates are wrong, you see!"

"Mr Walker." The magistrate stood up. The solicitors in front of her shuffled backwards. "If you can't keep calm, then I will hold you in contempt."

He stared at his solicitor. Her cheeks were red and her hair uncombed. "Tell them!" he shouted. "Tell them they've got it wrong."

"Remove him from the court, please," the magistrate said.

The policeman gripped Martin's arm and pulled him away.

CHAPTER SIXTY-THREE

THE ALLOTMENTS WERE EMPTY, THE ONLY LIFE THE CROWS pulling worms out of the rutted earth.

"Where did he go?" breathed Sam.

"I don't know," said Sarah. "Back to the farm, I hope."

Sam turned to her. "Are you alright?"

Her heart felt like it might burst and her legs felt hollow. "Yes."

"You look pale."

"I'll be fine."

What next? Did she have enough to take to the police herself? Bill hadn't told her which of his gang had actually killed those men. And without alternative suspects or a witness, Martin would have little chance.

She thought back to her own experiences on the road. Martin had been beaten up, but she'd faced worse. If it hadn't been for her father...

She felt the ground shift beneath her. She groaned and swayed a little, her head suddenly empty.

Sam grabbed her. "You're coming with me."

She blinked and leaned into him, gathering her breath. "No. I need to tell them. I need to talk to the police."

"What are you going to tell them?"

"That it wasn't Martin, of course." She swallowed.

"What about Robert's murder?" Sam said.

"That was different."

"They brought Ruth back, so they'll have charged Martin with that too."

She brought her fingertips to her forehead. It was beaded with sweat. Martin was under suspicion of three murders now.

"I have to talk to them," she croaked.

"You need to rest first."

She let Sam steer her towards his house, which was thankfully close to the allotments. She dreaded explaining herself to his family, but didn't have the strength to argue.

He propped her against him as he unlocked the door and pushed it open.

"Hello?" he called.

No reply. She felt a wave of relief flow over her, followed by nausea. She retched.

"Shit," Sam muttered. He grabbed a flowerpot next to the door and held it up to her face. She retched again but nothing came out.

"Sorry," she whispered.

"It's OK."

He guided her inside the house and onto the sofa. The house was cluttered and homely, dirty plates piled up next to the sink and books littering the floor between the sofa and the fire. There was another armchair, faded and green.

"I didn't take you for a reader," she said.

He held a book up. The cover featured a man with no shirt on. He was tanned and muscled. "Not me," he said. "My mum. Escapism."

She smiled weakly. Plenty of people needed a dose of escapism, here. Her own was found in the folds at the back of her cat's neck, which she liked to nuzzle.

She blinked to clear her vision, focusing on each part of the room in turn. There were pictures on the walls, framed watercolours which probably dated from before the floods. Surrounding them were rougher, less polished pieces of art on scraps of paper. Crayon, coloured pencil and one or two in paint.

"My sister's work," Sam said, spotting her gaze. "She likes to paint."

"Where does she get the paints?"

"There were some in the shop, from before. No one had claimed them. Mum's friendly with Pam."

Pam was the stern-faced woman who presided over the village shop. It was less a shop, more a distribution point, with people being allowed their allocated rations and no more. Sarah knew that Pam liked to help the families of the men who went out to work, who brought cash in. Ted had complained about favouritism often enough.

"They're lovely," she said.

"You think so?"

She nodded.

She pulled herself forward in the chair. Sam had placed a glass of water on the table next to her and she drank from it eagerly, the water hitting her empty stomach like a hailstorm. She belched.

"Sorry."

"Don't apologise."

She nodded and pulled herself to her feet. She was better now; the lightness had gone from her head and her body felt solid again, not as if she might pass through the nearest object.

She remembered her mother, standing in the hallway, calling after her. How long before her father came home?

"I need to go home."

"Do you want me to come with you?"

She shook her head.

"Has it occurred to you to tell your mum the truth?"

She stared at him. He was looking away from her, at one of the crayon drawings. It depicted a family; two parents, four children.

"What truth?" Her heart was racing.

His lips tightened. "About Martin."

Her mouth fell open. Did she want to tell the truth? Did she even know what the truth was?

"If you can't tell her," he said, "what about the police?"

"I don't have any evidence." She tugged on his arm and he turned to her. His eyes were red. "I shouldn't have told Bill to leave."

"That wasn't you."

"No. But what he told us… I don't know, Sam."

"He killed them. If not that, he was responsible for their deaths."

"I don't know."

"Sarah," he said, standing up. "You need to do something. You'll never forgive yourself if you don't."

She let him pull her up to her feet.

"I have to go home," she said.

"You're going back to your mum."

"No. I'm going to get the bike."

CHAPTER SIXTY-FOUR

THE HOUSE WAS STILL, NO SIGN OF HER MOTHER. SHE'D left the bike against the far wall after bringing it home the previous night, but would it still be there?

"Let's go round the back," she said. She gestured to Sam and he followed her round the side of Sanjeev's house, next door to her own. They flattened themselves against the back wall, feeling spray from the sea on their faces even this high above the waves. The sky was the washed-out grey of old towels.

She peered round the back window of Sanjeev's house. His younger brother was in the living room, crouched on the floor with what looked like a pack of cards spread out on the coffee table.

She smiled, wondering if she'd ever find normality like that.

She stepped out onto the grass and started to stroll towards her own house, past her neighbour's back windows. After a few paces she turned towards the boy. He was watching her, a card dropped to the floor.

She gave him a friendly wave and carried on walking.

Sam followed suit, hurrying to catch her up.

Anish was only sixteen years old; he wouldn't bother himself with the neighbours' business. She doubted he'd ever spoken to her mother.

At the corner of her own house, she stopped again. The bike was tucked under an overhang, right in front of a window.

"Do you want me to go?" asked Sam.

"No. I'll do it."

She reached forward and grabbed the rear wheel of the bike, which was closest to her. Gently, she pulled it towards her. She inched it to her slowly, until the handlebars were in her grasp.

There was no sign of her being spotted, no sign of the window being opened.

She turned to Sam. "Wish me luck."

He grinned. "Good luck. I'll be thinking of you."

"Thanks." She stood on tiptoe and kissed him on the cheek. He smelt of bread mixed with lavender and damp wood. "I appreciate your help."

He shrugged. "That's what friends are for."

She gave him a shrug in return, not meeting his eye.

She pulled the bike onto the path next to the house and swung herself into the saddle. The map was still where she'd left it in the bag tucked underneath.

"Can you pass me the map in the saddle bag?"

He rooted in the bag and brought out the map. Filey was only a couple of miles away; she'd do this in no time.

"Thanks." She folded the map and gave it to him to put back in its place.

She gave him a final smile and pushed off, clearing the front of the house. She glanced to her side to check if her mother had re-emerged; she hadn't. She let herself breathe again, aware that she had to focus on the bike now. She might be stopped on her way to the main road, challenged.

She considered. There was a field to the side of the village, leading to an old pathway. It snaked to the main road. It went in the wrong direction, but it would be safer than the public route of the Parade.

She turned into the side road leading to the beach, then pulled the bike onto the grass. It was a mountain bike so it coped with limited jolting and clattering.

She couldn't go fast; she had no experience with this sort of terrain. She'd had a bike back at home – at what had been home, once – but that had only been used on the road. Still, this couldn't be too hard.

"Sarah!"

She slammed on the brakes and scraped to a halt, almost skidding sideways. She turned to see her mother behind her, at the edge of the field.

"What are you doing?"

She stared back at Dawn. What could she tell her? What would she believe?

"Come back!"

She gritted her teeth. There wasn't time.

"Sorry, Mum!" she called. She turned the bike away and pushed off.

CHAPTER SIXTY-FIVE

"WHAT THE HELL WAS THAT ABOUT?" JUDITH STORMED
into the interview room, shoving the policeman out of her
way. He frowned after her and closed the door, leaving
them alone.

Martin stood up, kneading his fists on the table. "I met
Robert and the others on the eighteenth of February. I
know that because I was in a supermarket two days before,
and the—"

"A supermarket?" She threw herself into the chair
opposite him. "What does that have to do with anything?"

He sat down, trying to calm himself. "Look. They say I
killed those men on the first of March. But it was February
when it happened."

"You told me the dates tallied."

"I hadn't thought it through." He ran through their
first meeting in his mind. "And you didn't tell me the exact
date, anyway."

"They still have your prints on the knife."

"I know. I can't explain that. But I'm telling the truth.

If Cripps and Ali died in March, then they weren't the boys I was thinking of. I have no idea who they were."

"We just have your word for it."

"Wait." He stood up again, legs banging into the table. "Robert said something about losing two of their men. Kicking them out. I heard talk of it being rough. Maybe they killed them?"

"Was this in March?"

He slumped into the chair. "February. The day after I met them."

"So it doesn't help us."

"No."

"Alright. I'll talk to the CPS. We'll need to get your court appearance put back. But you didn't exactly do yourself any favours in there."

"Sorry."

"Don't apologise to me. It's not me who's looking at a jail sentence."

The door opened and Martin looked up. Judith turned in her chair. "Please, just a few more minutes. I have the right to meet my client in—"

Standing in the doorway was the detective who'd arrested Martin. Detective Sergeant Bryce. There were two uniformed officers behind him. No sign of his colleague.

"I said—" Judith began.

DS Bryce put a hand up. "That will have to wait. This concerns another case."

"Well, in that case you need to talk to me first."

"No. I don't."

Judith stood up. DS Bryce approached Martin. He gave him a wary look.

Martin looked back at him, his legs shaking. Had they found out who'd really killed those men?

"DS Bryce cleared his throat. "Martin Walker, I'm arresting you for the murder of Robert Cope."

CHAPTER SIXTY-SIX

DAWN WATCHED SARAH RECEDE INTO THE DISTANCE, wishing she was young enough and fit enough to chase her. Sarah hated her now; she'd tried to imprison her in her room and prevent her from talking to Bill.

Maybe she was wrong. Maybe she should let the girl find out the truth for herself.

She turned to see Sam running towards her.

"Sam! What's going on?"

Sam stopped running. "Hello, Mrs Evans."

"Don't *hello* me, Samuel. Did you and Sarah take that bicycle?"

His face was blank. "No."

She approached him. "Then how come I just saw her riding it across the Meadows?"

He paled. "I don't know, Mrs Evans."

She resisted an urge to cuff him. "Don't lie to me."

He plunged his hands into the pockets of his fleece. It was grey, a rip in the shoulder. "She went to talk to the police."

"She did what?"

"She wanted to tell them the truth."

"What truth?" She stepped towards him. He clearly wanted to back away but was too polite, or scared, to do so. "What truth, Sam?"

"It wasn't Martin who killed those boys. It was someone else."

"Someone else." She felt her chest stiffen.

A nod.

She swallowed the lump in her throat. "Exactly which someone else?"

His Adam's apple bobbed up and down. "One of Bill's men. Robert's men."

"Who told you this? No. Don't tell me. It was Bill."

He didn't argue.

"Why would she believe him?" Dawn asked. "Why would she believe any of them?"

"For what it's worth, Mrs Evans, I believed him too."

She felt her shoulders slump. "Why, Sam? Why would you, of all people?"

"Because she deserves to know the truth. She deserves to be happy."

"You can make her happy."

He licked his lips. "I don't think I can."

She put a hand on his shoulder. It was solid, damp. "You underestimate yourself."

He shrugged.

He was looking over her shoulder. He stiffened, his face registering surprise.

She turned. There was someone in the field, running in the direction Sarah had gone.

"Stop him," she told Sam.

Sam nodded then started running. The man wasn't expecting him so he caught up quickly. There were raised voices and waving arms, then the two men walked back to her.

"Bill Peterson," she said.

"Afternoon."

"My husband's got a lynch mob out after you."

His eyes widened. His face was heavily lined and he had a scar that snaked up from his wrist, disappearing under his heavy coat. He looked as if he'd seen pain, and loss. And death.

"You killed those boys," she said. "Didn't you?"

"No. But I know who did."

"I told him to leave," said Sam.

Dawn looked between them. "Why?"

Sam frowned. "We don't want killers here."

"He can help Sarah."

Sam made an involuntary noise. Dawn twisted her face at Bill.

"My daughter needs you."

"It wasn't me that killed them. It was two of the lads."

"Why?"

She felt herself shrink inside as Bill told her what had happened when they first came upon Martin. Such horror. She wanted to run home, to lock the doors and wait it out. That was what Ted would tell her to do.

If Ted found her out here, meddling, there would be consequences.

"You have to help her," she said. "She's gone off to the police, determined to protest Martin's innocence."

"What about Robert Cope? He killed him," said Bill.

"What kind of man was Robert Cope?"

"I think you know that."

"Not all of it."

"He had something deep in him, like a kernel of blackness. He enjoyed watching people suffer." A pause. "Including Ruth."

Dawn blinked back her horror. Her little girl had been caught in the crossfire.

"It sounds to me like Robert Cope was a man who deserved to die," she said.

"Possibly," said Bill.

"In which case Martin needs your help too."

CHAPTER SIXTY-SEVEN

Sarah passed a derelict supermarket as she rode into Filey. The petrol station forecourt next to it was overgrown and strewn with litter. The car park was crumbling into the ground.

She remembered these places; vast spaces full of food, household objects and a million things no one really needed. Pot pourri. Luxury chocolates. Dog food in little silver pouches. Such a waste.

She sped past it on her bike, trying to ignore the stench. It seemed that the local dogs used the place as a toilet; she could see a few of them now, chasing each other across the pitted tarmac.

She reached the edge of the town and slowed. This felt alien to her. Streets lined with houses, most of which looked occupied. Would the inhabitants know who she was, where she had come from? Would they run out of their front doors and chase her away? She'd heard her parents talking about the times the locals had invaded the village. Most recently it was just two teenagers scaring some of their kids and waving a misspelled banner. But four years ago it had been genuinely scary, villagers locking themselves up at night and the council sending guards out to patrol the edge of the village.

She hunched low on the bike, trying to be inconspicuous. She reached a traffic island and screeched to a halt. There was a sign, arrows pointing to the beach, the town centre, to Scarborough. But it had been torn from its moorings and lay on its side in the long grass at the centre of the roundabout.

She looked behind her, trying to gauge how many bends she'd turned. She was pretty sure the sea was to her right and slightly ahead. The road in that direction was wider than the others, with the houses set further back.

A car approached from behind and she pulled the bike off the road and behind a wall. The car crept past, its engine straining. It took the turning to the right. When it was out of sight she followed it.

The road sloped downwards now, giving her encouragement. She freewheeled along, enjoying the feel of the wind on her face. She'd been cold when she set off – bitterly cold, so cold she thought her bare hands might disintegrate – but the exertion had warmed her up. Her chest felt full and light at the same time. She was going to find Martin. She was going to get him released. What happened after that – she'd deal with that when the time came.

She reached another junction, traffic lights stopping her in her tracks. There was a sign to the civic centre, straight ahead. Maybe the police station would be there. She waited for the lights to change, despite there being no traffic other than herself on the road – it seemed her community wasn't the only one without access to fuel. When the light turned green, she pushed off, taking it slow so she could scan the buildings either side.

She came to a row of shops. Half of them were boarded up or in darkness. Half of what was left looked like they'd been closed for the day. Only a small few had dim lights on; a grocer's, a chip shop. The sea was approaching, in front of her down a steep hill. Maybe she'd gone too far.

She screeched to a halt as she came to the civic centre, almost losing the bike on the dip. In front of her was a vast beach, wider and shallower than the one at the village. She wanted to freewheel down the hill and explore, to see what such an expanse of unspoilt sand looked like.

But she had things to do. The sign for the civic centre also said Police. She leaned the bike against a wall. Thinking better of it, she pushed it towards the building and left it in front of a CCTV camera, making eye contact with the camera before leaving it. She had no idea if it would be working.

She pulled in a deep breath. Her chest felt tight and her stomach loose. She scanned the windows; was Martin behind one of them, or would he be deep inside, with no access to light? What rooms were lit looked more like offices than cells. And they wouldn't give prisoners a view of the street.

She dug her fingernails into her palm, ignoring the fact that they were ice-cold. She pushed the door open and went inside, trying to look as confident as she could.

She was in a generous hallway, with a potted plant in the corner and a few pictures of Filey on the walls. A woman sat at a long desk. She wore a green jumper and a pearl necklace that looked cheap. No uniform.

"Can I help you?" The woman smiled at her. She looked as if she rarely if ever saw people walk in here off the street.

"Yes."

Oh God. She should have prepared for this. She should have planned what she was going to say. She didn't even know what they were holding Martin for now, and if he'd been charged. Should she have sought Ruth out, asked her about her own experience here? Or would that be too cruel?

"OK. How can I help you?" the woman asked. Her smile was dropping.

Sarah put a hand on the desk. It was trembling. "You've got someone I know here. His name's Martin Walker."

"I'm sorry, but I'm not able to talk to you about who we may or may not have in custody."

Custody. It sounded nurturing and safe. It wasn't.

The woman squinted at Sarah. She had blonde hair that fell stiffly to her shoulders, like it hadn't been washed in a while.

"Sorry," Sarah said. "I've got evidence. About Robert Cope's death. And the others too, Zahir Ali and Jacob Cripps. I know Martin didn't do it."

"And you are——"

"I'm not his girlfriend."

"I just need your name."

"Oh." *Damn.* Now they thought she *was* his girlfriend, and would expect her to lie for him. "My name's Sarah Evans."

The woman opened a pad. "Sarah Evans. Can you give me your address please?"

"Six Turnberry Drive."

The woman glanced up at her, surprised. It was rare people from their village came to Filey, let alone to the police station.

"I was there," Sarah continued. "When Robert Cope died. And I know who killed Zahir Ali and Jacob Cripps."

The women nodded. "You'll need to talk to someone from CID."

"Can I see them now, please?"

"Hold your horses. Wait there, and I'll see what I can do."

There was a row of threadbare chairs behind Sarah. She turned and took the centre one, still unsure exactly what she could tell them.

CHAPTER SIXTY-EIGHT

"Sarah Evans?"

She stood up, smoothing her skirt. A man had emerged from a door to the back of the lobby. He was tall with dark hair that curled round his ears and a faded scar that ran up to his ear. He carried himself like someone who was used to stooping to get through doors. She recognised him from the farm, but he would never have seen her before.

"That's me."

She looked out to where her bike was still leaning against a thick hedge. The sun had come out and was illuminating it: *steal me*. She wondered who its real owner was. Would the police be able to tell?

"Come with me, please."

He led her through a blue door next to the one he'd come through. A woman came with him, the one who'd been with him at the farm. Sarah flashed her a greeting but the woman only frowned in return.

The man motioned towards a chair, one of four around a bare wooden table. On it was a tape recorder and in the corner of the room, high up, was a camera. She tried not to stare at it, wondering if Martin had been brought here. If he'd sat in here with a lawyer, or if he hadn't been given one.

"My name is Detective Sergeant Bryce, and this is Detective Constable Paretska. Please take a seat."

She did as she was told. The chair was cold and hard and it hurt her back. Her bum was sore from the cycling.

The two detectives sat opposite her. DS Bryce put his hands on the table and clasped them together.

"I gather you're here in relation to two murder cases we've been working on."

She swallowed the bile in her throat. "I was there when Robert Cope was murdered."

He frowned. "I was told you were too ill to talk to us."

"Who told you that?"

"Your father is Ted Evans?"

"Yes."

He nodded but didn't answer the question.

"And what's your connection to the other case?"

"Jacob Cripps and Zahir Ali. I know who killed them."

He leaned back in his chair. He had a mole under his right eye, the other side from the scar. It throbbed ever so slightly. "Were you a witness to that as well?"

"No. But I know who did it."

"Go on then."

"It was two men. Their names were Leroy and Mike."

"Leroy and Mike?"

"Yes."

"Anything more specific?"

She dug a fingernail into the back of her hand: *idiot*.

"No. But I know someone who can tell you more."

"And what are your grounds for saying this?"

"I've spoken to someone who was there. Bill Peterson."

"We've already interviewed Mr Peterson."

"And he told you he didn't know anything, I know. He was lying."

"So he was lying and you aren't?"

"Yes."

"And why should we believe your second-hand account?"

She frowned. She wished she had brought Sam with her; he would give her strength. He would stop her running out of the room, which was what she wanted to do. "It was Bill who told me."

"Why would he tell you that?"

"He realised it was wrong that Martin should be arrested for it."

"Very well. DC Paretska has been taking notes. If we think there are sufficient grounds, we may speak to Mr Peterson again. Now the other matter. You say you were there when Robert Cope was killed?"

"Yes." She pulled her hands off the table and clasped them in her lap. She tugged on her thumb.

"You were one of the women they abducted?"

She stared at him. So the police had been told about that. In which case, Martin would be a suspect.

"I was there."

DC Paretska pushed away her pad. "How come no one from your village will tell us the truth about those abductions?"

Sarah shook her head. "That's not why I'm here."

"But why? Those men grabbed you in the middle of the night and took you. God knows what they did to you on that farm. But none of you will talk to us about it."

"We don't have the best history with the police."

DS Bryce coughed. "I think we've been very helpful to you. Everyone has."

"Have you seen the way people round here look at us?

We have to keep our doors locked at night, for fear they'll turf us out of our beds."

"I think that's a bit extreme."

"Not for us, it isn't."

He sighed. "So. Tell us about Robert Cope's murder. You were at the farm?"

"Yes."

"And how did you get there?"

She hesitated. "On a bike."

"A bike."

"Yes. It's outside your police station now." She had to hope it hadn't been reported stolen. Maybe it *was* Ben's. Maybe it had been left behind by a holidaymaker, years ago.

"A bike." DC Paretska wrote in her pad. "How long did it take you to get there?"

"Four and a half hours."

The constable scribbled in her pad. She looked at her colleague. "It's about forty miles. That makes sense."

"And why did you go there?" asked DS Bryce.

"I didn't come here to answer questions about me. Just about the murders."

"We simply want to get a fuller picture," said DC Paretska. "Don't worry about it."

That was easy for them to say.

"So you were there on your bike. Why?" asked the sergeant.

"I was out hunting. For rabbits."

"Rabbits!"

She pulled at her thumb. That was stupid, lying to them.

"And you suddenly came across this farm and heard a commotion."

"No."

"No?"

"I was at the beach and some of the men grabbed me."

"Do you know which men?"

"I'm not sure, but I think it was Leroy and Mike."

"That's very convenient."

"They were the type."

"Was anyone else with them?"

"Yes. Bill Peterson."

"Not Martin Walker?"

"They caught up with him later. He tried to persuade them to let me go." She was digging herself in up to the neck now. They'd have asked Martin about this, and he'd have given a different story. "They took us both to Robert Cope."

"Where was Robert Cope when they took you to him?"

"In the kitchen. In the farmhouse."

"Which is where he was killed."

"Can I ask who told you about his death?"

DS Bryce smiled sardonically. "You can ask, but I'm afraid we can't tell you."

"Sorry," added his colleague.

She shrugged; worth a try.

"So what happened in the kitchen?"

"Robert Cope had a knife up to my face. He was threatening me with it."

"In what way was he threatening?"

"Twisting it against my skin." She brought her fingers to her cheek. "It dug in. He did it gently though, so as not to pierce the skin. Threatening."

"Then what?"

"He was shouting, arguing with Ben Dyer."

"Who'd got there how?"

Damn. It was Ben who'd used the bike.

"I didn't see him arrive."

"What were they arguing about?"

"Something that happened between them when they were teenagers. It didn't make a lot of sense."

"And Robert was holding the knife to your face while they did this?"

"Yes. He moved it to my forehead. He started to cut me. You can see the scar." She leaned forward to show them. DC Paretska drew a sketch in her pad.

"We'll need to photograph that," she said.

"No problem," said Sarah. Maybe they were believing her.

"And then what happened?"

"My father came running in."

"Your father?"

She felt an icy wave run down her back. "Yes. Ted Evans."

"And he'd come with you by bike?"

"No. He came on the boat. The village has a boat."

"What did Robert Cope do when your father came running in? What did your dad do?"

"They fought. Robert Cope let go of me and stabbed my dad's shoulder."

"We've seen that."

Good, she thought. Evidence. She needed more of that.

"And where was Martin Walker while all this was going on?"

"He was watching, from the other side of the room. They had him tied up."

"Did he manage to escape his bonds?"

"When my dad burst in, they let go of him. He threw himself in front of me, between me and Robert."

"Why would he do that?"

"I'm not sure." She could feel her cheeks flushing.

"You were a stranger to him, yet he leapt in front of a

man he already knew – a man who had a knife and was clearly dangerous – to protect you?"

"I guess he's that kind of person." She allowed herself a quiet smile.

"What happened between your father and Mr Cope?"

"Like I said, Robert put a knife in his shoulder. Dad collapsed to the floor and I fell onto him, holding onto the wound. Martin had thrown himself towards Robert, to protect me. Then Robert started on him."

"What do you mean, started?"

She felt the blood pulsing through her wrists. "He started lunging at him with the knife."

"And Martin responded to that how?"

"I couldn't see it all, but I heard a struggle and then it went quiet. When I looked up, Robert was slumped against the wall with a kitchen knife in his neck."

"Martin put the kitchen knife in his neck?"

"Yes. In self defence."

DS Bryce leaned over the table. Sarah pulled away. She willed herself to hold his gaze.

"So you're saying that Robert attacked Martin and Martin defended himself."

"Yes."

"Not that Martin attacked Robert in anger at what he'd done to you and your father?"

"No."

The detective chewed on his lips. He peered sidelong at his colleague's pad.

"And what about Ruth Dyer? What did you see her do?"

"Nothing." She swallowed, her throat tight.

"Nothing at all?"

"She took a ring out of Robert's pocket, after he was dead. Before that she was sitting in the chair opposite me."

"And how did she get there?"

"I'm not sure."

"You're not sure."

"No." She lowered her eyes. She should be better than this at lying, with the home life she had.

"Very well. Do you have anything else to add?"

"Will you let Martin go now?"

"I'm sorry?"

"He didn't do any of the murders. You should let him go."

"It's not as simple as that. You've only given us hearsay evidence on the Cripps and Ali killings. And as for what happened in that farmhouse, it seems no one in your village can agree."

He stood up and extended his hand. "That's all we need from you, Miss Evans."

She pursed her lips. "Is he here?"

DS Bryce raised an eyebrow. "I'm sorry?"

"Can I see him?"

"If you're talking about Martin, as I assume you are, then the answer's no."

"No he's not here or no I can't see him?"

A sigh. "You can't see him. Do you have anything else for us?"

She frowned, wondering if she could reword some of what she'd told them. Make it sound better.

"No."

He stood up again. DC Paretska walked to the door and held it open.

"Thank you for coming to us," she said.

"Does this change anything?"

"We will consider what you've told us about Robert Cope's murder. But as for the others – you weren't there. It would be better if we could speak to someone who was."

"Didn't you talk to Bill, when you arrested Martin?"

"He wasn't exactly forthcoming," said Bryce. "Now, thank you once again." He gestured towards the door.

She shuffled through, feeling hollow. If anything, she'd made things worse for Martin. She traipsed to the main exit, spotting the bike through the glass doors. Once again she wondered where it had come from. Why had Bill not told her about it earlier?

She pushed back through the doors.

"Hello?" she called.

The woman at reception gave her a puzzled look. A door opened and DC Paretska emerged. She looked tired.

"I'll get him," Sarah told her.

"Sorry?"

"Bill. He'll tell you. Come to the village. He's there."

CHAPTER SIXTY-NINE

SARAH SPED ALONG THE COUNTRY ROADS, HER LEGS GOING as fast as she could push them. How long ago had Sam told Bill to leave the village? Two hours? He'd only have got a few miles on foot.

She made for the village, wheels flying. She almost hit a man who was walking along the side of the road, keeping to the grass verge.

She flew past him then slammed on her brakes. Shouldn't Bill be going the other way?

She turned. The man had disappeared.

"Bill?"

Nothing. She dropped the bike and walked back to the spot where she'd passed him.

"It's me! Sarah. From the village."

He pushed his head over the hedge. "I know where you're from. What are you doing?"

"I've been to the police." She leaned over, balling her fists on her knees. She was out of breath. "They don't believe me."

"No surprise there then."

She gulped down a lungful of air and straightened up. "They've got Martin. We have to help him."

"We're no help to him now."

"That's not true! You can tell them what happened. How those boys died."

"And Robert's death?"

She clenched her jaw. "You can tell them Martin was defending himself."

"That's what you said?"

"Yes. Why were you walking this way? Were you following me?"

"I worked it out."

"Worked what out?" She felt the handlebars slacken in her grip.

"Who killed them. Zahir and Jacob."

"But you told me. It was your men."

He cocked his head. "They'll know you're lying. The police."

"Please, Bill. Martin's a good man. He deserves your help."

"And what makes you think I am?"

"What?"

"A good man. You've seen what I've done. It was me what took you."

"You apologised. You felt guilty."

He shrugged. "I still did it."

She stared at him, betrayal swirling around in her head alongside despair. "I don't care. People change."

"Like your dad?"

"Even my dad."

She heard a wailing sound in the distance. They both turned towards it. It was faint but unmistakeable; police cars, approaching them.

Bill grabbed her arm and pulled her behind the hedge.

She stumbled through and pushed him off, brushing herself down. The sound passed. She peered over the hedge to see three cars, two of them marked.

"Why did you do that?" she asked.

"Why the hell do you think?"

She breathed out through her nose. "Please, Bill. I told them to go to the village. They want to talk to you. You can set things straight."

"Straight?"

She nodded.

"What if I tell them the truth, about Jacob and Zahir?"

"That's what I need you to do."

"And then there's Robert. Martin stuck that knife in him—"

"He did it for me!" she cried. "And you've said yourself that Robert deserved it."

"That doesn't mean Martin should have—"

"Who else?" she cried. "You? Would you have defied him? No! But Martin did."

He raised a hand as if to push her back through the hedge and then thought better of it.

"I heard you talking to him," he said. "About Lincoln. How you and he almost met."

She stared at him. "You wouldn't."

"Why wouldn't I?"

"Please, Bill. He was defending me."

"That seems to happen a lot."

"Please."

He sighed. "You go back to the village. Tell them to wait for me. I'll catch up."

"It'll take you hours."

"I'll hurry."

She gave him one last look, her nostrils flaring, then mounted the bike and pushed off towards home.

CHAPTER SEVENTY

DAWN HAD BEEN BUSYING HERSELF WITH PEELING POTATOES and carrots. Ted had returned home briefly, stormed upstairs and then gone out again, carrying what looked like a lump of wood. She wondered how many people he'd talked into his way of thinking, how many of them were going after Bill.

He was gone now: they wouldn't find him. He'd told her he'd go back to the farm. But she didn't trust him.

She heard doors slamming outside. She tensed, expecting Ted to come barging through the front door. She crept upstairs and peered out of the front window, her heart racing. Could Sarah be back?

There were three cars parked in the square. Two police cars, and one unmarked. They stood quietly in the gloom, no one near them.

She pushed her face to the glass, trying to see along the row of houses. Where had they gone? Had they taken Sarah to Ruth?

Had they found Bill?

The door to the back of the village hall slammed and

three men ran out. Ted, Harry, and another man she didn't know. She put her hand to her chest and waited. If Ted came this way she would hurry downstairs and boil the kettle.

Instead, he headed for the police cars. He peered inside each of them in turn, hands against the glass. Either they were empty or their occupants weren't about to talk to him.

He turned back to Harry and spoke to him. Harry shook his head and put a hand on Ted's arm. Ted shook it off. He turned to the house, staring up at it.

Dawn froze. The house was in darkness but her face was close to the window. He didn't know she came up here, wouldn't expect to see her. But still.

She retreated as slowly as she could, hardly daring to blink. He frowned then looked towards Ben and Ruth's house. Dawn let out her breath again.

She slid down the stairs and into the kitchen. She lit the gas under the kettle and made a pot of tea. She placed it in the middle of the table, taking time to adjust it just so, then poured herself a cup. She sat down, closing her eyes as she drank. Her heart was racing and her skin felt like it had something crawling over it.

She heard another slamming door and muffled shouts. She put her mug down and went to the front door, where she leaned against the wood.

There was a rap at the door, almost knocking her to the ground. She smoothed her hands on her apron and opened it.

"Ted," she said. She wanted to berate him for forgetting his keys but didn't want to enflame his mood.

But it wasn't her husband.

"Mrs Evans?"

"Er, yes. That's me."

Two people stood on her doorstep. A short, chubby policeman, the one who'd asked her name, and a taller, willowy man in a faded black suit. A detective, she assumed.

"We need to speak with your daughter, Sarah Evans."

Her lips were dry. "She's not here."

The detective turned away from her door. More police were out there; four more. Two of them were talking to Ted and Harry. She wanted to go to Ted's side, to calm him.

"She hasn't come back yet?"

But she was with you, Dawn thought. *Why haven't you got her?* She looked past him, towards the Parade. It would be getting dark soon. No time for a young girl to be out alone.

She pulled her cardigan tight around her. "I'm afraid not."

The man nodded. "We'll be here for a little while. Please tell her to find us when she arrives home."

"Yes."

"Have you seen a man called Bill Peterson?"

Dawn blinked back her surprise. "Not recently."

"When did you last see him?"

"About two hours ago. He was leaving the village."

The police officers exchanged glances.

"Do you know which way he was going?"

"I thought he might be coming to you."

"No."

"Sorry. That's all I know."

The detective gave her a stiff smile. "If you do see him, or if your daughter comes home, please let us know immediately."

"Err…yes."

They moved away, heading next door to Sanjeev's. No one answered the door so they continued along the row of houses, nearing Ruth's. Dawn hadn't seen Ruth since her return from Filey; she hoped she was all right. Ruth was a good doctor; kind, gentle. She didn't deserve any of this.

She looked towards the Parade again before closing the door. Ted had disappeared back into the village hall, with Harry. The angry mob he'd gathered earlier seemed to have dissipated.

She could make out movement in the distance. Two shapes, moving up and down. The shapes got larger and closer, and coalesced into two bright yellow shoes, pedalling a bike towards her.

Sarah.

CHAPTER SEVENTY-ONE

DAWN RAN OUT OF THE HOUSE TOWARDS HER DAUGHTER. "Sarah!"

Sarah panted her way towards her. She was pale and her thin jacket was soaked through. The bike came to a stop and Dawn threw an arm around her.

"We haven't got time, Mum."

"Are you alright? What did they say?"

Sarah narrowed her eyes. "You didn't want me to go."

"That doesn't mean I didn't worry about you. Let's get inside."

Sarah looked towards the cars. "The police are here."

"Don't worry about that."

"Sarah!"

Dawn turned to see Ted running towards them from the village hall. He was alone. Sarah squared her shoulders.

"Where the fuck have you been?" he hissed.

"I went to Filey, Dad."

"I tried to stop her," said Dawn, "but she wouldn't—"

"What the hell are you playing at, girl?"

"I went to see the police."

"Why the hell would you do a stupid thing like that?"

"To tell them the truth about Martin."

He raised his hand to cuff her. Sarah threw her own arm up to stop him and he withdrew, muttering.

"Get inside," he said. "We don't want the whole bleedin' village listening in."

Dawn tugged Sarah towards her. She tried to push from her mind what Ted might do once they were hidden inside.

She glanced up and down the front of the houses as Ted opened their front door. The two police who'd spoken to her had gone into one of them; Sheila and Colin's, she thought. There was no sign of the others.

She and Sarah fought each other as they stumbled into the house, Dawn batting at her daughter in an attempt to smooth her hair and clothes, and Sarah desperate to pull away from her grip. At last Ted separated them.

"What's this about Bill Peterson and the police?" he said.

"He's got evidence, Dad," she said. "He can help."

"Rubbish. They want to arrest him."

"He didn't do it, Dad."

"Didn't do it? He slung you over his back and carted you off to that farm, the bastard. He should be in jail."

"I don't want to press charges."

"Of course you don't. But we can sort him out. The village. We look after our own."

Dawn looked between them, scared.

"Ted..." she said.

Ted batted a hand at her: *go away*. She frowned.

"Ted, you need to listen."

He turned to her. There were tight red circles high on his cheeks and his eyes sparked with anger. "What?"

"We don't know what he's going to tell the police," she said.

"So? They can all dig themselves into the shit for all I care."

"Ted. We need to make sure he tells them Robert's men did it."

"What are you on about, woman?"

Sarah stepped forward. "There were two boys. Zahir Ali and Jacob Cripps. They attacked Martin. The police think he killed them, but really it was Robert. His men, anyway."

Ted looked from Sarah to Dawn. His forehead was creased. "What were their names?"

"Zahir Ali and Jacob Cripps," Sarah said. "Did you hear anything about them, when you came after me, to the farm?"

"No." His eyes were on Dawn.

"I think you should let him," Dawn said, her voice tight.

Ted took a step towards her. His eyes were red-rimmed and his face pale. "Don't tell me what to do."

"Please, Ted…"

He hit her on the arm, one, twice, three times. She closed her eyes. He grabbed her other arm and started to pull her towards the living room.

"Dad! Stop!" Sarah cried. He ignored her.

Dawn threw her hands up in front of her face. He would be careful not to leave a mark, with the police sniffing around. But he was angry. Maybe scared.

He flung her onto the sofa. "Stay there! Don't go out and don't meddle in things that don't concern you again!"

Dawn drew her knees up to her chest. She lay still, waiting for more blows.

She saw Sarah above them. The girl grabbed her

father's shoulder. He spun round. He pushed her to the ground.

"You!" he spat at her. "This is all your fault. If you hadn't brought that little shit here——"

There was a knock at the door.

"What now?" said Ted. He glared at Sarah, then Dawn. He marched towards the hallway. Dawn watched him, trembling.

CHAPTER SEVENTY-TWO

"WE'VE BEEN TOLD THAT YOUR DAUGHTER HAS RETURNED home."

Sarah stepped forwards, pushing past her father. "Hello, Detective Bryce."

"Hello again. Where is he?"

"Bill?"

"You said he was at the village. We've had various reports that he's left."

"That's because we drove him out," said Ted. "We could drive you out too, if you don't stop bothering us."

"Dad." Sarah turned back to the detective. "Let's go outside."

She stepped past her father onto their path. She looked towards the Parade; no sign of Bill.

Behind her, Ted was leaning against the door, glaring at the two police detectives. Sarah pulled the door closed, ignoring his complaints.

"Come with me," she said. She led them across the square to the JP. It was open but deserted, just Clyde behind the bar reading a book. He looked up as they entered and started busying himself behind the bar, looking flustered.

"Why have you brought us in here?" DC Paretska asked. "Is he here?"

Sarah shot Clyde a questioning look. He shook his head.

"I wanted to get away from my parents. And into somewhere warm. He's on his way."

"How do you know that?"

"He promised me. I saw him on my way back. He was on foot and I was on a bike. He said he'd catch up with me." She looked out of the window. It was dusk now, darkness descending. Lights-on would start soon and last for just an hour.

"You believed him?"

"Yes." Should she have trusted him? "He might have gone back to the farm though."

DS Bryce pulled a mobile phone out of his pocket. Sarah stared at it, and could sense Clyde doing the same. She'd never had a mobile, and he probably hadn't for years. She thought they'd disappeared.

"He's on the main road, either heading for Filey, or towards Scarborough. He won't be far away."

Sarah felt her hand tremble. "What will you do, when you catch up with him?"

"We'll ask him to corroborate your story."

She nodded. She'd been so sure Bill would help her. Back at the farm, after Martin had gone, he'd been good to her. He'd talked to her about her parents, reassured her about Martin. Given her the bike.

She'd been too trusting. Her parents were right; this was her weakness. She'd even trusted Martin, and she had no way of knowing if he really was innocent.

"We'll be off now then," said DC Paretska. "We'll let you know if we need to interview you again."

"Yes. Of course."

She watched them push through the door of the pub and disappear into the gloom outside. Then she had a thought.

She slammed into the door, banging her knee. They hadn't gone far.

"Wait!" She ran out, limping.

DC Paretska turned. Her colleague ignored her and continued walking to the cars.

"Wait!" she called again. "There's someone else you can talk to."

CHAPTER SEVENTY-THREE

Ted stepped away from the door, eyeing Dawn. She met his stare.

"Does she know?" she said.

"Does she know what, woman?"

"That it was you who killed them."

He advanced on her. "Don't talk bollocks."

"I'm not, Ted. You know I'm not. Zahir and Jacob. Those were their names. Sarah didn't hear. But you did."

"I heard nothing of the sort."

"How many times have you hit her?"

He glared at her. "Don't you dare accuse me."

"How many, Ted?"

"Just the once."

"I saw that. But you pushed her, just now. I think that's not the only time."

She backed into the wall, next to the door. Her hair brushed against her crucifix. She reached behind her and pulled it off its hook.

"Put that damn thing down, woman."

"It gives me strength."

"Strength for what?"

"Just… strength."

His shoulders slumped. "You can't tell them. You can't tell her."

"I think she knows."

"Please, Dawn. What will you do without me? You won't be able to keep this house you're so proud of, for starters."

"I hate this house."

He puffed out his chest. "Dawn."

She felt for the door handle behind her. He would kill her, if he thought she was going to tell.

"I won't say anything."

He stepped towards her. He put a hand on her cheek. She stiffened but didn't push it away. "Really?"

She swallowed. "Really."

"Good."

There was banging at the door. "Dad! Mum! Let me in!"

She turned to the door and pulled it open, hoping Ted hadn't seen the lie in her eyes.

CHAPTER SEVENTY-FOUR

SARAH RAN TO HER HOUSE, LEAVING THE DETECTIVES behind her. She had no idea if they would follow. She slammed on the door, annoyed with herself for forgetting her key.

"Dad! Mum! Let me in!"

Her mother opened the door, her face grey and washed-out. She was clutching her crucifix. Sarah paused, wanting to ask her if everything was all right, but there wasn't time.

Her father was in the living room. He sat on the sofa, his hands on his knees. He looked awkward, sitting upright and staring into space.

She looked between her parents. Dawn had her shoulders pushed back and was looking more angry than Sarah had ever seen her.

"Dad, I need you to help me," she panted.

Ted blinked a few times as if coming out of a trance.

"Dad?" She sank to the floor in front of him, trying to make eye contact. "Dad, I need your help. With the police."

His face darkened. He looked at her steadily, his pupils dilated.

"Dad?"

She turned to her mother. "Is he alright? What's happened?"

"Nothing, dear." Dawn put a hand on her shoulder. "Nothing you need worry about."

Sarah frowned. Ted pushed himself up and walked past her. He stood by the back windows. "What's up?"

She stepped towards him, then stopped. He may be looking odd, frail even. But he was still Ted.

"You were with me," she breathed. "At the farm. In the kitchen."

He gave her a condescending look. "No I wasn't."

"You were. At the end. When Robert died. You saw it."

Ted put a hand to his shoulder. All his anger and bravado had made her forget he was injured. Was that it?

"Is your shoulder alright, Dad? It's not infected?"

Something passed across his face and he removed his hand. "No, love. No, I'm fine. Now what are you asking me again?"

"You saw what happened when Robert died. You saw what he was doing."

His features sharpened and he was the same rodent-like man again, raising his chest up and glaring at her.

"Don't talk bollocks, girl. I was bleeding on the floor, wasn't I?"

"The police don't know that."

Dawn gasped. Ted raised a corner of his mouth. "You want me to lie to the police."

"I want you to tell them Martin was defending us all. Including himself. You saw Robert with that knife. He was threatening me. He threatened Martin too."

Ted cocked his head. "He did?"

She nodded, her lips tight. She ignored Dawn's look of shock.

"He did," she whispered.

Ted stared at her for a moment. She held the stare, challenging him. Daring him. Ted had probably lied to the police before, but would he do it for her? For Martin?

"That's not the only thing you need to tell them," said Dawn.

Both Ted and Sarah span towards her.

"What?" said Ted.

"Mum, please," said Sarah.

"You know what I'm talking about, love," said Dawn. "It was going to catch up with us eventually."

Sarah looked at her father. He was staring at his wife with an expression she'd never seen before. It was fear.

He looked down at his hand and tugged at his wedding ring. For a moment Sarah thought he might pull it off.

"No," he said. "They deserved it."

There was a knock at the door. Ted turned to it. "Bastards," he muttered. He threw his shoulders back and went to it.

"What is it?"

DC Paretska was standing outside, raindrops beading her shoulders. She looked past Ted to Sarah.

"He's back," she said.

CHAPTER SEVENTY-FIVE

"Can we come in?"

"Of course," said Dawn. She headed into the kitchen and lit the stove. She was still reeling from what had happened between her and Ted.

She could escape him now. Armed with her knowledge. But if it didn't work, if they didn't believe her, what would he do?

Could she do this?

She crossed herself, muttering a short prayer. She needed guidance. What she was considering was wrong. *Till death us do part.* But what her husband had done was worse.

The two police detectives clattered into the house. The man was tall and gangly, with a permanent stoop. He wore a long black coat that made him look ill. The woman, younger, more nervous, wore a blue leather jacket that reminded Dawn of the times before the floods. The way Sarah had followed fashion.

"Would you like a cup of tea?" she asked.

The woman shook her head. The man hesitated for a moment them smiled. "That would be lovely."

They weren't alone. Behind them, looking dirty and awkward, was Bill. She'd told him to leave, and now here he was back again. She felt her chest rise and fall with the effort of not telling him how she felt about him.

She poured hot water into the kettle and rummaged in a cupboard for mugs. They only had three.

She met Sarah's eye. Sarah gave her a reassuring look. "Not for me, Mum."

Dawn smiled at her. All this horror, and she was still embarrassed not to be a proper hostess. What kind of woman was she?

They came into the kitchen, bulky coats and cold breath filling the space. They pulled out seats at the table and Ted joined them. Dawn looked at him, her mind ticking over. When he met her stare she looked away, her breath shallow. Sarah and Bill hovered behind them. Sarah was watching her father, looking puzzled.

The man looked at Ted. "My name's Detective Sergeant Bryce, this is Detective Constable Paretska. We just want to ask you all a few questions."

Ted grunted. Dawn busied herself with the teapot, relieved when the man refused milk; the goats here weren't made of the stuff.

"Sit down with us," the woman, DC Paretska, said. Dawn frowned then lowered herself into a seat opposite the man.

The man cleared his throat. "Bill, we need to ask you a few questions."

Bill shuffled forward. "About Robert Cope's death."

The detective turned in his chair. He motioned with his head for Bill to come closer. Bill shifted around the room until he was facing Dawn. He looked at the back of Ted's head. Ted stared ahead, glaring at Dawn.

"And two other murders," said the detective.

Sarah leaned forward. DC Paretska – nice looking girl, thought Dawn, couldn't be older than twenty-three – arched an eyebrow.

"Bill gave the order for them to be killed. Because Robert Cope told him to," said Sarah.

Bill eyed her. "Robert told lots of people to do lots of things. Do you want to know what he told Martin to do with you?"

Sarah flushed. Dawn lifted herself up in her seat, wishing she could comfort her daughter.

"Did he?" asked Bill.

Sarah glared at him. "Did he what?"

"Did he rape you?"

Ted roared and pushed his chair back. He grabbed Bill by the neck. DS Bryce was on his feet instantly, pulling Ted off. Dawn watched open-mouthed. When Ted had been bundled back into his seat, she looked at Sarah. Sarah was avoiding her eye.

"No," said Sarah. "He didn't."

Bill looked at her as if he knew something he wasn't telling. Dawn could feel her chest caving in. She felt a tear run down her face.

"Robert told Martin to hurt you, but he didn't. He helped you get away instead." Bill looked at Sarah. "If I was as strong as him, those boys would still be alive."

DS Paretska opened her pad. "Mr Peterson, can you tell us when it was you last saw Jacob Cripps and Zahir Ali?"

Bill twisted his mouth, thinking. "It was February. After the floods."

"Any idea of the date?"

"Yeh. The nineteenth. After Valentine's Day - that was when they got carried away."

"Carried away?"

"They went for some women. In a shelter. Tried to chat them up. It got nasty."

"In what way nasty?"

"One of the women had a can of mace. Don't worry, those lasses didn't get hurt."

"And then what?" DC Paretska was chewing her pen. Dawn glanced at Ted, who was shifting in his seat. Muttering.

"We roughed them up a bit. A lot. Kicked them out. They were in quite a bad way. But we didn't kill them."

DS Bryce rubbed his forehead. "None of this is making any sense."

Bill stared at him. "Tell me about it."

The detective looked at him. "Cripps and Ali were found almost three weeks after you say you kicked them out of your group. They'd only been dead a few days. They didn't die from what you did to them. They had other injuries. Severe ones. They'd bled out."

Bill gave a slow nod. Dawn let out a whimper. Sarah was staring at her, her eyes widening. Dawn shook her head at her daughter. If the girl touched her now, she would cave in.

"It was Ted," Dawn whispered.

"Mum…" Sarah muttered. Ted was glaring at Dawn, his face red.

She shifted away from her husband.

"They attacked Sarah. Broke into her tent. Outside Lincoln." She felt herself shaking. "Ted caught them. He – he hurt them."

DS Bryce turned to Ted. "Is this true, Mr Evans?"

"The little shits deserved everything they got," Ted muttered. Sarah gasped. Dawn held her breath.

"Go on," the detective said, his voice low.

Ted lifted his face to stare at the man. "They tried to rape my girl. I wasn't going to let them do that. I defended her." He turned to Sarah and sneered. "Like she says Martin did for her."

"Mr Evans. Did they attack you? Did they provoke you?"

"Yes, they provoked me!" Ted stood up and his chair fell to the floor. Dawn stared at it, chewing a fingernail.

"They attacked my bloody daughter. If that isn't provoking, I don't know what is. I sliced their bloody dicks off."

DS Bryce nodded at his colleague. She stood up and moved beside Ted. She put a hand on his shoulder.

"Ted Evans, I'm arresting you for murder."

Ted's eyes widened. "What?"

"What about Robert?" Sarah cried. "Bill, tell them the truth about that. Please."

Dawn swallowed and looked across the table at Bill. "I was holding Martin," he said. "I had him restrained, with some electrical wire. I let him go when Robert attacked Ted here. Then Robert went for Martin. He was going to stab him, he had a flick knife. Martin grabbed a kitchen knife and defended himself."

Sarah stood up. "I was there too. He's right."

She turned to Dawn. Dawn blinked back tears, staring at Ted. She felt light, airy, like she might float away.

CHAPTER SEVENTY-SIX

SARAH STOOD WITH HER ARMS WRAPPED TIGHTLY AROUND herself. Her father was just feet in front of her in the back of the police car, his eyes on the seat in front of him. In the front, the two detectives were muttering to each other.

They handled this wrong, Sarah thought. *They should never have let us all be in a room together.* Now they had no way of untangling what was a lie and what truth.

Her mother was behind her. Her face was grey, her jaw set. Sarah put a hand on her arm but Dawn shook it off.

She slapped the roof of the car to get DC Bryce's attention.

"How long before Martin's released?"

"It's not as simple as that," he said. "We'll need to speak to all the other witnesses. Jess and Ruth Dyer. And we're looking for the other men. The ones Bill was with in that farm."

"They're gone."

"We'll find them."

"If you don't, what happens?"

"That depends on the witnesses from the village."

She stiffened. She hardly knew the Dyers; what would they say? They'd do what they needed to to protect Ruth.

"But we'll be dropping charges against Martin on the murder of the two boys," said DS Paretska. She was looking at Dawn.

Dawn moved in behind her, her breath on her neck. "Don't worry," she whispered.

Sarah snapped round. "What?"

"I spoke to Jess. It's going to be alright."

"Are you alright, Mum?"

"No. But I will be."

"You were very brave."

Her mother's eyes hardened. "*Thou shalt not kill.*"

Sarah heard a door closing behind her and turned to see the Dyers coming out of their house. Ben, Ruth and Jess. Ruth looked pale, Ben angry. Jess stared at the police car, her jaw set.

The detectives were watching. Sarah looked back at them. DS Bryce turned and spoke to her father, while DC Paretska was beside him.

The cars drove off, rear lights receding to nothing at the top of the Parade. She realised that a crowd had gathered to see what was going on. The Dyers – Jess, Ruth, and Ben too – watched in silence. Sarah gave them a nod. Jess returned it.

CHAPTER SEVENTY-SEVEN

"HERE. I FOUND YOU A SAUCEPAN."

Sarah opened the box she'd brought and lifted its contents into a cupboard. A saucepan, two plates and two bowls. Two sets of cutlery.

Martin watched her as she moved, his cheeks glowing. She knew what he was thinking.

She placed the empty box on the floor and kicked it towards the door. "What else?"

"Jess said she had some bits and bobs she could spare."

"Sonia's," Sarah said.

"Who's Sonia?"

"Jess's mum. She died not long after they got here. I never saw her much."

"Oh. Sorry."

She grabbed his hand. It was warm. "It's alright. You weren't to know."

"Hello? Anyone home?"

They turned to see Dawn at the top of the stairs leading up to the flat. She carried a teapot.

"Mum! You can't spare that."

"We've got two. Every new home needs a teapot."

Sam came out of the bedroom. "I've got your lamp working, mate. Right snug it is." He winked at Sarah. Then he spotted Dawn and blushed.

"Oh. Mrs Evans. I'm sorry."

Dawn laughed. "I was young once too, you know."

Sam's face went from pink to deep red.

"Welcome to our village, Martin," Dawn said. Sarah looked at him; she knew how nervous he was about getting to know her mother.

"Thank you, Mrs Evans."

"Please stop calling me that. You too, Sam Golder. Makes me feel old."

"Right. Yes," said Martin, looking even more clumsy and awkward than he had a moment before. Sarah knew it would take time for either Sam or Martin to call her mother by her first name.

Sarah grabbed the teapot. "Let's get the kettle on."

A few minutes later they were sitting on what seats they could find. Dawn occupied the sole armchair and Sarah was on its arm. Martin perched on a box while Sam leaned against the wall.

"Lovely brew," said Sam.

"I'm sorry about everything you went through," said Dawn, looking at Martin. "About what my husband did."

Martin looked at Sarah's mother, his cheeks flushing.

"Thank you," he said. "I appreciate what you did."

"It wasn't just for you. Sarah here, too."

"Why?" asked Martin.

"Because Sarah deserves better than I had. She loves you."

Sam was fidgeting by the door.

"Sorry, Samuel," said Dawn.

"'S alright, Mrs Evans."

Dawn raised her eyebrows at him. He said nothing.

Sarah exchanged glances with Martin. She thought of the way he'd kissed her when she'd gone to fetch him from the police station. They'd dropped charges on Robert's murder after Jess had corroborated Sarah's story. And Ted was awaiting his court appearance for the murder of Cripps and Ali. "How did you know, Mum?"

"A mother knows." Dawn tapped her nose. "And I had a tip-off from Sam here. You owe him."

Sam blushed. "No, it's not like that."

Sarah stood up, being careful not to walk into her mother's mug on the floor. She went to Sam. "Is it true, Sam?"

He shrugged and looked at her through lowered lashes. "I saw you together. You *worked*. And I could see the effect you have on him."

Sarah looked back at Martin, who was staring at Sam. "What effect?"

"You make him better." Sam sniffed. "If he hadn't met you, he'd still be one of Robert Cope's lackeys."

Martin paled. "He could be right. I owe you, Sam. And you, Sarah. All of you. This entire village. I'm so grateful for this flat."

Sarah looked at her mother. They had been offered another month in that big house, but Dawn had rejected it. They'd moved to a smaller cottage, away from the sea. Dawn had filled the surfaces with ornaments, flowers from the dunes, anything she could find. Sarah wondered how long she would stay there; her mother needed her, for now. But not forever.

Martin coughed. "Let's take a walk."

Sarah smiled up at him then looked at her mother. "We won't be long."

Dawn waved at her. "You go. We'll carry on making this place nice. Won't we, Samuel?"

"Well," said Sam. "My mum's expecting me home in—"

"I'm sure she won't mind waiting."

Sarah pulled Martin down the stairs and onto the street outside. He grabbed her hand and they walked towards the sea, their arms swinging between them. They passed people on the way; some said hello, while others looked wary. It would take time.

They stopped at the clifftop. She stared out to sea, thinking of their journey back here, from the farm, in separate boats. Then their journey back there, together. She hoped she'd never see that boat again.

She leaned her head on Martin's arm. He felt soft, and warm.

He wrapped his arm around her. "I love you."

"I know," she replied, her heart lifting. "I love you too."

— ◊ —

Find out what happens to the villagers next in the third book in the series, *One of Us*.

And you can read *Underwater*, the prequel stories to this book, for FREE at rachelmclean.com/underwater.

READ THE PREQUEL

Find out how the villagers arrived in Yorkshire in the prequel, *Underwater*.

'Hurricane Victoria, they called it. Such a British name. So full of history, and patriotism, and shades of Empire.'

Little did they know it would devastate London and send an exodus of refugees north.

In this companion set of prequel stories to *Thicker Than Water* and *Sea of Lies*, discover how the Dyer family are forced to leave London as it descends into chaos. **Will they reach Leeds and their eventual coast destination safely?**

To read *Underwater* as well as *After The Flood*, a story about what happens to Martin's mum after he leaves her behind in a flooded house, join my book club at rachelmclean.com/sol.

Happy reading!
Rachel McLean

ONE OF US - THE FINAL BOOK IN THE VILLAGE TRILOGY

'Leave, or die.'

Jess Dyer has won safety for her sister-in-law Ruth and proved her worth as the leader of her refugee community.

Sarah Evans has stood up to her parents and discovered who she can trust.

But the villagers still aren't welcome. When the local population expresses its anger, can Jess keep everyone safe? Can she hold it together as Steward when someone she loves dies?

And how will Sarah react when her partner Martin receives death threats?

One Of Us is a gripping thriller about community and acceptance - buy it now and complete the trilogy.

Catawampus Press

catawampus-press.com

Printed in Great Britain
by Amazon

32838289R00198